W9-DCO-062

2021

THE **ESCAPE**

Center Point
Large Print

Also by Lisa Harris and available from
Center Point Large Print:

Missing
Pursued
Vanishing Point
A Secret to Die For
Deadly Intentions
The Traitor's Pawn

**This Large Print Book carries the
Seal of Approval of N.A.V.H.**

US MARSHALS | 1

THE ESCAPE

LISA HARRIS

CENTER POINT LARGE PRINT
THORNDIKE, MAINE

This Center Point Large Print edition
is published in the year 2021 by arrangement with
Revell, a division of Baker Publishing Group.

Copyright © 2020 by Lisa Harris.

All rights reserved.

This book is a work of fiction. Names, characters, places,
and incidents are the product of the author's imagination
or are used fictitiously. Any resemblance to actual events,
locales, or persons, living or dead, is coincidental.

The text of this Large Print edition is unabridged.
In other aspects, this book may vary
from the original edition.
Printed in the United States of America
on permanent paper.
Set in 16-point Times New Roman type.

ISBN: 978-1-64358-838-4

The Library of Congress has cataloged this record under
Library of Congress Control Number: 2020950391

THE ESCAPE

ONE

There is a razor-thin edge between justice and revenge, where the two easily blur if left unchecked. Five years after her husband's murder, Madison James was still trying to discover which side of the line she was on—though maybe it didn't matter anymore. Nothing she did was going to bring Luke back.

Her pulse raced as she sprinted the final dozen yards of her morning run, needing the release of endorphins to pick up her mood and get her through the day. At least she had the weather on her side. After weeks of spring rains, typical for the Pacific Northwest, the sun was finally out, showing off blue skies and a stunning view of Mount Rainier in the distance. Spring had also brought with it the bright yellow blooms of the Oregon grape shrubs, planted widely throughout Seattle, along with colorful wild currants.

You couldn't buy that kind of therapy.

Nearing the end of the trail, she slowed down and grabbed her water bottle out of her waist pack. Seconds later, her sister, Danielle, stopped beside her and leaned over, hands on her thighs, as she caught her breath.

"Not bad for your second week back on the trail," Madison said, capping her bottle and putting it back in her pack. She stretched out one of her calves. "It won't be long before you're back up to your old distances."

"I don't know. I'm starting to think it's going to take more than running three times a week to work off these pounds." Danielle let out a low laugh. "Does chasing a toddler around the house, planning my six-year-old's birthday, hosting our father for a few days, and pacing the floor with a colicky baby count as exercise?"

"That absolutely all counts." Madison stretched the other side. "And as for the extra weight, that baby of yours is worth every pound you gained. Besides, you still look terrific."

Danielle chuckled, pulling out her water bottle and taking a swig. "If this is looking terrific, I can't imagine what a good night's sleep would do."

"You'll get back to your old self in a few weeks."

"That's what Ethan keeps telling me."

Madison stopped stretching and put her hands on her hips. "Honestly, I don't know how you do it all. You're Superwoman, as far as I'm concerned."

Danielle laughed. "Yep, if you consider changing diapers and making homemade play-dough superpowers. You, on the other hand, actually save lives every day."

"You're raising the next generation." Madison caught her sister's gaze. "Never take lightly the importance of being a mom. And you're one of the best."

"How do you always know what to say?" Danielle dropped her water bottle back into its pouch. "But what about you? You haven't mentioned Luke yet today."

Madison frowned. She knew her sister would bring him up eventually. "That was on purpose. Today I'm celebrating your getting back into shape and the stunning weather. I have no intention of spending the day feeling sorry for myself."

Danielle didn't look convinced. "That's fine. Just make sure you're not burying your feelings, Maddie."

"I'm not. Trust me." Madison hesitated, hoping her attempt to sound sincere rang true. "Between grief counseling and support from people like my amazing sister, I'm a different person today. And I should be. It's been five years."

"Despite what they say, time doesn't heal all wounds."

Madison blinked back the memories. Five years ago today, two officers had been waiting for her when she got home to tell her that they were sorry but her husband had been shot and pronounced dead at the scene. They'd never found his killer, and life after that moment had never been the same.

9

Madison shook her head, blocking out the memories for the moment. She started walking toward the parking lot where they'd left their cars. She'd heard every cliché there was about healing and quickly learned to dismiss most of them. Her healing journey couldn't be wrapped up in a box or mapped out with a formula. Loss changed everything and there was no way around it. There was no road map to follow that led you directly out of the desert.

"Did you go to the gravesite today?" Danielle asked, matching Madison's pace.

"Not yet."

She slowed her pace slightly. Every year on the anniversary of Luke's death, she'd taken flowers to his grave. But for some reason, she hadn't planned to go this year. And she wasn't even sure why. She'd been told how grief tended to evolve. The hours and days after Luke's death had left her paralyzed and barely functioning, until one day, she woke up and realized time had continued on and somehow, so had she. She wasn't done grieving or processing the loss—maybe she never would be completely—but she'd managed to make peace with her new life.

Most days, anyway.

"You know I'm happy to go with you," Danielle said.

"I know, but I'll be fine. I'll go later today."

Danielle had been the protective older sister for as long as she remembered.

Her sister took another sip of her water and stared off into the distance. "Want to head up on the observation deck? The view of Mt. Rainier should be stunning today."

"I need to get back early, but there is something I've been needing to talk to you about."

"Of course."

Madison hesitated, worried she was going to lose her nerve if she didn't tell her sister now. "I've been doing a lot of soul-searching lately, and I feel like there are some things I need to do in order to move on with my life."

"Okay." Danielle cocked her head to the side, hands on her hips. "That's great, though I'm not sure what it means."

Madison hesitated. "I've asked for a transfer."

Danielle took a step back. "Wait a minute. A transfer? To where?"

Madison started walking again. "Just down to the US Marshals district office in Portland. Maybe it sounds crazy, but I've been feeling restless for a while. I think it's time for a fresh start. And I'll be closer to Dad."

"Maddie"—Danielle caught her arm—"you don't have to move away to get a fresh start. And there are plenty of other options besides your moving. The most logical one being that we can move Dad up here. I'll help you look for a place for him like we talked about, and we'll be able to take care of him together—"

Madison shook her head. "He'll never agree to move. You know how stubborn he is, besides—he visits Mama's grave every day. How can we take that away from him? It's his last connection to her."

"He needs to be here. You need to be here."

Madison hesitated, wishing now that she hadn't brought it up. "Even if Daddy wasn't in the equation, I need to do this for me. It's been five years. I need to move on. And for me that means finally selling the house and starting over. I've been dragging my feet for too long."

"I'm all for moving on, but why can't you do that right here? Buy another house in a different suburb, or a loft downtown if you want to be closer to work. Seattle's full of options."

Madison's jaw tensed, but she wasn't ready to back down. "I need to do this. And I need you to support me."

"I get that, but what if I need you here? I know that's selfish, but I want my girls to know their aunt. I want to be able to meet you for lunch when you're free, or go shopping, or—"

"It's a three-hour drive. I can come up for birthdays and holidays and—"

"With all your time off." Danielle shook her head. "I know your intentions are good, but I'd be lucky to get you up here once a year."

"You're wrong." Madison fought back with her own objections. "I'm not running away. I'm just starting over."

Danielle's hands dropped to her sides in defeat. "Just promise me you won't do anything rash."

"I won't. I've just been doing some research."

Danielle glanced at her watch. "I hate to cut things off here, but I really do need to get back home. I didn't know it was so late. Come over for dinner tonight. I'm getting Chinese takeout. We can talk about it more. Besides, you don't need to be alone today. I'm sure the anniversary of Luke's death is part of what's triggered this need to move."

Madison frowned, though her sister's words hit their target. "You know I love you, but I don't need a babysitter."

"Isn't it enough that I love your company?" Danielle asked.

"I was going to spend a quiet night at home."

"Maddie—"

"I might be your little sister, but I'm not so little anymore. Stop worrying. I'm good. I promise. I just need a change. And I need you to support my decision."

"Fine. You know I will, even though I will continue to try and change your mind. We could go house hunting together. In fact, remember that cute house we walked through that's for sale a couple blocks from my house? It would be perfect—"

"Enough." She reached out and squeezed Danielle's hand. "Whatever happens, I promise I'll still come up for the fall marathon, so I can beat you again—"

"What? I beat you by a full minute and a half last year."

Madison shoved her earbuds in her ears and jogged away. "What? I can't hear you."

"I'll see you tomorrow."

She flashed her sister a smile, then sprinted toward the parking lot. She breathed in a lungful of air. Memories flickered in the background no matter how much she tried to shove them down.

For her it had been love at first sight. She'd met Luke in the ER when she went in with kidney stones. He was the handsome doctor she couldn't keep her eyes off. Ten months later they married and spent their honeymoon on Vancouver Island, holing up in a private beach house with a view of the ocean. As an ER doc and a police officer, their biggest marital problem had been schedules that always worked against them. They'd fought for the same days off so they could go hiking together. And when they managed to score an extra couple of days, they'd rent a cabin in Lakebay or Greenbank and ditch the world for forty-eight hours.

Their marriage hadn't been perfect, but it had been good because they'd both meant the part about for better or worse. They plowed through rough patches, learned to communicate well, and never went to bed angry. Somehow it had worked.

When they started thinking about having a family, she'd decided that she'd pursue teaching criminal justice instead of chasing down criminals after the first baby was born so she could have a regular schedule and not put her life in danger on a daily basis. And Luke looked for opportunities to work regular hours.

But there'd never been a baby. Instead, in one fatal moment, everything they planned changed forever.

Madison's heart pounded as she ran across the parking lot, trying to outrun the memories. Five years might not be enough time to escape the past, but it was time to try making new memories.

Tomorrow, she was going to call a Realtor.

She was breathing hard when she made it back to her car. She clicked on the fob, then slid into the front seat for the ten-minute drive back to the house she and Luke had bought. It was one of the reasons why she'd decided to move. The starter home had become a labor of love as they'd taken the plunge and moved out of their apartment to become homeowners. A year later, they'd remodeled the kitchen and master bath, finished the basement, and added a wooden deck outside. Everything had seemed perfect. And now, while moving out of state might not fix everything, it felt like the next, needed step of moving forward with life.

Inside the house, she dropped her keys onto the kitchen counter and looked around the room. She'd made a few changes over the years. Fresh paint in the dining room. New pillows on the couch. But it still wasn't enough.

No. She was making the right decision.

She started toward the hallway, then stopped. Something seemed off. The air conditioner clicked on. She reached up to straighten a photo of Mount St. Helens that Luke had taken. She was being paranoid. The doors were locked. No one had followed her home. No one was watching her. It was just her imagination.

She shook off the feeling, walked down to her bedroom, and froze in the doorway as shock coursed through her.

There. On her comforter was one black rose, just like she'd found every year at her husband's grave on the anniversary of his death. But this time, it was in her room. In her house. Her heart pounded inside her chest. Five years after her husband's death she still had no solid leads on who killed him or who sent the flower every year. If it was the same person, they knew how to stay

16

in the shadows and not get caught. But why? It was the question she'd never been able to answer.

She'd accepted Luke's death and had slowly begun to heal, but this this was different. Whatever started five years ago wasn't over.

TWO

Jonas Quinn drove through Seattle's Queen Anne neighborhood, surprised at how familiar the city felt. And how good it felt to be back. He'd grown up here, skiing Mount Baker with his father and visiting the fishmongers at Pike Place Market on the weekends with his mother. He knew he'd come back one day, but settling down had always been off the radar. Now the idea was actually tempting.

The piercing whir of sirens sliced through his thoughts. Jonas glanced in the rearview mirror and caught sight of the flashing lights as an ambulance turned into a parking lot behind him. He blew out a slow breath of air, intent to calm the sharp flood of adrenaline. Triggers had lessened the past year and a half, and mandatory counseling had put a safety plan in place to ensure he knew how to cope with flashbacks. But nothing could erase the memories of a fugitive apprehension gone wrong.

Or the immeasurable loss that had followed.

Forcing the memories aside, he pulled into the last parking spot outside the building, grabbed the flowers he'd bought earlier, then headed toward the entrance. Two minutes later, a smiling Glenda Michaels was ushering him into a third-floor condo.

"Welcome back to Seattle, Jonas."

"Thank you." He smiled back and handed her the flowers. "If I remember correctly, carnations used to be your favorite."

"They still are, and these are beautiful. Thank you so much." She shut the door behind them. "Carl will be out in a minute. You'd think he could go into work late without getting calls."

"Unfortunately the job never ends." Chief Deputy Carl Michaels strode into the room, then pulled Jonas into a hug. "It's good to see you, especially knowing you're here for good this time."

"It's good to see you as well. It's been too long," Jonas said.

"Agreed."

"Everything okay on the phone?" his wife asked, looking between the two men.

"It will be. Just a last-minute issue on a prisoner transport, but we're not going to talk about work right now. Jonas doesn't officially start until tomorrow." Michaels patted him on the back. "How are you?"

"Slowly settling in. Glad I'm here."

"So no regrets on moving up here?" Glenda asked.

"Are you kidding? Yesterday, I spent the day

19

hiking Rattlesnake Ledge and breathing in the mountain air. Moving here was definitely the right decision."

Michaels's smile widened. "I knew the day you left you'd be back."

"Looks like you were right," Jonas said.

Michaels might have been the man who'd hired him, but he was also a longtime family friend who'd taken him under his wing when Jonas's father died. And now he was someone who would bring a bit of familiarity to this new season.

Jonas took a long look at his new boss. The man had aged since he'd seen him last. His hair was now completely gray and there were signs of a slight paunch around the middle. But Carl Michaels wasn't the only one who'd exchanged a "normal life" for a high-stress career. As satisfying as the job was, law enforcement came with a long list of unavoidable stressors.

"I hope you're hungry," Glenda said, pulling Jonas back into the present, "because breakfast is ready."

"I am, and from the smells of whatever you're cooking, I know I'm not going to be disappointed."

"I hope not." Glenda signaled for him to follow her through the living room that was exactly as he remembered with its vintage decor that highlighted her love of antiques. "I thought we'd eat on the balcony. I made smoked salmon eggs

Benedict and roasted red potatoes. Favorites of yours if I remember correctly."

Jonas grinned. "Why do you think I took this job? I understood that your cooking was part of the deal."

"Ah, so now the truth comes out." Glenda laughed. "Well, we're glad to have you back. And I know your mother's happy as well. The two of you go make yourselves comfortable outside. I'll be out there in just a second with the rest of the food."

Jonas followed Michaels out to the balcony with its stunning panorama of the Space Needle and Elliott Bay in the distance.

"I never get tired of this view," Michaels said. "Moving here is going to do you good."

"I think so, though that will all depend on how much time off my boss will give me. I hear he's a slave driver."

Michaels chuckled as he poured orange juice from a pitcher into three glasses. He handed a glass to Jonas. "Hopefully, he won't be that bad."

Glenda returned with the food and a minute later, they'd said a prayer and were filling up their plates with the smoked salmon smothered in hollandaise sauce, roasted potatoes, and berries. Jonas couldn't remember the last time he'd had a home-cooked meal.

He took a bite of the salmon. "This is delicious."

"I figured you could use a bit of fattening up after living as a bachelor for so long." Glenda's smile faded. "I know the past couple years have been tough. Carl told me about that fugitive arrest that went south."

Jonas attempted to shrug off her concern as he dug into the food, but if he closed his eyes, he could still replay every moment of that day.

"Any lingering physical effects?" Glenda asked.

"I have some limited nerve damage in my arm from the bullet, but therapy has helped."

"I'm glad to hear that. And on a lighter note, what about your move here?" she asked. "Feeling settled at all?"

"I'm almost unpacked. Carl gave me a couple days before I start working. This move has been a long time in coming, but for one reason or another has never seemed right until now."

"I know I've been working for years to get you to return," Michaels said.

"So has my mother."

Glenda filled up his half-empty orange juice glass. "Where are you living?"

"For now in a studio apartment that my mom owns not too far from here. She's been renting it out for years and it happened to come up vacant just when I needed a place. I'm planning to live there until I can decide if I want to rent or buy, and in the meantime, I'll give it a fresh coat of paint and a few upgrades."

Glenda's brow rose. "Still not ready to buy a house and settle down?"

"I'd like to say this is my last move, but time will tell," he said.

Flexibility had allowed him to focus on a career that took him from the courthouse to training fugitive task forces across the country. He loved the constant change in scenery, and the rush of adrenaline that kept him on his toes.

"Have you been out to visit your mother since you've been back?"

Jonas stabbed another bite of fish and sauce. "I'm planning to head to Bellevue to see her over the weekend."

"It's hard to believe it's been almost three decades since your father and I were beat cops together here in Seattle," said Michaels.

"It is." Jonas nodded. "I miss him."

"I miss him too. He was a good man."

There wasn't a day that went by when Jonas didn't think about his father and the heart attack that had taken him away too soon. His dad had joined the police force right out of college. Michaels joined a couple years later. Eventually, both men joined the US Marshals. Jonas was seven when he decided he was going to follow in his father's footsteps, and he'd never looked back.

Michaels's gaze shifted past Jonas toward the water. "And now, I'm about to celebrate twenty years as a US Marshal. It's hard to believe."

"Speaking of celebrations," Glenda said, "I'm helping to plan our church's twenty-fifth anniversary party in a couple weeks. It might be a nice way for you to meet a few people. The city's changed significantly over the past ten years, and I'm sure you don't know very many people anymore."

"Glenda . . ."

Jonas caught Michaels's warning glance at his wife. "Am I missing something?"

Michaels turned toward him. "Let's just say my wife likes to play matchmaker, and our very single niece will be there—"

"It was just a thought." Glenda held up her hands in defeat. "When you're new to a city, a few friends can only help."

Jonas shifted in his seat. "I'll be honest. The last thing I'm interested in right now is dating. I'm here to work, and I'm pretty sure there will be plenty of it."

"Yes, but you have to do more than work," she said. "You need a social life."

Jonas frowned. Eighteen months should have been long enough to move on from Felicia, but he'd found it impossible to take that first step.

Glenda pushed her chair back. "I forgot I have a pot of coffee brewing if you'd like some."

"I would," Jonas said. "Thank you."

She stood up and headed back inside. "Though I still say you need a social life."

"I'm sorry." Michaels set his fork down and leaned forward as soon as Glenda had stepped inside the condo. "My wife doesn't know the details of what happened."

"Forget about it. She's like my mother. Wants to make sure I'm okay. I can understand that."

"Do you ever talk to Felicia?" Michaels asked.

"She made it clear that things were over between us a long time ago."

Michaels nodded. "I remember meeting her one time when she was up here visiting her grandmother. She was a good deputy marshal."

"She was." And at one time, she'd been the woman he thought he'd spend the rest of his life with. But one pivotal moment had changed all of that.

Michaels's phone rang and he pulled it out of his pocket. "Sorry. I need to take this."

Jonas finished his last few bites while Michaels took the call.

"Is everything okay?" Jonas asked a moment later when the older man came back to the table.

"Actually, no." Michaels set the phone on the table. "You told me you wanted to hit the ground running. We've got a transport leaving in an hour, and I need you on it. Two felons, both in for murder, are being expedited back to Denver.

25

We need these guys put away, though if you need more time off—"

"No, honestly, I meant it when I said I was ready to jump in."

"That prisoner transport I was working on just fell through. Mason's down with the flu and Cody's wife is in labor."

"Seriously, you can count me in," Jonas said, "though I take it I won't be the only marshal on board."

"There will be two pilots, and I'm going to call in another marshal. Madison James."

"Madison James?" Jonas asked. The familiar name took him by surprise.

"You know her?"

"I do, actually. I worked with her briefly three, maybe four years ago. Back when I was training task forces. I didn't know she was a marshal now."

Madison James was one of those officers he'd never forgotten. She'd been completely focused on her work, to the point of never socializing outside their training. Friendly, yet reserved and dead accurate in everything she did. And where she might have lacked physically from her five-foot-five stature, her intellect made up for it. He'd been impressed with her skills back then and had wondered from time to time what happened to her. No doubt another few years on the job had honed her skills even further.

"You don't look happy," Michaels said, "but she's one of the best. Which is why I'd like to partner her up with you."

"I'm not unhappy, just surprised. She was good. Maybe one of the best I've ever trained. For some reason, though, I always felt . . . like she didn't like me."

"But you liked her?"

Jonas let out a low laugh. "Please don't tell me you're trying to play matchmaker like your wife."

Michaels grinned. "Never."

"I'll admit, in different circumstances, I might have liked to have gotten to know her better, but I think I was just impressed with her skills. She's very good."

Jonas pushed his plate away from the edge of the table. The shoot house where he'd trained Madison was a live-fire facility where he worked with local law enforcement officers in high-risk situations, teaching them how to work as an effective team.

"She never interacted outside our training sessions," Jonas said. "Never talked about anything personal. Which was fine, though, because her instincts—as well as her aim—were always spot-on."

"I'd forgotten the connection, but you were training her when that shoot house murder happened, weren't you?"

27

Jonas nodded. "I was."

"That story hit the news cycle all across the country," Michaels said. "On top of that, I'm assuming you knew her husband was killed the year before you trained her."

"I didn't know that." The revelation surprised him, but it also made sense as to why she'd been so reserved. "It will be good to see her again. We'll make a good team."

"That's what I like to hear. She might not have the years of experience you do, but her ability to read people and get them to talk is amazing. Just a routine transport to Denver and back. You'll be back in the city before you know it."

Jonas frowned. *Just a routine arrest* was the last thing Felicia had told him when their task force banged on the door of a man with their final warrant for the day. Truth was, there was never anything routine when dealing with felons. He of all people knew that.

THREE

Twenty minutes later, Jonas stepped into Michaels's office at the US Marshals district office, just ahead of Madison. Her shoulder-length brown hair was a couple inches longer, but she hadn't changed much since he'd seen her last.

"Jonas reminded me that the two of you have already met," Michaels said.

She shot Jonas a half smile, one that didn't quite reach her honey-colored eyes, as if she were trying to place him. "Jonas Quinn. Of course."

He held out his hand and shook hers. "It's been a long time. I wasn't sure if you'd remember me."

"I couldn't exactly forget you. Best training I ever had."

"Glad to hear it," he said. "I didn't know that you'd become a marshal until Michaels told me, though I'm not surprised. Congratulations."

"Thank you, and you . . . I thought you lived back East?"

"I just moved back, actually."

"Jonas used to live here, which is why he and I go way back." Michaels grabbed a stack of papers off his desk. "His father and I were close friends on the force."

"Welcome home, then," she said.

"Thank you." Jonas shoved his hands into his pockets. "How long has it been? Three years—"

"Four," she said, too quickly.

He caught a glimpse of pain in her expression and regretted his comment. If she'd still been dealing with the death of her husband during the training, she wouldn't have forgotten the time frame.

"After working under you, my basic training at the academy seemed like a breeze," she said.

"Somehow I doubt that, but clearly I wasn't the only one you impressed," Jonas said, glancing at Michaels.

"You're right," Michaels said, "but unfortunately catching up is going to have to wait for another day." He handed her a copy of the file. "You'll be moving two federal prisoners by air, leaving in forty-five minutes. They're both deemed highly dangerous, so you're going to want to watch your backs."

Madison glanced at Jonas. "Forty-five minutes is cutting it close. We're going to need to go over the prisoners' paperwork, check the plane before the prisoners board—"

Michaels shot her a wide grin. "Which is why I'm sending in my best."

Madison nodded at the compliment. Both of

them had been trained to handle any situation that might evolve in their line of work, but that didn't erase the adrenaline rush that always came with an assignment. You could never assume anything with a high-risk transportation. Never let your guard down. From searching the plane for any contraband to studying prisoner posture, they had to expect that the prisoners' mindset was to escape.

Theirs was to ensure they didn't.

Madison flipped open her file. "So what have we got?"

"Paul Riley was arrested for robbing a diamond exchange and has three cases of armed robbery, and most recently, murder. Damon Barrick was arrested for the murder of a local couple outside of Denver and is being sent back there for his trial. Both carry flight risks, which is why I chose the two of you to transport them.

"Two pilots, two prisoners," Michaels continued. "Flight will be just under three hours. You'll touch down in Denver at 1400 hours, where your plane will be met by US Marshals from the local office who will then escort them to the courthouse. I've got you both scheduled on a red-eye flight back here tonight."

His phone rang and he grabbed it off his desk. "Your ride is waiting."

On the way to the airport, they checked their weapons and went over the flight plan and every possible variable they could think of. The paper-work Michaels had given them contained each prisoner's ID, medical history, and security data, essential information to ensure they hadn't over-looked any details. At the airport, the prisoners went through another pat-down before being secured on the aircraft. In a few moments, the pilot had the go-ahead for takeoff.

Even with the time crunch, Jonas preferred to keep to the same routine each time he flew as an assurance he didn't forget anything important. Thankfully, Madison still seemed just as diligent and focused as he remembered.

He secured his seat belt while they waited for air traffic control to give them the green light. Ten minutes passed and they were in the air. Jonas studied their two passengers, who were restrained with handcuffs and ankle and waist chains. Although he didn't anticipate any problems with the transport, their job wouldn't be done until the marshals in Denver took over.

Madison shifted in her seat across from him, her body language indicating she was just as alert as he was. "How long have you been back?"

"Arrived a couple days ago. I'm looking for-ward to the change of pace."

"I get that, though this is probably going to be my last flight out of Seattle."

"You're retiring?" he asked, surprised at her admission.

"Relocating. I've asked for a transfer to the Portland office."

"Really? Why's that?"

"Personal reasons."

He studied her expression but couldn't read her. Neither was he surprised by her answer. Clearly she was just as guarded as when he'd worked with her before, making him wonder what secrets were hidden behind those light-brown eyes.

"Sorry," he said. "I didn't mean to pry."

She shook her head, indicating it didn't matter, but she didn't offer any personal information either. "Michaels said you're from here?"

"Grew up in Olympia. Left a decade ago, and did a bit of moving around because of the job." He shrugged. "But I'm pretty sure I'm back for good."

"This part of the country has a way of staying with you, doesn't it?"

"Let's just say when I'm not working, I plan to spend my days off hiking, fishing, and eating seafood."

"You actually think you're going to have days off?" She let out a low laugh. "When's the last time you had a vacation?"

"2010," he said without breaking a smile. "My plan, though, is to put in a few more years of work, retire early, and open a bait and tackle store on the coast."

"A bait and tackle store?"

"Sounds relaxing, doesn't it?"

"Yes, which means you'd be bored to death." She glanced at the prisoners. "You do *this* for a living."

"A man can dream, can't he?"

The plane rumbled beneath them.

"Sorry about the rough ride, folks." The pilot's voice came over the cabin's intercom. "There's no need to be concerned, this is going to get a bit choppy over the next few minutes. We're going to lower our altitude and see if we can avoid some of the turbulence by flying around the storm."

Jonas got up quickly, double-checked that their prisoners were secure, then sat back down across from Madison. "You okay?"

"I'm not a fan of rough weather, especially while up in the air, but who is?"

Jonas glanced out the window, figuring from the time that had passed since they left that they were somewhere over Idaho. He'd forgotten just how beautiful this part of the world was. Endless miles of evergreen trees, mountains, and canyons. The last time he visited his mother, he'd never imagined returning permanently, but now that he was back, the timing seemed perfect. And despite the dark storm clouds moving in around them, he was excited about this next chapter in his life.

Jonas grabbed the armrest as the plane dipped again. He double-checked that his seat belt was securely fastened. He wasn't ready to admit out loud that the turbulence had him on edge, but it did.

He looked behind him. From the look on their passengers' faces, they felt the same.

Paul Riley's face had paled, and a panic settled in his eyes as he gripped the armrests. "I need off this plane."

Barrick leaned forward. "He's panicking. You need to do something."

"It will settle down soon. We'll all be fine." Jonas tried to sound calm.

Riley tugged on his shackles. "I need to get off this plane."

Jonas caught Madison's gaze. He had no idea whether this was a stunt or real panic but getting off wasn't exactly an option.

Barrick's voice rose a notch. "He's having a panic attack."

Madison leaned over her armrest. "Take a deep breath and try and calm down. The pilot's working to get us out of the storm. It's just some turbulence."

Riley looked unconvinced. "I'm going to throw up."

"Take a deep breath," Madison said. "We're going to be fine."

"You don't know that. If we crash—"

"It's just bad weather," Jonas said. "The pilots are used to navigating around storms like this—"

35

"But that isn't always enough." Barrick linked his fingers together. "Japan Airlines Flight 123 in 1985—520 dead. Turkish Airlines Flight 981—346 people dead. In 2014, Malaysia Airlines Flight 370. Vanished over the ocean with 239 people on board, and more recently—"

"Barrick, be quiet. You're not helping." Jonas got up and crouched down next to Riley. "I want you to listen to me. Thousands of planes take off every day and land successfully at their destination. We're going to get there safely."

Never mind that the upcoming trial would probably leave both of them in prison for life.

Riley shook his head. "You don't know that. Small planes are even more dangerous than commercial air—"

"Flying is the safest form of transportation there is. You'll be fine."

Riley sucked in a breath of air and nodded, but he still didn't look convinced.

The plane dropped again. Jonas grabbed on to the seat back next to him as the pilot came over the speaker once more, asking them to take their seats. Jonas fought to push down the panic bubbling inside him as he stumbled back up the aisle, quickly sliding into his seat.

The pilot's voice crackled again on the intercom. "Please prepare for a crash landing."

A crash landing? Surely the pilot wasn't serious. They were in the middle of nowhere with two prisoners. The plane took a nosedive, confirming the fact that this was no joke. One of the men behind them let out a long groan. Jonas grabbed Madison's hand, then closed his eyes and braced for impact.

FOUR

Madison drew in a deep breath and imme-diately felt a stab of pain shoot through her rib cage. She opened her eyes and forced herself to not panic. An eerie stillness surrounded her. It was quiet. Too quiet. There was no sound of an engine running. No voices. Just the smell of something burning and the quiet groans of the metal aircraft.

Sunlight streamed in from behind her as she tried to focus on the situation. She unbuckled her seat belt, then slowly stood up, needing to figure out what had happened. Where they were. And why it was so quiet. She pressed her hand against the back of the chair to steady herself, pressing her lips together at the pain. She held up her arm. Nothing seemed to be broken, though her wrist looked slightly swollen. She pulled up the bottom edge of her shirt and found a bruise forming.

But she didn't have time to worry about it right now. Seconds seemed to drag by. There were six people on this plane and nothing but silence. She couldn't be the only one who had survived the crash.

Metal creaked beneath her as she turned around

and discovered the source of the light. The aircraft had been snapped in half and the back section—where the prisoners had been—was gone. But that wasn't the most disturbing part. The front—where she stood—wasn't on the ground.

She tried to not panic as she struggled to put together the scenario in her mind. They'd crash-landed in a forest. And the plane—at least half of it—was hovering somewhere above the ground. One false move . . .

She shoved aside the thought and moved slowly to the other side of the aisle where Jonas sat motionless. "Jonas. Jonas, are you okay?"

He answered with a moan. "I think so. How long was I out?"

Jonas's voice flooded her with a sense of relief. "Not long, I don't think." She fought to clear her mind. They needed to make a plan to get out of here. Needed to see if the pilots and prisoners were injured. Needed to get off this airplane before it took another dive and ended up on the ground this time. And they were also going to have to get help.

Madison checked her pockets to find her phone, but it wasn't there. She searched the area around her seat, then felt her heart sink when she caught sight of it. She unwedged her broken phone from beneath a piece of twisted metal. The screen was shattered and blank.

Great. "What about the pilots?" Jonas asked, pulling her back to the crisis at hand.

"I don't know. I have to go check on them, but we're lodged in a tree. Do you know where your phone is? Mine's crushed."

"I'm not sure where it is, but we've got to get out of here ASAP. We're still responsible for those prisoners."

"True, but the tail of the plane is on the ground. It was snapped in half."

Jonas sucked in a breath. "We're lucky to be alive."

She nodded. "I'll check on the pilots if you check on the prisoners."

"Madison . . ."

She turned around. "What's wrong?"

"I don't know. I can't move. My leg is pinned beneath the seat in front of me somehow."

"Don't panic. We'll get you out."

"And if this airplane decides to quit defying gravity first?"

She took careful steps but managed to maneuver herself until she stood right beside him. She studied the seat. The chair in front of him had twisted on impact. She moved in front of it and pulled as hard as she could, but it didn't budge.

A tree limb snapped somewhere beneath them, and the plane shifted. Her stomach lurched.

"How high up are we?" he asked, straining to look out the window from his seat.

"I'm guessing about twenty to thirty feet off the ground."

"And I'm stuck beneath a strip of metal."

"That about sums it up. It shifts slightly when I push on it, but then I can feel the plane shift as well. Let me check on the pilots. If they're alive, they'll be able to help."

"Careful. Any movement is going to mess with the integrity of the plane. If the weight shifts, and the plane falls . . ."

He didn't have to finish his sentence, though at the moment, the plane dislodging from its current location was only one in a long list of problems they were facing. She took another step. The plane creaked beneath her but didn't move.

"Be careful."

"I will."

Another step toward the front of the plane gave her a better view out the window where she could see the broken-off section below them. Her stomach turned again.

"Riley's still in his seat, but considering the angle of his neck and the fact he isn't moving, he might be dead."

"And Barrick?"

She felt a shiver slide down her spine as she shifted her gaze to where Barrick had been sitting. "The way the back of the plane fell, I can't see his seat."

She couldn't panic. Not yet. He was shackled

41

and couldn't have gone far. More than likely, he'd been thrown from his seat and was dead like Riley. She moved cautiously to another one of the windows and searched the ground for signs of him as far as she could see through the dense forest. But there was no sign of the man.

"I can't see any footprints from this angle," she said, turning back to Jonas. "But I can't be sure."

"We're going to have a serious problem if Barrick managed to vanish. This guy is desperate—and smart. We both read his file. He used a toothbrush to make a shiv and killed a fellow inmate, and that was after he murdered two people."

She nodded. "So worst-case scenario he's alive and escaped, but even if that's true, he couldn't have gone far. More than likely he's injured, and on top of that, he's shackled."

She slowly approached the cockpit, worried about what she was about to find. If the pilots were alive, or at least conscious, she should have heard them.

The cockpit door had buckled in the crash, but it was surprisingly easy to open. Blood covered the front of the pilot. A tree branch had shattered the window and impaled his copilot. Nausea bubbled in her gut, reaching up into her throat. She checked the pulse of each man but there was nothing. Just lifeless faces staring back at her. A satellite phone lay on the floor between them, the screen crushed.

She fumbled for the radio and pressed the button. "Mayday, Mayday, Mayday. This is JPATS prisoner transport flight 342 en route from Seattle to Denver. Can anyone hear me?"

She counted to ten, waiting for a reply. Nothing.

"Repeating, Mayday, Mayday, Mayday, this is flight 342 en route from Seattle to Denver with United States Marshals. We have just crashed. Location unknown. This is a prisoner transport plane. Pilots are both dead and possibly one prisoner has escaped. Need assistance."

The radio buzzed, then went silent.

"Jonas," she called out to her partner. Her heart was beating frantically. "I can't get through on the radio."

"Try again."

Panic threatened to engulf her. She was used to high-stress situations. Ones that put her life at risk on a daily basis. In an early-morning raid, there was never any way to know what was going to be on the other side. Whether they'd be met with live rounds of fire or a submissive suspect. This was no different. She just needed to stay focused and remember her training.

"Mayday, Mayday, Mayday." She repeated the information, praying that someone would hear her. There had to be someone out there listening. Or maybe someone had seen the plane go down? Except she had no idea where they were. It was possible that no one had seen the crash.

"They're dead, aren't they?"

She stepped back into the cabin, nodding. There was no time to feel sorry for herself. "Communications are out. There's no way to send a message."

"I found my phone," Jonas said. "There's no signal, but there should be an emergency beacon on the plane."

He was right. The airplanes sent messages during the flight including latitude, longitude, altitude, and airspeed. The authorities would track them here and send someone to rescue them.

"They'll track us using breadcrumb data," Jonas said. "On top of that, sensors will automatically transmit a distress signal when the crash is registered."

"But we can't stay here. If Barrick managed to escape, we have to go after him." She stared at the seat that had him trapped. "But first we've got to get you out of here."

"Are you injured?" Jonas asked.

She brushed off his concern. "Just a few bruises. I'll be fine."

She stood in front of him again, trying to determine exactly what had happened. The bar from the seat in front of him had jammed across his leg, pinning him down. She tried pulling on it from in front of the seat but couldn't get enough leverage to move it. She tried slowly from another angle. The plane shifted beneath her, dropping several feet before stopping again.

Her shoulder slammed into the side of the plane, knocking the wind out of her.

"Madison?"

Stillness surrounded them. Her fingers gripped the seat in front of her. Seconds passed. The plane creaked beneath her. She realized she was holding her breath, waiting for the plane to fall again.

He reached out and put his hand over hers. "Are you okay?"

"No. We need to get out of here. Another drop like that could kill us."

Their options were limited, but what was she supposed to do? She couldn't get him loose without moving the seat, and that meant the risk of the plane falling again.

"We need something to pry this seat forward," she said, turning carefully to see if anything in the cabin looked useful. She came up short.

"You could to go to the cockpit again and see if there's a crash ax."

"It's too unstable."

"We don't have a choice. We need some kind of leverage to move this seat off of me." He gave her a weak smile. "Go on."

She turned back around, careful not to move too quickly. A minute later, she'd found it and returned to the cabin.

"Where do you think we are?" she asked as she jammed the ax into a spot where she could get the leverage she needed to free him.

"I'm thinking we have to be over Idaho."

She secured the ax's position and used her forearm to wipe sweat from her brow. "Okay, so what do you know about this part of the country?"

"It's full of national parks and is one of the least densely populated states. The landscape is rugged—well, you can see that for yourself."

A shiver slid through her. "Which means we could be hours or days from human contact."

"Unless we happened to land somewhere right outside a town. There's still a chance someone saw the crash."

She pulled on the ax with all her strength, careful not to strain her wrist or make any sudden movements that might further dislodge the plane.

The seat groaned under the pressure.

"Gently," Jonas cautioned.

"I'm doing my best."

"You're doing great. Just another half an inch or so, and I think I can get out."

A few seconds later he was free.

"Is your leg injured?" she asked.

He pulled up his pant leg in order to see. "It looks as if I'm going to have quite a bruise, and the skin is scraped up pretty badly, but nothing feels broken."

"Good." She grabbed her backpack, then handed him his. "I think the only safe way out—if you can call it safe—is through the cockpit."

Their weight any farther toward the back of the plane would be too dangerous, causing the metal death trap they were in to shift and drop.

"For now, all that matters is that we locate our second prisoner."

They moved slowly, one at a time, out of the shattered cockpit window, careful to avoid the shards of glass covering the confined space. She tried not to make any sudden movements while Jonas took her hand to help her out. Outside the plane, she made her way toward the trunk of a tree, thankful for the thick branches that had kept them up so far. From the treetops, though, all she could see was the surrounding thick forest. Which meant the likelihood of running into a hiker seemed slim.

A couple minutes later, they'd both managed to climb down the branches and make it onto the ground.

She brushed off her pants, then grabbed her backpack and headed toward the downed section of the plane, careful to avoid walking directly beneath the craft they just escaped. Riley still lay motionless in his seat, but Barrick . . .

"Jonas." She spun around to face him. "Barrick's gone."

FIVE

Jonas stared at Barrick's empty seat. Their worst-case scenario—one they tried to avoid at all costs—had just become a reality. He studied the darkening clouds connected to the storm they'd just passed through. Not only did they have no idea where they were, but the storm churned above them, and as soon as the sun set, the temperatures were going to drop significantly.

At the moment, bad weather felt like the least of their worries. There was a dangerous man out there, and if he found them first, Jonas had no doubt he'd kill again.

"Riley's definitely dead," Madison said, walking back toward Jonas. "Looks as if he has a broken neck."

"He probably died upon impact."

But he knew what she was thinking. Paul Riley was no longer a risk and no longer a part of the equation. The Marshals Service typically only transported prisoners on the smaller planes when they were thought to be especially dangerous. Like Damon Barrick. And they had no idea where he was.

Jonas studied the tail section of the plane. The

49

impact had twisted the metal, splitting the plane in two. But it was where Barrick had been sitting that captured his attention. Not only had the man managed to survive the crash, he'd escaped.

"He clearly managed to get out of his seat belt," he said, "but there's blood on the seat, so we know he was injured."

"But not badly," Madison said. "There's not enough blood."

Madison rested her hands on her hips and stared out through the surrounding forest. "In our favor is the fact that he's still shackled and wearing orange. That will slow him down and make it harder to vanish."

But they also knew enough about the man to know he was resourceful.

Madison crouched down and studied the soft dirt next to the tailpiece. "This has to be him. Fresh footprints. He took off this way"—she pointed toward the woods—"and should be pretty easy to follow. He can't be more than a few minutes ahead of us."

"And he's going to be moving slowly," Jonas said. "But there's also a good chance he's looking to ambush us. He could have taken something from the plane, but he's going to want our guns and supplies, because he knows we're coming after him."

"I think we should also leave a trail of our own." She pulled a bandana from her pack and started ripping it into strips. "That way if help makes it here, it will be easier for them to follow us. Especially if we end up getting lost."

He frowned, but knew it was a possibility. He stared out at the densely wooded area as they walked, leaving the plane and three dead bodies behind. An icy shiver slid through him. It was a miracle they were alive.

"How's your leg?" she asked.

"Manageable."

They paused their hike for a moment while she dug some pain medicine out of her backpack and handed it to him. "This should help."

"Thanks."

"What would you do if you were him?" Jonas asked. It was the question he asked himself every time he hunted a fugitive.

"I'd find a way to get out of my shackles and into a change of clothes, then I'd get as far away from here as possible."

"He'll need to find a hiker or try hitching a ride," Jonas said before downing the medicine. "He'll also need money and a cell phone, and if he had everything on his wish list, a weapon as well."

"I agree," Madison said. They started walking again. "The good thing is, like us, he has no idea where he is, and maneuvering in shackles won't be easy."

"Which gives us the advantage. He'll need to

find a trail and stick to it. It would be far too hard to maneuver in his condition off one of the designated routes out here."

"You said you thought we were over Idaho?" she asked.

Jonas let out a low chuckle. "That's my best guess. The flight plan took us over the corner of Washington, then across Idaho and Wyoming. Because of the thick forests, I'd say we have to be in one of the national forests. Either Payette or Salmon-Challis. Possibly a corner of Yellowstone, but I don't think we were that far."

"That's what I'm thinking, but we still could be miles away from a road or main trail." She tied another scrap of her bandana to a tree limb. "He'll need to find the nearest town."

But they had no idea which direction the main trail lay.

They continued in silence for another five minutes, with no sign of their fugitive.

"Did you do any hunting growing up?" he asked, breaking the quiet that had settled between them.

"My father was a hunter. He didn't have any boys—and my sister refused to go camping—so I became his sidekick." She readjusted the strap on her backpack. "He taught me how to judge yardage and to age and identify tracks, with the goal of spotting the deer before it spotted me."

"Why am I not surprised. You were the one

with the almost perfect scores at the shoot house. The one I'd never want to be on the wrong side of the law against."

"What about you? You were always my toughest competition."

Jonas shook his head. "Believe it or not, I shot my first gun in basic training. My mother hated weapons growing up. She didn't even want me playing with Nerf guns."

She caught his gaze, an amused gleam in her eyes. "And she let you join the military?"

"Let me?" he countered with a grin. "I was eighteen. She didn't exactly have a choice. But in my defense—or perhaps hers—today she's my biggest supporter."

Her expression softened into a smile. "Good. She should be."

"Though if she finds out where I am now, she won't be too happy."

"I'm guessing she's like my sister. Always worried about you."

"Exactly."

He studied the terrain around them, his frustration growing as he focused on the trail. Where was Barrick? He couldn't have gotten far ahead of them.

Unless they were following the wrong trail.

"We should have caught up with him by now," he said.

"I know."

The thick foliage they were passing through opened up ahead of them, making it easier to see farther. But there was still no sign of the man. No flash of orange in the distance. No unexplained movement. It was as if he'd vanished.

Jonas stopped next to a thick ponderosa pine and picked up one of the cones. "Are you sure he went this way?"

"It's clear he's trying not to leave a trail, but yes, I'm sure."

"Then where is he?"

She hesitated. "I don't know."

"He could have doubled back at some point. We could have missed it."

"It's possible. The last footprint I saw was behind us."

There were dozens of ways to confuse trackers. He could have set up a false trail. He'd know that where the ground was hard, it was more difficult to read the tracks. The man was smart. As long as he stayed out of their line of sight, he would be safe, which meant his goal would be to put as much distance between them as quickly as possible.

Unless Barrick had decided to hide. No movement. No noise. Jonas continued studying the terrain around them. Barrick would assume they would keep up their search, which was exactly what they were doing. They could have easily walked right past him. Or they could be facing some kind of ambush. Neither thought made him comfortable. In their line of work, plans and details ensured they always had the upper hand. This situation had taken that away from them.

They slowed their pace slightly, guns drawn, and every muscle tense. Barrick was out here. He would do anything to avoid going back to prison. That fact was undeniable.

And he and Madison stood between Barrick and freedom.

Still, as smart as the man might be, no one left an invisible trail. And though Jonas might not have the hunting experience Madison did, he still knew how to track someone.

He moved forward on the balls of his feet, testing the ground with each step as he searched for his footing. His reaction time had to be automatic, because he wasn't the only one planning out his next move. They were both trying to plan three steps ahead, with alternate plans if something went wrong.

Madison held up her hand, motioning for him to stop.

"What is it?" he asked.

"I'm not sure. It might have been an animal." She crouched in front of him. "There. Did you hear that?"

"I did. He has to be ahead of us."

He scanned the tree line, trying to figure out

what they'd heard. Storm clouds rumbled in the distance. A bird called out from above them. But besides the wind sweeping in from the west, there was a stillness around them unheard of in the city.

A white-tailed deer scampered past them, its tail up.

Something had triggered its movement.

A second later, he heard something whiz past him. Madison cried out and dropped to the ground beside him. He ducked down next to her and scanned the perimeter again, still not seeing anything. He rolled her over onto her back. A trickle of blood ran down the side of her face where she'd been hit. A rock lay a foot to her left. He grabbed the orange bandana from her pocket to use to stop the bleeding, careful to stay low to the ground.

"Madison?"

Her face had paled, and she wasn't responding.

"Madison!"

Nothing.

He put his hands on her shoulders and squeezed lightly. "I need you to answer me."

She opened her eyes, squinting at the light. "My head."

"Are you dizzy?"

She nodded, closing her eyes again.

He crouched beside her, needing to make a visual inspection before he made a decision.

Barrick was nearby. They knew that now. Waiting for another opportunity to strike.

"Can you sit up?" he asked.

"I'm just so dizzy."

"Then don't try it. Not yet."

Orange flashed to his left.

He wasn't going to play into Barrick's hand.

Madison met his gaze. "Go after him, Jonas."

"That's what he wants. To separate us."

She managed to sit up, her gun clasped between her fingers. "I just need a minute to catch my breath, but I'll be fine. Do a perimeter check and see if you can track him. We can't lose him."

He stood up, decision made, but he still wasn't happy.

"I'm not going far. I'll be right back, because Barrick isn't the only problem we're facing. This lightning storm's heading our way, so we're going to have to take cover soon."

Small drops of rain had begun to fall. Streaks of light flashed in the distance, followed by rumbles of thunder. Jonas felt his heart race. They were both armed, but that wasn't necessarily enough. Barrick's likely plan was to pick them off one at a time in order to stop them. And if he got ahold of their weapons and gear, the man would be unstoppable.

But Jonas wouldn't let that happen. Not on his watch.

SIX

M adison gripped her weapon with both hands and leaned against a tree, her adrenaline pumping as it began to rain. If Barrick did come after her, she had to be ready. She scanned the surrounding vegetation. Her head still hurt, but at least everything was finally coming back into focus. She scanned the tree line around her, irritated that they hadn't anticipated his move.

Something rustled behind her. She jumped to her feet, searching for the source of the noise, then paused. Maybe Jonas was right and separating had been foolish. There were too many places for Barrick to hide while they searched. But where? Where was he?

He was clearly nearby and probably watching her. A shudder slid through her as she strained her eyes for a glimpse of something other than trees. Behind her was a drop-off leading to the river below them. All she could see in front of her was the unending lines of trees. She needed to anticipate his next move, but how?

Everything they did as marshals was strategic in order to ensure the safety of everyone involved.

She had to rely on her skills, her teammates, and her faith in God.

But this—she hated not having a solid plan and feeling out of control. Madison pressed her hand against her forehead. Why was it so hard to focus?

Like when Luke died.

Memories of that day invaded her thoughts, refusing to leave her alone. Finding out he was dead, the visit to the morgue, the funeral, and the sleepless nights that followed. His death had thrown her well-ordered life off-kilter and left her reeling, because there was nothing she could do to change that situation. No going back to the morning she'd told him goodbye. No more chances to tell him she loved him. Only the feeling that she no longer had control over anything.

Just like today.

There was no plan. No backup on its way. It was just her and Jonas facing a violent fugitive and the elements with no idea where they were or how far they would have to go to reach the nearest main road or cell phone towers. No idea when help would find them.

The ominous sound of a rattlesnake shifted her attention to the left. She scanned the ground and found the source coming toward her through the underbrush. Her heart pounded. Give her a morning raid in the middle of the city to arrest a hardened criminal any day, or even an encounter with a bear, but a snake? A shiver sliced through her. She hated snakes.

She took a step back and pointed the gun in the snake's direction. "Stay right where you are. I'm moving out of your way."

She moved back another step. To her left, she could hear water rushing through a twisted ravine below her. To her right was more dense foliage. Her father had always told her that her fear of snakes was irrational. She should respect them, yes, but fear them, no. Snakes didn't want to encounter her any more than she wanted to encounter them. But his assurances had never taken away the phobia. Her father had always taught her simply to not approach snakes, which she clearly wasn't going to do, and to back away slowly.

She took another step, turned at a noise, then saw the orange flash a second too late. Barrick slammed into her from behind. Madison managed to catch her balance, but he came at her again, this time hitting her hard against her jaw with his fist. Biting back the pain, she lunged forward. His arms were still handcuffed, but he'd managed to get out of his leg shackles. She rammed her elbow into his throat, then without giving him time to recover, swung her knee hard into his groin. He let out a groan, then came at her quickly, knocking her weapon out of her hand.

Panic ensued. She watched the snake slither off, but where was her weapon? Frantic, she shoved Barrick into a thick tree trunk, then searched the ground around her. Barrick stumbled away from her, but her own head still felt fuzzy. She might be able to beat him in hand-to-hand combat, but if he got ahold of the gun, it was over.

A glint of metal on the ground to her left caught her eye. She fumbled for the weapon but was a fraction of a second too late. Barrick grabbed it, faltered for a moment, then aimed it at her.

"Don't scream, don't move, or I will shoot you." Barrick took a step forward. "Give me your backpack."

"Whatever your plan is, it won't work. They'll trace the plane. Trace our phones. Already they will have ensured that access out of the forest is blocked off. There's nowhere for you to run. Every law enforcement officer in the surrounding states will have your photo in front of them. Not to mention that your face will be on every television across the neighboring counties. If you kill a government official, you'll get the death penalty."

"Not if they don't find me. They'll have to search thousands upon thousands of acres, and I could be anywhere. A needle in a haystack."

She gripped the pack between her fingers, still not willing to give him what he wanted. Still trying to figure out a way to get her gun back.

"That might be true, but do you know how many people get lost in this wilderness and never make it out?" She wiped a drop of rain from her cheek, needing to find a way to create doubt. To regain the upper hand until Jonas came back. "You didn't know the flight plan. You have no idea where we are. Choose the wrong direction, and you'll be dead before you ever find a way out of here."

"Shut up and just give it to me. Now, or I will shoot you."

"And if I give it to you? How does this end?"

If she did what he was demanding, he wouldn't need her anymore. On the upside, if he fired her weapon again, there was a good chance Jonas would hear it and might be able to find her, but she'd probably already be dead by then. So what choice did she have?

She forced her mind to focus. The river was below them, currents that might allow her to escape. She was a strong swimmer. She also didn't want him getting the bag, which meant her only real option was to run.

Madison took her chances and slid down the embankment beside her, hoping her sudden move took him off guard. It was steeper than it looked, forcing her to grab for a tree limb as she tumbled down the sharp slope, trying to slow her descent. Her pack got stuck on something, so she dug her feet into the ground to stop and grab for it, but she fell another ten feet before she could reach it. The river rushed toward her and a moment later, she plunged into the water.

The icy river pressed in around her as she struggled to find her way back to the surface. Tumbling forward, she grabbed on to a large rock and managed to find her footing. An eerie quietness surrounded her as she came up for air. She hovered behind the rock—still in the water—looking up at the ridge where she'd come from. Had he followed her?

A bullet slammed into the water nearby, answering her question.

She slid farther into the water. She was shaking from the cold, but she couldn't think about that right now. Couldn't go back for her pack. Not with him shooting at her. She glanced behind her, keeping her head out of the water just enough to see. The other side of the river's shoreline was a good twenty yards away. From there, she could quickly slip into the woods, but if she swam across the water, Barrick would see her and she'd be fair game.

Unless she stayed under the water.

A plan slowly formed. There was a small cove next to an outcropping of rocks on the other side. If she swam far enough underwater, then came out a dozen feet downstream, she should be able to make it. The current wasn't too strong at this point, and the water was deep enough to hide her. But hiding from Barrick would make it more difficult for Jonas to find her. The farther she went away from him, the harder it was going to be for them to get back together. On top of that, being out here alone left her vulnerable. She was already wet, the temperatures were dropping because of the storm, and now she had no fresh water or supplies. But what other choice was there? She was unarmed, with no real way to defend herself, and Barrick was unwavering.

Decision made, she slowly pushed herself away from the rock, and looked up again to see if she could spot Barrick. She caught a flash of orange. He was trying to make his way toward her at a point where the slope was not quite as steep.

With little time to get across, she took in a deep breath and dove down into the water. If she didn't cross in one breath, she would be an easy target. On top of that, the murky water might help camouflage her, but it also was going to make it harder to judge where she would come out on the other side. She kicked against the current, but her pant leg snagged against something. Panic ensued as she tried to pull away. Her lungs burned. She couldn't be more than halfway across, which meant she couldn't come up for air. Not yet.

Frantic, Madison managed to get the fabric loose, then continued swimming to the other side. By the time she came out of the water on the opposite shoreline, the wind was blowing harder, and she was out of breath. The frigid air bit at her skin. She didn't have time to worry about herself though. She searched for Barrick, but there was no sign of him. Had he decided she wasn't worth getting rid of? Or was she missing something? For the moment, there was no way to know. She scurried up the incline, praying he'd somehow missed her. She was wet and cold, and she needed to find Jonas.

SEVEN

Jonas heard the gunshot behind him and froze. As much as he wanted to believe that shot had been Madison defending herself, there was no way to know who'd pulled the trigger. But what he did know was that he never should have left her alone. Running as fast as he could through the underbrush back to where he'd left her, he searched through the dense trees for a sign of Barrick's orange prison clothes. A branch scraped his arm, but he barely felt the sting. He had to find Madison and make sure she was okay.

The river flowed below him, as he located the large tree he'd pegged as a marker on the narrow trail. Another twenty feet and he should find her. He rushed through the last of the thick forest and entered a small clearing. Empty. He studied the ground where he'd left her, pausing at the sets of footprints. There were three now. Hers. His. And Barrick's. A wave of panic surfaced. Barrick must have found her, and it looked as if there had been a fight. But what had happened next?

He moved to the edge of the incline where brush and undergrowth had been disturbed. There was no way to know who had won, but from the way the brush had been crushed, it looked as if at least one of them had gone down the hill.

Jonas scurried down the incline as fast as he could, making sure he didn't lose his balance in the process. He stopped at the water's edge and searched the river, but there was still no sign of Madison or Barrick. Thunder rumbled, echoing in the distance and making him question what he'd heard. Thunder or a gunshot? Lightning flashed again. If Barrick was smart, he'd be long gone by now.

Jonas continued forward, following the tracks where the ground had been disturbed, while keeping an eye out for any movement.

He stopped a moment later, searching the ground again for clues as to what had happened and found two sets of tracks. Barrick and Madison. They'd both been here, but where had they gone?

Jonas scanned the shoreline, then shifted his gaze to the river. The smaller set of tracks disappeared into the water. If Barrick had over-powered her and grabbed her gun, was it possible he pushed her into the water? Or had she tried to escape from him and swum across?

As determined as he was to find Barrick, his priority right now had to be Madison. As capable as she was, going up against Barrick wouldn't be easy. Jonas had made a foolish decision in leaving her behind.

Felicia's face ripped through his thoughts. He thought back to the moment that shot rang out. The moment he'd run to get help. And then the moment he realized he'd made the wrong decision. She might have forgiven him, but he'd never been able to shake the guilt.

It didn't matter that hindsight was 20/20, like they said. Maybe he couldn't change the past, but he could change this situation. He could find Madison.

He shoved away the memories, because he'd been down that road before, and it led to guilt that had never gone away. Which is why she had to be okay. He picked up his pace, moving as quietly as he could through the undergrowth while looking for signs of movement or flashes of orange. If she'd swum across, she'd be on the other side. If Barrick had pushed her into the water . . .

He followed along the river toward a shallow bridge that crossed to the other side. The only reason she would have run from him was if Barrick had somehow gotten the gun. And she could have used the water as cover. A sharp crack of thunder shook the ground as he tried to calculate where she would go. She had no map. No GPS. No way to know where she was.

Jonas continued up the river, searched the surrounding woods, not wanting to put himself, or Madison, at further risk. His responsibility had been to watch for signs of an ambush and yet somehow, he'd missed it.

A spot of color caught his eye in the distance, and he jogged down the trail, ignoring the pain in his leg, while trying at the same time not to worry about her. He slowed his pace as he neared a tree with a cloth strip hanging from one of its branches. Someone had been here recently. *Madison.* She'd used her bandana earlier to leave a trail of bread crumbs for the rescue team.

He ripped the cloth off the limb and wadded it up between his fingers, irritated because there was just as good a chance that this was a trap. Barrick could be here, waiting to ambush him. Just like he'd ambushed them the first time.

A flash of movement pulled his attention to the left. He lifted his gun and moved cautiously in that direction. If she'd been shot—if she was injured—there was no quick way out of this wilderness. No calling for backup, and he didn't have many supplies in his pack.

A figure flew toward him. Jonas ducked, barely missing the brunt of the blow from the thick branch being wielded as a weapon. Recognition flickered as the figure stumbled backward.

"Stop. Madison, it's me."

He caught the vulnerability in her eyes as she held the log above her head. A small laceration on her cheek showed the place where Barrick had hit her with the rock. For a moment Barrick, the plane crash, and everything they'd gone through the past few hours vanished. She was okay, and that's all that mattered.

He pulled her into his arms, surprised at his emotional reaction, and pressed her against his chest. He wasn't normally like this. He had a job to do and he did it. It was what made him a good marshal. Emotional involvement had a tendency to make people miss things. He'd learned that the hard way.

"I never should have left you. I'm so sorry." He took a step back but kept his hands on her shoulders. "Are you okay?"

"Just a few scratches."

"You're wet and shaking. You went into the river."

She nodded. "But I'm fine."

He rubbed his hands up and down her arms. "What happened?"

"He came at me from behind. He probably grabbed my pack, and he's got my weapon. He tried to shoot me. I managed to get away from him, but he's still out there. Looking for us."

Jonas frowned. "He got what he wanted. If he's smart, he's running, because if I find him . . ." His jaw tensed, but then he saw the expression on her face. He couldn't blame her for Barrick's escape. "Take a deep breath. We're going to find him, and we're going to get out of here."

"The only good thing is that he doesn't know this area."

"Yes, but unfortunately we don't know this area either. And now that he's armed, he's going to have an advantage."

"I'm sorry."

"Stop." Jonas pulled a wet wipe out of his bag and handed it to her so she could clear her face. "I'm more worried about you right now. How do you feel?"

"Besides being cold?"

He peeled off his jacket and wrapped it around her shoulders. It wasn't heavy, but at least it would help block the wind.

"Thank you." She hesitated, then started walking in the same direction they'd gone before. Hopefully it would lead them to a road. "But this shouldn't have happened. He got the jump on me, has my pack and weapon. We need to find him."

"Madison, wait." Jonas hurried after her. "I'm pretty sure you have a mild case of hypothermia and with the temperatures continuing to drop, it's just going to get colder—"

She spun around and faced him. "He has a weapon, Jonas. If he doesn't come after us, he'll find someone else. He's desperate."

He looked at her, then diverted his eyes to the ground. "I know. More than likely, his next move is to head out of here as quick as he can, but he's facing this storm as well."

"How did you find me?"

"Tracked you from where I left you. There's a bridge not too far downriver. Made my way across, saw one of your fabric clues, and found you."

"I'm glad."

"Me too." He shoved back any remaining misplaced emotion. "I never would have forgiven myself if anything happened to you."

"It wouldn't have been your fault. None of this is your fault. And I'm the one who let him get away with my weapon."

"We can forget about any blame or lack of blame for the moment. The situation is what it is. I think our priority has to be making a shelter to wait out the storm in, then getting help once we find our way out of this forest."

"And how do we find shelter with no idea where we are?"

Jonas ran his hand through his hair. "We're quite a qualified team, remember? I'm pretty sure we can figure this out."

"Advantages, I suppose, but I don't think Barrick's finished with us." She looked worried.

"We'll be extra careful, and in the meantime, I've got some food and water in my pack. Let's find a place to warm up and get some rest, then once it's daylight, we can travel downriver and find help."

He was doing his best to sound positive, but he

struggled to stuff down his worry as they began hiking. The list of possible issues played through his mind. If they could hear the thunder this loud, the lightning was within striking distance. They needed to stay away from peaks and higher terrain. Even trees with large trunks could be dangerous. Trees could be shattered, lightning strikes could discharge ground currents, and a fire could erupt in an instant. The bottom line was that there was no safe place to be outside in these conditions, and finding safe shelter wouldn't be easy in the middle of hundreds of thousands of acres of wilderness.

Wanting to keep their minds off their circumstances, Jonas changed the subject, trying to speak above the sound of the wind. "I had an uncle who lived out in the middle of nowhere. Used to go hunting at least once a year and was always telling me about people he met and places he stumbled across. Abandoned buildings and centuries-old ghost towns where men and women once searched for silver and iron. He took me on a couple trips when I visited him."

"I'm sure your mom loved that," she said.

Jonas smirked. "He made me promise that I'd never tell her."

"Do you know why she was so against guns?"

"Besides the fact that I probably wasn't the most responsible teen?"

"I can see how that might have been a factor.

I can only imagine the kind of trouble you got yourself into."

"Thanks." He laughed.

"I was just kidding."

"You're not that far off."

There was a long pause in the conversation. "When I was sixteen, I found out that my grand-father—her father—died in a hunting accident. She was there when it happened. That moment changed her life."

"Wow." She stopped and caught his gaze. "I'm sorry. I can't even imagine the trauma."

"Me neither."

Another flash of lightning struck, followed by thunder that shook the ground.

"We need to find shelter and get out of this storm," he said, the anxiety rippling through him again.

Because at this moment, he wasn't sure which was more dangerous—Barrick or the harsh wilderness surrounding them.

EIGHT

Barrick was close. She could feel it. He'd managed to outsmart her by getting her gun and backpack, and now her gut told her he wasn't finished. Not knowing where they'd crashed, or how long it would take to find their way out, meant that going after the rest of their supplies made sense. She glanced through the thick trees, searching for where he might be hovering in the underbrush or watching them from the ridge ahead. Jonas, on the other hand, believed the man was long gone. That it would be far smarter for him to avoid another confrontation and he was probably trying to get as far away from them as possible. Maybe he was right, but at this point, there was no way to know for sure.

A small branch snapped beneath her boot as she hurried to keep up with Jonas. They both knew that leaving the plane had been a gamble. With the GPS marker inside the craft, it was only a matter of time until the authorities found the crash site. But time wasn't something they had on their side. Their job was to find Barrick and stop him. But now they were facing another problem. From her calculations, the storm was less than a mile away. Already, the rain was falling harder, but it was the blinding flashes of lightning that worried her the most, because these storms also carried the potential for forest fires. And they were about to be stuck in the middle of the woods with no shelter.

She shuddered as a flash of lightning ripped across the sky.

"I'm telling you, he's long gone, Madison. Or at the least, he's found a place to wait out the storm."

"I know I'm on edge, but we can't assume he won't try and ambush us again. He holds the advantage, and he knows it."

"I agree, but not only is it going to be impossible to track him in the dark but you're soaking wet. We've got to get out of this weather and get you dry, before your body temperature drops. It could easily get down into the thirties or forties tonight with this storm."

Her hands clenched at her sides. Maybe Jonas was right. If Barrick was close by, more than likely he would have already made another attempt to ambush them and get what he wanted. And the rain and wind were both getting stronger, blocked only by the dense foliage around them that still didn't stop the drops of cold rainwater slipping off the leaves and sliding down the back of her neck. She'd appreciated the warmth of Jonas's jacket, but it was soaked now. Another bolt of lightning lit up the sky, followed by a crash of thunder.

"How's your head?" he asked.

"It's fine. Stop worrying about me."

"I didn't say I was worried."

She nudged him with her elbow. "You didn't have to. I can hear it in your voice."

"I just—"

"Jonas, I'm fine. I've faced a whole lot worse than this."

"Hmm . . . A plane crash in the dense wilderness, an afternoon swim in one of the rivers, and an armed felon who very well might be hunting us."

She let out a low chuckle. "Okay, point taken. Maybe I haven't experienced anything quite this dramatic, but I have been involved in some pretty intense fugitive hunts over the past couple years."

Which was why she knew firsthand the dangers they were facing. She shivered as a drop of water slid down her cheek. "We could try and find some drier branches to make some kind of shelter."

"I was just thinking the same thing," he said. "As long as we're out of the open as much as possible, we should be okay. Wet, but okay."

They hiked another few minutes in silence, searching for some kind of semiprotective space where they could wait out the storm.

Something caught her eye ahead of them that

didn't fit in with the surrounding woods. "Wait a minute."

Jonas stopped beside her. "What is it?"

"There's something up ahead. It looks like a cabin."

Or at least she hoped it was a cabin. She hurried ahead of him, her boots squishing in the mud with each step, but she barely noticed. In a small grove of trees was a cabin. Madison blew out a relieved breath at the thought of getting out of the rain. A minute later, the last stair creaked as she stepped onto the front porch. Jonas wasn't far behind.

She turned to him. "How old do you think this place is?"

"I don't know, but there are a lot of empty cabins in the Northwest."

Inside the one-room cabin was a bed frame but no mattress. There were a couple broken chairs and some rusty cast-iron pots, but it didn't look as if anyone had been inside the place for months.

She stopped in the middle of the wooden floor. "I don't think these walls are going to stop a bullet if Barrick comes after us, but they should keep us dry. What about a fire?"

"The fireplace doesn't actually look that bad, and there's a pile of logs on the porch that are hopefully still dry." He crouched down in front of the wall of stone. "After what you've been through, I want you to sit down and rest. I'll have a fire going in a few minutes."

He returned a minute later with a large armful of wood. "This should last us most of the night."

"Perfect."

Another bolt of lightning flashed. Jonas dug a box of matches out of his backpack. A second later, a crash of thunder confirmed the storm was hovering right on top of them.

"And you don't by chance happen to have any food in there as well, do you?" she asked.

"Normally, no, but I still have some things from my flight to Seattle, because I wanted more than peanuts for lunch and never unpacked it." He pulled out a ziplock bag and grinned. "Looks like we're in for a fire and a gourmet dinner. I've got a package of beef jerky, a couple protein bars, and some trail mix—plus a couple bags of airline peanuts."

"Sounds like I ended up with the right partner for this trip." She pulled off the wet jacket and laid it out next to her, still shivering from the cold.

He reached into his bag, pulled out a small notebook, and added the crumpled pages as tinder. Another few minutes and he had a decent fire going. Madison leaned toward the fireplace, grateful for the warmth of the flames.

"What made you decide to move back to Seattle?" she asked.

"I grew up there and my mother lives in Bellevue." Jonas checked the chimney flue and the draft, before piling some logs inside the fireplace. "I guess it's something I knew I would do eventually, but it was always far in the future. Michaels contacted me a while ago and planted the seed about moving back, and well, here I am."

She held her hands closer to the fire. "Did you miss it, being away?"

"To be honest, most of the time I'm so busy I don't really think about settling down and planting roots."

"You had to have missed something."

"There are a few things. Like Pike Place Market," Jonas said. "Every time I visited my mother, we'd always spend a Saturday morning there. She would look at the crafts, and I would eat. Chinese street food, French crepes, Persian kebabs. Hands down, the best is the seafood chowder."

"I love going there as well, though I'm not a huge seafood fan."

"And you live in Seattle?" He laid down a couple more sticks, then sat down next to her and held his hands toward the flames. "You've got to be kidding. When I lived in the city, one of my favorite restaurants was located just down the street from me and served the most amazing clam chowder in a sourdough bread bowl. I used to go at least twice a month. In fact, one of the reasons I decided to move back to the Northwest was the seafood."

"You moved back for a bowl of clam chowder?"

"Well, when you put it that way, yes."

She laughed. "Seattle does have more to offer than just seafood, you know."

"True."

"That's what's so wonderful about living in the city. It doesn't matter what I'm hungry for. Chinese, Vietnamese, pizza, or even a hot dog from a street vendor—"

"Wait a minute. You'd pass up chowder for a hot dog."

Her eyes widened. "Have you tried one with cream cheese and onions?"

He shook his head. "No, but I'll make you a deal. Once this case is over—and it will be soon—I'll celebrate with you by eating one of your cream cheese hot dogs, if you let me take you out to one of my favorite little restaurants and promise to try their chowder."

She paused. Was he asking her out on a date?

"Just as fellow marshals and colleagues," he said, seeming to backtrack when he realized the implications of his offer.

"It's a deal then. Hot dogs and chowder." She scooted another inch closer to the fire. "And here's another thing to celebrate. I think I can feel my toes and fingers again."

"Just glad we're facing a spring thunderstorm and not a winter snowstorm." Jonas unzipped the food bag and held it out for her to choose what she wanted. "I bet when you decided to go into law enforcement, you never imagined a situation quite like this."

"True." She grabbed one of the granola bars. "You go in hoping to make the world a better place and you end up lost and soaking wet in the middle of the wilderness with airplane peanuts and power bars."

Jonas laughed. "What does your family think about your career choice?"

"Both my father and grandfather were police officers, and on top of that, I had two uncles in the military and a third who was a firefighter. When my dad ended up having two girls, I don't think he knew what to do with us, especially when Danielle had no interest in guns and hunting. So it's always been just mine and his thing." She stared into the crackling flames as Jonas grabbed another thick branch to toss on top. "It's been a long time since we've gone out together though. His health has been deteriorating over the past year."

"I'm sorry. I really am. I know how tough that is."

"He does love that I'm a marshal though."

"I have to say I was surprised when I found out."

"Honestly? You're the one who inspired me to become a marshal."

"I find that a bit hard to believe. I always thought you didn't like me."

She let out a low laugh. "You were tough, but I knew if I wanted to stay alive in this job, I needed to learn everything I could. You were the best instructor I'd ever had."

"I'm not sure about that. I did notice that I never had to push you. In fact, you were the one pushing the rest of the class to keep up with you." He picked up the beef jerky, opened the pouch, and offered her a piece. "I'm sure I wasn't the only reason behind your career change."

She reached for a piece of the meat, hesitating with her answer. "I was ready for a change, and at the time the Marshals seemed like the perfect challenge. It still is."

Jonas dropped the pouch into his lap. "I feel as if I owe you an apology."

"What do you mean?"

"Michaels told me today about the death of your husband. I wish I would have known back then."

She shook her head. "That training was exactly what I needed. I was pretty much existing on autopilot back then. It gave me a reason to get out of bed. But if I'm being honest, I did almost drop out at one point. In fact, everyone told me

I should, but I knew I'd never get back out there again if I did."

"I still wish I would have known. I pushed you harder than anyone in that class because you had more focus and skill than everyone else. But I was also completely insensitive. You should have said something."

Madison shivered as the wind howled through the cracks in the cabin walls. Rain pounded against the roof. But except for a couple steady drips on the other side of the room, the inside was still fairly dry and warm.

"That's one of the reasons why I made sure you didn't know. I was there to train. I didn't need you feeling sorry for me and slacking off on my training. I knew if I was going to get everything I wanted out of that experience, I couldn't have anyone babying me. People die when they aren't prepared."

"I wouldn't have babied you," he said.

"Really? I find that when I tell people my husband was murdered, it tends to get me a lot of sympathy. They immediately see me as fragile and vulnerable."

"Trust me, I never saw you fragile or vulnerable."

She smiled. "Thanks. Sometimes I tend to push myself too hard—at least that's what my sister says, but it was something I needed to do."

"Did they find your husband's killer?" Jonas

shook his head. "I'm sorry. You don't have to talk about it."

"No, it's fine. It's been long enough that I'm okay talking about him, but no. They never found his killer."

A flash of lightning struck close by, lighting up the sky. A second later the door flew open and slammed against the inside wall of the cabin.

NINE

Jonas grabbed his handgun and rushed to the door, managing to slam it shut before too much rain blew in. He looked to where Madison still sat by the fire. He knew what she was thinking. What they'd both been thinking. That despite the storm, Barrick was still out there. And even though it made sense to him that the man would get as far away as possible, there was still a chance Madison was right and he was close by, waiting for an opportunity to strike. They couldn't afford to let their guard down.

He looked out one of the front windows, but all he could see was dark shadows stirring. "I'm pretty sure that was just the wind."

She grabbed one of the wooden chairs that sat lopsided across the room and jammed it under the doorknob.

"Good idea," he said. "That should keep it from flying open again."

She nodded, before sitting back down in front of the fire.

"You okay?" He sat down beside her, noting a change in her expression he couldn't quite peg. "You look far away."

"Yeah."

She didn't say anything for a long moment as the fire crackled in front of them. He added a couple more of the logs, feeling guilty over his too personal questions.

"I really don't mind talking about my husband, it's just that today's the anniversary of Luke's death."

He hesitated, not sure how to respond. "Wow, I'm sorry. This has been one tough day for you."

"I thought working would help me forget, but there are some things you just can't run from."

"I've been told once or twice that I'm a good listener. If that would help."

He waited silently for her response, while lightning flashed in the distance.

"It was an otherwise normal Tuesday." The fire cast a yellow glow across her face she stared into the fireplace. "It's funny how I can remember so many little details, like what day of the week it was. Luke was an ER doctor and had just finished a twelve-hour shift. He called me on his way to the parking garage. Told me he was going to pick up some takeout and meet me at home as soon as I got off work. We'd both had a long day and were anxious for the chance to unplug for a few hours. I got home about an hour after we spoke. There were two officers from my precinct waiting in my driveway with the news. Luke had been shot twice in the chest in the hospital parking garage."

"I can't imagine how hard that had to have been."

"Sometimes it still seems surreal. Like I'm going to wake up and discover it was all nothing more than a bad dream. My father drove up from Portland to stay with me, and my sister was there, making sure I was eating and taking care of myself, but I was numb for weeks. My captain insisted I take some time off from work, which of course, I fought him on. I guess I thought if I just kept moving—if I was too busy to feel the pain—I'd somehow skip to the other side of grief. But I quickly learned that grief wasn't optional."

Jonas frowned. Was that what he'd tried to do?

"In the end, they classified his murder as a robbery gone wrong, but they never had any solid leads. His killer stole his wallet, then left him bleeding out next to the car. All for twenty bucks. A woman found him and called 911, but by the time she got to the hospital, he was already gone. I didn't even get to say goodbye."

"I really am sorry. I know pain like that doesn't ever completely disappear."

"No. I know I've healed on so many levels, but when I think I've taken another giant step forward, some kind of trigger—like the anniversary of his death—tries to smack me back."

He tossed another log on the fire, realizing he

needed to tread carefully. She was strong, there was no doubt about that. But sometimes the illusion of strength could be used as a veneer to hide the chinks in one's armor. He'd learned that firsthand.

"You're trained to track people down for a living," he said, "so I suppose it's safe to assume you did your own investigation."

Madison let out a soft laugh. "I think my sister used the word *obsessed*. The first year was the worst. I tracked down every lead the police had and searched for my own, but there was never anything. The surveillance cameras were out in the garage. There were no witnesses other than the woman who called 911, and she didn't see the actual shooting. No physical evidence we could match to the case. No personal connects we could find to any of his cases where a patient might have a grievance toward him. Nothing ever panned out."

"It's not completely surprising. A third of all murder cases are never closed."

"And yet, my job is to track down felons, and five years later, I have no idea who killed my husband. It's something I wake up to every morning and go to bed with every night." Her eyes looked glassy. "I should have found his murderer years ago."

He understood the need for resolution from his own life, and how not finding closure could interfere with moving forward. "Closure's important."

"It is." She fiddled with one of the buttons on her shirt. "There's another piece of the puzzle that you'll find odd."

"What's that?"

"I haven't even told my sister this, but every year, someone leaves a single black rose on his grave on the anniversary of his death."

"That is odd. And you think it's the killer?"

"It would make sense, but what's the point, other than to ensure I remember his death? And it's not as if I'm going to forget."

"Any card or note with it?" he asked.

She shook her head. "Nope. Just the rose."

"There can't be a lot of florists who sell black roses. It seems like it wouldn't be too hard to trace it."

"They're definitely not as popular as your typical flower, but you'd be surprised how many places sell them. And because you can order them online, narrowing it down has been impossible." She shrugged. "It just makes an already hard day harder."

"You should have taken the day off and spent it with your family," he said.

"Like I said, staying busy has always been my answer to grief."

"Did you find a flower today?" Jonas asked.

She nodded. "I haven't had much time to

process it yet, but this year . . . this year it was on my bed."

"Wait a minute, Madison. Someone was in your house? If this is your husband's killer—"

"I know. I need to find them."

"Yes, but you also need to go to the authorities."

"I will. I'm just worried that nothing will come of it again. I never felt my life was in danger, and we've always thought it was a random robbery."

"Leaving a black rose on the anniversary of your husband's death isn't random. And leaving one in your bedroom? That's personal and it's a threat. Someone is trying to mess with your head."

"I know."

"And it means that whoever killed your husband sees this as personal. Very personal."

"I promise I'll file a report when I get back and have my locks changed, but there's not much I can do about it right now." She waved her hand in the air as if she could dismiss it just as easily. "I feel like I've just laid my whole life story out in front of you, and I still don't know much about you."

He dumped the small bag of peanuts into his hand and shrugged, popping a few into his mouth. "Probably because there isn't much to know."

"I doubt that's true. You can start wherever you want. Favorite travel spot. Favorite food besides seafood chowder. Taken or single."

"Let's see. Thailand, sushi, and single."

"Interesting. Thailand's on my bucket list. I suppose I shouldn't be surprised about sushi, though I am about the single status."

He shot her a wide grin. "Because I'm such a great catch."

"One could do worse, I suppose."

"Thanks. I think. Let's just say I'm sure there's someone out there for me, but I've never met anyone willing to put up with both me and my job."

"So the job always wins? That's kind of sad. Lots of marshals find a way to juggle both."

"With the right woman." He hesitated. "Maybe one day."

"You've never come close?"

"Once, but that's a story better left for another day."

She gestured to the empty cabin around them. "You have something better to do right now? I just told you things I've never even told my sister."

He stared into the fire, wondering how he was going to get past her inquisitive nature.

"Fine. I won't push, but I do have another question for you then," she said.

"What's that?"

"Were you serious about opening up a bait and tackle shop?"

"That's your question?"

"The idea intrigues me. You're a US Marshal,

and you've spent your whole career putting your life at risk chasing down felons."

"So you think it's too far away from my character? That I'd be bored?"

"Yes, actually. I see you as the kind of person who will be a hundred before you retire."

"Maybe, but people change. Grow. Look for different adventures. I love what I do, but I'm not sure I want to do this my whole life. Don't you ever think of doing something a little less dangerous? To settle down with a regular nine-to-five job and live a normal life? Or is normal simply overrated?"

He tried to gauge her response in the firelight. He knew how hard it was for people like them to have anything close to a normal life. Just to become a marshal was fiercely competitive, and once you were in, there was no typical day, other than the fact that it was going to be long and grueling.

"I don't know," she said. "My sister just had a baby. She stays home with her three kids, has what I'd call a normal life, and loves every minute of it."

"Then tell me what you do for fun, besides chasing after bad guys."

She let out a swoosh of air. "Now that's a tough one. I like to run. Hang out with my sister's family. Their kids are still young, but definitely old enough to spoil."

"I bet they love you."

"Probably not as much as I love them. I'm also involved in a nonprofit that is working to stop sex trafficking in the area. That might not be fun, but it is fulfilling."

"What about rest?" he asked.

"Rest? I know God had a reason for that day of rest, but I struggle to find time for it." She shifted slightly and caught his gaze. "Once again, you've angled the conversation back to me. What about you? What do you do for fun besides eat chowder and dream of opening a tackle shop?"

He let out a low laugh. "Working out and motorcycling. I have a bike and have found it's a great way to wind down."

"Luke and I used to take at least one trip every summer on a bike with a group from church."

"Have you taken any trips recently?"

"No. When you're not a couple anymore, it's easy to get lost in the shuffle."

"I'm sorry."

"It's a journey. I'm coming to realize that sometimes life is hard, and that's okay. I've had to give myself permission to grieve, especially on days like today that somehow manage to bring back all the memories—both good and bad."

"There's some great places to ride outside Seattle. The Chinook Pass Scenic Byway, the Yakima River Canyon—"

"Now that's not a bad idea. You could always

be a guide. Do tours, rent out bikes and fishing equipment. I can definitely see you doing that rather than standing behind a cash register selling worms."

"Maybe, but it really doesn't matter. I'm not exactly ready to retire. Not yet anyway."

"Even after this fiasco?"

He chuckled. "Even after this."

He yawned and she followed suit.

"You're making me tired."

"Maybe that's good," he said. "I'll take the first watch. Tomorrow's going to be a long day."

She looked around the room. "And something tells me it's also going to be a long night."

Water continued to drip in various spots around the room, but at least the spot they'd chosen was still dry.

He added a couple more logs to the fire. "I'll lean against my bag. You can lean against me."

For a second he wanted to take his words back. Somehow the invitation seemed too . . . intimate. "I'm just trying to ensure we both are at least somewhat comfortable and warm."

"It's fine." She smiled. "And, Jonas, thank you."

Getting comfortable, though, proved to be an effort in futility. He settled in on the hard, wooden floor that wasn't exactly even, while she snuggled up next to him.

A minute later, she was softly snoring.

He was glad she'd be able to forget the day, even if it was only for a few hours. Glad she'd been able to share with him about the significance of today. But why hadn't he been able to talk about Felicia? Just when he thought he was past everything that had happened, he found himself frozen when trying to talk about her. Memories of their last encounter blurred his thoughts.

He'd met Felicia outside her physical therapy class that afternoon. He'd planned to give her a ride home, hoping she might agree to stop for lunch on the way. Nothing had turned out the way he'd expected.

"How did it go?" he asked her, knowing how ready she was to lose the wheelchair.

She started down the extra-wide hallway beside him. "My therapist said I'm making progress."

"That's great! I talked with a guy I met down in the cafeteria. His name is Matt Johnson, and he works with some cutting-edge technology for amputees."

"Stop trying to fix me, Jonas." She huffed, picking up speed as they headed toward her room. "Like it or not, this is how I'm going to be the rest of my life."

He hurried to keep up with her. "But there are so many advances. I've been reading about people without limbs who have climbed Mt. Everest, played professional baseball, people who've become runners, even pilots and airplane—"

"Enough." She stopped in the hallway and angled her chair toward him. "You're not the one who lost a leg."

"And I can't imagine how terrifying it's been." He crouched down in front of her and took her hands. "But you're not alone. I promised I'd be here every step of the way with you, and I meant it. You can't give up—"

"I'm not giving up, but you keep thinking you can fix this. That you can somehow make it okay. But you can't, because things will never be the same again. I'll never have two legs." She blew out a breath. "Before all this, I was training for the Ironman."

"There was a double amputee who completed—"

"Stop. You don't get it. I don't care how many people finished, or ran, or whatever. This is me. I lost my leg. I'll never be able to compete like I did before and nothing you can do will ever fix that."

"I get it, but while a lot has changed, how I feel for you hasn't." He caught the distant look in her eyes and straightened his posture. He took a step backward. "What about us?"

She shook her head. "I'm sorry. This is something I have to do on my own."

"I'm not going to let you push me away."

"Don't come back, Jonas."

"Why? This doesn't change anything for me. I still want to marry you."

"Do you? I'll never know if you're just marrying me because you feel sorry for me, or if you really love me."

"You know I love you. You know I want to marry you."

"I'll never be sure. Why didn't you ask me before the accident? Why are you suddenly wanting to ask me now?"

"Because I love you—"

"No, it's because you think you can make me whole, but I have to learn to be whole without a leg. Without you." She avoided his gaze. "I'm sorry, but I'm leaving."

"What are you saying?"

"I'm moving back to Texas to live with my parents. There's a rehabilitation center near their house that has agreed to work with me."

"Felicia—"

"It's over, Jonas."

"You don't mean that."

"I'm sorry, but I do."

"Felicia, please."

Tears were streaming down her face, but he recognized the stubborn set of her jaw and the emptiness in her eyes as she looked at him. "I really am sorry."

She spun her wheelchair around and rolled back down the hallway toward her room, the wheel he'd tried to fix still squeaking.

He couldn't fix it. Just like he couldn't fix her.

A crack of lightning brought him back to the present.

Eighteen months had passed, and he still wondered what had happened to her. If he ever allowed himself to fall in love again, he'd decided it was going to be someone with a normal job without the high stress of his work. Like a kindergarten teacher or a gym instructor. Someone who he didn't have to worry about not coming home at night. Or maybe his career choice meant falling in love and getting married simply wasn't going to happen.

He shifted his gaze to Madison, who was still sound asleep. He resisted the urge to brush a strand of hair off her forehead, not missing the irony in the unwelcome thought. He'd chosen this life because it gave him a sense of purpose. Made him feel as if he was doing something positive in the world every day by making the world a better place. He had also learned that he didn't have to have someone in his life in order to be complete. Maybe that would change one day, but for now, his life was fine the way it was.

He must have dozed off for a while because the sound of something creaking outside woke him. The step. He shook Madison gently, then signaled for her to be quiet when she opened her eyes. Apparently, he'd been wrong about Barrick.

TEN

Madison scrambled to her feet at Jonas's silent nudge, the heaviness of sleep gone in an instant. The rain had finally stopped, and the light coming in from the window told her that the sun had just begun its ascent above the horizon. But her only thought at the moment was that Barrick was out there.

Jonas moved to the window, then signaled for her to cover the area behind the door. She grabbed a thick log from beside the fire, then moved into position, pulse racing, her body geared up to fight. There might be two of them against one of him, but not having her weapon put her at a tactical disadvantage. On the other hand, they'd trained together, making it easier for her to know what Jonas was thinking. The intruder couldn't know for certain that they were in here.

A second later, the handle jiggled. When the door didn't open, someone tried to kick it in. The chair she'd jammed beneath the handle last night rattled but held. They kicked against the door again. This time, the entire frame shook. A third time, the chair cracked, and the door flew open. Jonas fired off a shot while she caught the bottom edge of the door with her boot, stopped its momentum, then kicked it closed. The man cried out in pain.

"It's him." Jonas grabbed a piece of the chair and shattered one of the windows, keeping his body behind the frame as he took aim and fired off three quick shots.

Barrick responded with three of his own shots from outside, two that managed to penetrate the door and slam into the back wall.

"Do you see him?" she asked.

"He's retreated to the tree line."

For now.

She stood still in the middle of the cabin. The storm was gone and now an eerie silence seemed to surround them.

"I'm pretty sure I hit him," Jonas said.

"How bad?"

"I couldn't tell, but we need to get out there and track him down."

"We're sitting ducks," she said.

"I know. How many rounds do you think he has left?"

She searched her memory. "Probably nine."

She glanced again at the window. If they left the cabin, he'd have a direct shot at them, but they couldn't stay holed up there. Something on the porch caught Madison's eye. "There's blood here."

"He was definitely hit," he said. "He was also

out of his handcuffs." Jonas grabbed his back-pack. "I'll cover us while we run across the porch, right, toward the back of the house."

She nodded, pulled open the door, and ran. The pop, pop, pop of Jonas's pistol echoed through the morning air. Barrick fired back. She caught her breath at the back of the cabin as Jonas ran up to her.

"You okay?"

"Yeah." Madison turned around in the soggy ground and studied him. "Jonas, wait, your arm."

"What?" Blood ran down his arm, right below his shoulder. "It's just a graze. I'm fine."

She reached up to check it, but he stopped her.

"I'll clean it up later. We need to go after him. Now."

They stayed low as they ran across the grass toward the tree line behind the cabin, hyperaware of any movement. Madison studied the ground in front of them. With all the rain last night, it would be hard for him to hide his tracks. The injury from Jonas's bullet was another disadvantage that would slow him down. What they would have to be careful about was another ambush.

"Jonas, I've got something." A breath of relief shot out of Madison's lungs as Jonas crouched down beside her. "After last night's storm I wouldn't expect to find fresh prints from a hiker on this trail, so this has to be him. Look here. He tried to miss this patch of mud, but he hit it with the heel of his boot."

"You're right. That's got to be him."

"He's headed north out of here." She studied the trail, making sure she didn't miss anything. "So you think he gave up on us?"

"I certainly would at this point."

"And this time I agree."

They paused by a cluster of trees to catch their breath and Jonas offered her another power bar. She took it but couldn't help but wish for a large espresso with an extra shot of caffeine to go with it. She needed it today, if only to warm her up. But that would have to wait. They had a fugitive to track down.

Even though they'd found a trail after about an hour of searching, Madison was worried they were going in circles or at the very least going deeper into the forest. Still, she was certain they were close on Barrick's tail despite the fact that he was trying his best to leave no trace. The rain had made that impossible.

They just had to catch up with him.

"How's your arm?" she asked, breaking the silence that had settled between them.

"The bleeding seems to have stopped and the pain is minimal."

She glanced at him. "What are you thinking?"

"Just going over in my mind what we read

103

in his file. We know he's violent, but he's also charismatic and manipulative."

"Which won't do him any good out here. He's a city boy, out of his element, and his options are limited."

"True, but he has spent some time hunting. I don't think we can totally dismiss his ability to survive temporarily out here. And if he runs into people, he has the ability to manipulate the situation to his advantage."

Madison frowned. "Then we need to get to him first."

But where was he?

A scream pierced the morning air.

Madison froze momentarily, trying to determine which direction the cry had come from, then rushed down the trail, with Jonas right behind her. At a bend in the trail, Jonas pulled out his gun. A woman in her thirties, dark hair pulled up into a ponytail, was hovering over a man wearing only a pair of briefs. An orange jumpsuit was jammed into the bushes.

The woman put her hands up and stumbled backward. "Please, please don't shoot us."

Madison held up her hand. "We're US Marshals, and we're here to help. Where's the man who did this to you?"

"I don't know. He took off running."

Jonas handed Madison his backpack. "Stay here and help them."

Madison knelt down beside them. "Can you tell me what happened?"

"He . . . he came at me from behind." She was nearly hyperventilating.

Madison put her arm on the woman's shoulder. "What's your name?"

"Amy."

"And your partner?"

"My husband, Keith."

"Good. Amy, I need you to take a deep breath. In and out. Slowly. You're going to be okay. Keith, I don't want you to move, but can you talk to me?"

"Yeah." His eyes were open, but there was a large bruise forming on his cheek. "I think I'm okay. He just knocked the wind out of me and my head hurts."

Madison pulled out the first aid kit from the pack. "Did he hit you?"

"He punched him in the face and stomach," Amy said. "What's a prisoner doing out here?"

"Plane crash," Madison said. "We were on a prisoner transport."

"A prison transport?" A look of fear registered in her eyes. "Are there other prisoners out here?"

"No. He was the only one."

The only one who survived.

"We're trying to track him down. Can you tell me exactly what happened?"

"I didn't even hear him coming. He grabbed

me, held a gun to my head, and told me not to make a sound, then forced my husband to take off his clothes. He put the clothes on, snatched our backpacks, then he just ran."

"What was in your backpacks?"

Amy rubbed the bridge of her nose with her fingers. "Just basic supplies for a day trip. Food and water, sunscreen, Keith's phone, insect repellent, and a first aid kit. Stuff like that."

"What about weapons?"

"My husband had a knife and a gear repair kit." Amy blew out a sharp breath. "He also has our car keys."

Madison carefully checked the husband over for injuries, still aware of her surroundings, but Barrick was long gone. He'd got what he needed, a clean set of clothes so he no longer looked like a prisoner, more supplies, and the keys to a vehicle.

"What about a map?" Madison asked.

"There was one in my pack, but I have a grid map in my pocket. He didn't take that, or my phone."

"So he could find his way out," she said.

Amy nodded. "He left heading east along this trail. If he keeps going that way, he'll hit one of the main roads leading out of here."

"How far?" Madison asked.

"We're about, I don't know, an hour from where we parked our car." Amy glanced at her husband. "What are we supposed to do if he takes our car?"

"As soon as we get somewhere with cell coverage, we'll send someone to help you," Madison said. "I'll leave you with the rest of our food, but hopefully you won't have to wait long."

"Barrick's moving quickly," Jonas said after doubling back. "I think we both need to go after him."

Keith moved to get up. "I think I can start walking out of here."

Jonas helped the husband to his feet. "Are you sure?"

"Yeah, I think so. I feel like I've been hit by a brick, but no dizziness or shortness of breath."

Jonas dug a pair of shorts and a T-shirt out of his backpack. "It won't keep you particularly warm, but it will help. And you can take my jacket."

"I couldn't do that."

"Yes, you can. It's fine." He removed his badge then handed over the jacket.

"What if he comes back?" Amy asked.

"I don't think he will," Madison said. "If he thought you were worth something to him, he wouldn't have let you go. He knows we're right behind. At this point just be thankful you're alive."

"We could use your map though," Jonas said.

"Of course." Amy pulled out the map from

her back pocket. "Do you even know where you are?"

Madison glanced at Jonas, then shook her head. Amy handed her the map. "Welcome to Idaho."

They parted ways with the hikers before heading down a trail. Madison jogged beside Jonas, hoping they could catch up with Barrick and unable to forget that the man who had killed someone with a shiv now had both a gun and a knife. She'd seen the desperation in the man's eyes when he'd tackled her near the river. As far as she was concerned, he'd killed before, and he'd kill again.

"So much for being creative," she said. "He decided to do things the old-fashioned way."

"So what would you do now if you were him?" Jonas asked.

It was a scenario she'd played out a hundred times. Get into the fugitive's mind. Figure out their next move. "Time is crucial. Get as far away as possible as quick as possible. He'll take the car, but not for very long. He knows we're behind him, so he also knows we'll probably expect him to take the car."

"His options?"

"He drives it until he can find another car." She shrugged. "Or he could hitchhike. People are trusting for the most part. He's no longer in his prison uniform, which means he has the ability to blend in. He also doesn't particularly look like a felon, which is another plus for him. And because we're so isolated, he knows it's going to take law enforcement time to get here."

Jonas held up his hand for her to stop.

"What is it?" she asked.

"Nothing. I thought I heard something, but I think I'm just getting paranoid."

Something he had every right to be. They kept moving at a slow jog while she waded through possible scenarios in her head. What she did know was that Barrick would do whatever it took to ensure he wasn't caught again.

"What if Barrick decided not to head to the end of the trail like we're assuming?" she asked.

"What do you mean?"

"I glanced at this map." She stopped at the edge of a clearing, pulling out Amy's map. "There should be a ranch located just across this valley at the edge of the forest. I can see a couple out-buildings, and it looks like there's a trail leading that direction ahead. What if he went there?"

"It is closer, and if nothing else, they should have cell service, so I can call for backup."

They followed the trail toward the ranch through a narrow ridge with outcroppings of rocks on either side.

Someone shouted from above them. "I've got my rifle aimed at you. Weapons on the ground, then hands in the air and don't move."

Madison glanced at Jonas, then hesitated as

three more men stepped out of the brush in front of them, each one armed.

The tallest, heavily bearded and aiming his rifle at her heart, rested his finger on the trigger. "Hands in the air now, both of you, or I swear, I'll shoot you."

ELEVEN

Madison felt a shot of adrenaline rush through her as the men circled tighter around them, each one holding his weapon steady on her and Jonas. Somehow their shortcut had just landed them in the middle of a hornet's nest.

"I mean what I said," the man repeated. "Hands in the air or I will shoot."

She studied the face of the man who was clearly in charge, then slowly raised her hands. Jonas set his gun on the ground.

"I don't know what's going on here," Jonas said, "but you need to know that we're with the US Marshals—"

"We already know who you are, and you certainly aren't marshals."

She glanced at Jonas, trying to put the pieces together. "We're US Marshals, searching for a man who escaped a prisoner flight transport after a plane crash. We tracked him here."

"An escaped convict?"

Madison nodded. "Have you seen him?"

A second man cocked his rifle and took a step closer to her. "I'd say our escaped convicts are right in front of us, Simon. There were two on the plane. And his descriptions match perfectly."

"Wait a minute," Jonas said. "Whose descriptions?"

"We were just paid a visit by US Marshal Jonas Quinn, who told us about the plane crash and how you'd escaped," Simon said.

Madison fought the sick feeling bubbling inside her. So that's what Barrick had done. Used the papers in her backpack and passed himself off as a federal marshal. What had Jonas said about Barrick? He was charismatic and manipulative? His evaluation had clearly been spot-on.

"We're not the prisoners," she said, "and every minute we spend arguing with you gives him more time to get farther away. His name is Damon Barrick, and he murdered three people. If he said he was a lawman, he lied to you."

"And we can prove it," Jonas said, slowly reaching for his backpack.

Simon frowned and cocked his gun. "He told me you'd say that."

"He was lying," Jonas said. "And you're making a big mistake. Is he still here?"

"My son's taking him to the sheriff's office right now so they can coordinate the search. Guess they won't have to do that now." Simon spit. "Told me to be sure to call him if you happened to show up, which I'm about to do. From what he said, the entire state's looking for you."

"He won't be coming back for us, and he's not

112

headed to the sheriff's office," Madison said. "He played you and is long gone by now."

"We'll see about that." Simon grabbed her arm and pulled her to a horse that was tied up just around the corner of the trail with three other horses. "Hope you can ride. Phil, tie them up so they don't do anything foolish like escape again."

It was less than half a mile to the ranch house that was located on the far side of the ridge. None of the men said anything while they rode. Any questions from Madison went unanswered, making her even more irritated. If they lost Barrick now, picking up his trail again would be next to impossible.

A middle-aged woman wearing jeans, a flannel shirt, and cowboy boots met them on the front porch of the two-story house nestled next to a grove of trees and a large barn. "You shouldn't have brought them here."

"You've got nothing to worry about." Simon climbed down off his horse, then ordered the two of them to get down. "Once I get ahold of the marshal, all of this will be over."

"So he's not answering his phone?" Jonas asked.

Simon frowned. "Cell reception out here's spotty, especially with these storms we've been having. I'll get ahold of him."

Madison tried to keep her frustration at bay.

They were getting nowhere with these people. Then a new plan popped into her head. "How old is your son?" Madison asked.

"Eighteen, but he knows this land like the back of his hand," the woman said. "They took one of our vehicles, convinced you'd both headed toward town."

"Linda—"

"There is something you need to understand." Madison cut Simon off, then leaned forward and caught the woman's eye. "I don't know what he told you, but Damon Barrick is no lawman, and if he has your son—"

"Enough," Simon shouted. "This is what's going to happen. You're both going to sit down on this porch, shut up, and we're going to wait for the marshal to return. The rest of you can get back to work. I've got them covered."

The men nodded, then headed off the porch toward the barn.

"Ma'am, I was serious when I said your son is in danger." Madison ignored Simon's glare. "That man who was here, Damon Barrick, has already murdered three people. It's why he was in prison and why he was being transported to Denver."

"Go back inside, Linda, and don't listen to them. They're trying to scare you."

"And it's working." Linda hesitated in the doorway. "Simon, if they're telling the truth, then Will's in danger—"

"He's fine."

"Will's your son?" Madison asked.

Linda took a step forward. "He's my son, and if he's in danger—"

Simon locked eyes with his wife. "I said, enough."

Linda shook her head at her husband. "No. What if they're right?"

"They're not. He had the paperwork proving who he was. You heard him. He told us there was a plane crash yesterday and that the two of them escaped in the aftermath. We're not falling for their games."

Madison gauged her words carefully. "Barrick can be charming in order to get what he wants. It's what makes him so dangerous. I don't want your son to be one of his victims."

Linda's face paled as she disregarded her husband's orders and sat down on the padded chair across from them. "You're telling me my son is out there with some . . . some cold-blooded killer?"

"Yes."

"He could use him as a hostage."

"It's very possible."

"Linda—" Simon's voice sounded a little less confident.

"Sir, we can prove to you who we are," Jonas said. "Look in my backpack. Barrick's file—and his photo—are in there. I was supposed to give it to the agents in Denver when we handed him off to them, but he escaped after the crash with my partner's backpack."

"He gave us all the proof we needed. We saw his marshal papers."

"Those were my papers," Madison said.

Her jaw tensed as she caught the panic in Linda's eyes. Barrick had to have known his plan would eventually fall apart, but all he'd needed was a vehicle and a good head start. And he already had both.

"He lied to you." Madison leaned forward. "Every minute you keep us here is another minute your son is in danger. Barrick planned all of this. Knew if we fought here among ourselves it would buy him more time to get away. It's a game to him, and you're playing right into his hand. Just open up the bag and look at the blue file."

Simon scowled and started to object again, but Linda grabbed the pack, unzipped it, and pulled out the file.

"Open it up," Jonas said. "His photo is right there."

"Simon, this is his photo. They're telling the truth." Linda moved in front of her husband and shoved the papers into his hands. "Look for yourself. He lied to us and now our son . . . You put our son's life in danger."

"Linda—"

"No. You need to let them go. It's my son out

116

there and I won't lose him because you were too stubborn to listen. You were a fool to believe him. And now, if anything happens to Will—"

"Ma'am," Madison said. "For now we just need to worry about finding your son. Do you have another vehicle we can use?"

Simon stepped up beside them. "Yes, but I'll have to fill it up with fuel. It shouldn't take more than a few minutes."

"How much of a head start did they get?" Jonas asked.

"By now . . . fifteen, maybe twenty minutes." Simon untied the bindings around both marshals' hands.

"Which means we need to get moving," Jonas said, stretching out his arms. "Have you tried to call your son?"

"I've tried calling both of them, but they're not answering. They're probably in a dead zone."

Madison caught the man's worried expression, wanting to believe his explanation as much as he did, but she knew the truth. Barrick wasn't coming back, and Will's life was in danger.

"We need to call both our boss and the local authorities and give them a heads-up on what's going on," Jonas said, pulling out his phone. "Good. I've finally got service. We're going to need a BOLO out on your vehicle and Barrick's photo sent out to every law enforcement in the county."

"And if I can borrow a cell phone, I'll call our boss," Madison said.

Simon motioned to his wife. "Give her your phone, Linda."

"It's charging in the house, but I'll go get it."

Simon pulled his own phone out of his back pocket as Linda hurried into the house. He turned toward Jonas. "I'll send you the sheriff's personal number."

"How far away is town?" Jonas asked.

"It's fifty-five miles from here. We're on the outskirts of the Frank Church–River of No Return Wilderness and there's nothing but wilderness to the south and west."

"We're going to need a guide."

Simon nodded. "Anything you need.

Jonas stepped away when someone answered.

"And while the two of you make your calls, I'll go get my truck."

Linda returned and handed Madison her phone, then offered her a smile. "I could get you some food."

Madison punched in her boss's number. "I appreciate the offer, but we don't have time to wait."

"When's the last time you ate?" Linda asked.

Madison hesitated as she waited for the call to connect. "Besides airplane peanuts and a power bar?"

"It will take Simon a few minutes to get

the truck gassed up. The least I can do is send something with you. I've got some roast left over from last night."

"We're fine—"

"I know, but I'm not, and I need something to do with my hands. It won't take more than a few minutes to whip up a couple sandwiches."

Madison nodded as she was prompted to leave a voice message.

"Michaels, this is Madison. I'm guessing you're already alerted to the fact that our plane went down in the Salmon-Challis National Forest. We just now have cell phone access. Jonas and I are fine, but the pilots are dead as well as Paul Riley. Damon Barrick is currently on the run. Please call us as soon as you can on this number."

She hung up, frustrated by yet another delay. She was beginning to understand the woman's need to do something. Feeling restless herself, Madison stepped into the house to find Linda. She found the woman in the kitchen. "What can I do while we wait for the vehicle?" she asked.

Linda looked up from her spot by the fridge. "Would you mind slicing the bread?"

"Of course not."

"I want to apologize for my husband." Linda busied herself by pulling roast and cheese and condiments out of the refrigerator. "He's very protective of his family and this ranch."

Madison grabbed a knife from the counter and

began slicing the bread. "You were both only trying to do what you thought was right. I understand."

"You're very kind." The woman continued assembling the sandwiches. "There's something you need to know about my son."

Madison paused and looked up at her.

"He's resourceful and intelligent, but he's also autistic."

"I know something about that," Madison said.

"He is high-functioning, and most of the time people don't even really notice, but he does have some social and communication skills issues. Simon never should have let him get involved." Linda caught Madison's gaze. "I need you to find my son. Please. Promise me you'll find my son."

"I will." Madison looked over when Linda's phone pinged, then she snatched it off the counter. "I'm sorry. This is my boss." She stepped into the living room and answered the call. "Michaels?"

"Madison, our search and rescue team just found the plane. Are the two of you okay?"

"Yes, but we've got a problem."

"Besides two dead pilots and a dead prisoner?"

"Barrick's got a possible hostage."

There was a short pause on the line. "Where is he now?"

"I don't know where he is, but I know where he's been." She stood in front of the large windows overlooking an incredible view of the mountains. "He managed to escape the crash and made it here to a local ranch, where he posed to the owners as a marshal. He's headed toward Claymore Falls with their son in one of their vehicles."

"I'll put the US Marshals office in Boise on alert, but have you been in contact with local authorities?"

"Jonas is talking with them right now. We're about to head out."

"Keep me updated on what's going on, and I'll work on things from my end."

"Use Jonas's number from now on. We'll be in touch with any updated information."

Simon burst through the front door as she hung up. "I've got the truck ready."

"Good. We need to move."

Jonas stepped into the house behind him. "The sheriff's heading toward Deadwood Crossing where we'll meet him. If we're lucky, we'll find Barrick and Will somewhere in the middle."

A minute later, they were squeezing into the single cab truck.

Simon turned the keys in the ignition and offered his apologies. "She might not be pretty on the outside, but she's a workhorse."

"As long as it gets us there, that's all that matters," Madison said, maneuvering her legs to avoid the stick shift.

The scenery along the winding dirt road was stunning. Almost enough to momentarily make her forget that she wasn't here for the view.

"Madison?" Jonas brushed his hand against her arm. "You okay?"

"Just frustrated and trying to figure out how this happened. If I hadn't let him get my pack and my weapon—"

"You'd probably be dead, and even if you had managed to avoid that happening, he would have simply come up with plan B."

"And then there's my sister."

"You need to let her know what's happening before this hits the major news cycles." He handed her his phone. "Call her."

She nodded, knowing he was right, then punched in her number. The call automatically went to voice mail.

"Danielle, this is Maddie. I want you to know that I'm safe, and there's nothing to worry about, but there's been a hiccup in our plans. I'll call again when I have a chance."

"A hiccup?" Jonas asked, as she handed the phone back to him.

"She worries. A lot."

He laughed. "At least she knows you're safe."

"I was supposed to be home tonight. We had a family dinner planned. It's my niece's birthday. She's turning six."

"I'm sorry you're going to miss it."

"Me too, though it isn't the first time. My family understands, for the most part."

"She's got to think you have a super-cool job."

"More like she worries about me constantly."

"I think it's a super-cool job."

"Funny."

Simon's phone rang on the dashboard.

"Why don't you get that," Simon said. "It's probably the sheriff."

Jonas grabbed the phone and put the call on speaker. "Sheriff? What's going on?"

"We just found Simon's vehicle."

TWELVE

W here are you?" Jonas asked.
"We're at the number seventeen mile marker on Highway 101," the sheriff answered. "Half a mile after the turnoff."

Jonas glanced at Simon. "How far away are we?"

"We're about two minutes away," Simon said. "I need to know if my son's okay."

Jonas caught the panic in Simon's voice. "Sheriff, did you hear that?"

"I did, and I'm sorry, but there's no one in the truck," the sheriff said.

"What do you mean there's no one there?" Simon asked. "My son was in that vehicle!"

"I realize that. We're doing an initial perimeter sweep of the area to see if we can track them down."

Silence hung on the line for a few seconds, until Jonas finally spoke again. "Make sure your men know who we're dealing with. Barrick is armed and dangerous. Call me back if you have any updates."

"Roger that."

Simon pressed down on the accelerator as

he flew down the gravel road. "If I would have questioned the man more, or taken a closer look at the paperwork he had—"

"This isn't your fault," Jonas said. "We'll find him."

"You don't know that."

"Your wife told me that your son's extremely resourceful and knows this land well," Madison said. "That could give him a huge advantage."

"Is that a nice way of telling me what his odds are against a murderer?"

"Of course not, I just meant—"

"I know what you meant. And yes. He can hold his own in most situations." Simon gripped the steering wheel. "I'm more worried about who the other guy is and what my son is up against right now. Do you think he's desperate enough to murder someone else?"

Jonas held on to the armrest as they accelerated. "I think he's just been given a chance to run, and we stand in the way of his possible freedom."

"Making my son first in that line."

"Yes. But it's more likely that his goal right now is focusing on getting as far away from here as fast as he can."

"Which means he's going to need another vehicle," Madison said.

"I don't know," Simon said. "There aren't a lot of cars that come past here."

Jonas braced himself against the window as

Simon made a sharp turn onto the main road.

"We're almost there."

He understood the man's frustration, because he was dealing with his own. But as much as Jonas wanted to, he could make no guarantees that Will would be okay.

A minute later, they caught sight of the sheriff department's vehicles parked along the edge of the road, lights flashing.

Simon slammed on the brakes, jumped out of the vehicle, and ran straight for the sheriff. "Where's my son? He's got to be out here somewhere."

"Simon—"

"My son was in that truck, Sheriff. He can't be that far."

"I know, and right now I need you to listen to me. There's already a search underway. We will find your son, but we're going to need help." The sheriff turned to Jonas and Madison and quickly made formal introductions. "It's not often that we have US Marshals show up, and I have to say I'm glad you're here."

"And it's not often that transport planes crash in the middle of your forest and we're forced to chase down a fugitive," Jonas said. "We appreciate your cooperation."

"I've been on the phone with your boss and he's updated me on the case. Anything you need, you've got. We need to find this guy."

"Agreed," Madison said.

"I've got four of my officers doing a perimeter sweep, but I'd like to show you what happened."

They followed Sheriff Hill to where the front bumper of Simon's other truck had smashed into a tree off the side of the road and both the driver's and passenger-side doors had been left open.

"It looks like the driver lost control and swerved off the road."

"The air bags weren't deployed. We think it happened on purpose."

"You think my son caused the wreck?" Simon asked.

"That's what my initial investigation of the crash site points to. There are no skid marks until right before the crash, making it look as if the driver was caught off guard. We believe Will probably pulled on the steering wheel, then made his escape."

Jonas walked around the truck. The sheriff's evaluation seemed logical, but where were Barrick and Will?

Madison interrupted his thoughts. "There's blood on the driver's seat."

"It's also along the driver's side window where the glass is broken," the sheriff said.

"Were there any weapons in the truck?" Jonas asked.

"We keep a handgun in the glove compartment," said Simon.

Jonas popped it open. The space was empty.

"I know my boy. If he realized that man wasn't who he said he was, he'd find a way to escape, even if it meant crashing the truck."

Madison backed away from the vehicle and turned toward the thick tree line. "There are two sets of footprints leading into the woods, but it doesn't look like they were running together."

"My men are following them right now. Initially, they did a swift search of the location, but so far they haven't found either of them."

Jonas turned back to the sheriff. "What kind of backup can you get us?"

"We've got an APB out to all surrounding counties. I've also called in our backcountry team who patrol this area regularly, and if we need it, we can call in our search and rescue team. They're volunteers, but they work closely with our department and know what they're doing."

"Good." Madison nodded. "Put them on alert, though I personally am leery about sending civilians into a possible hostage situation."

"I understand, but I'll have them ready." The sheriff's radio buzzed and he picked it up. "Hold on. What have you got, Emmett?"

"We've swept the initial perimeter, and we lost the trail."

"Then I want you to come back here. We need to implement a broader sweep."

"Copy that."

The sheriff laid out a map on the hood of his car. "Technically, the two of you are in charge, which is fine, because I for one would definitely like your input."

"Good, but you are the one who knows the land. Where have they already searched?"

"On the map—here and here." The sheriff pointed to the immediate vicinity around the crash.

"You're right. We need to increase the search perimeters toward town," Madison said, pointing to the map, "as well as set up roadblocks at these three locations."

"Agreed. Consider it done."

"What about air support?" Jonas asked.

"I can set it up right now, and even get our K9 unit out here."

"Good."

"Don't you think you should look farther off the road?" Simon asked.

"We can't count it out at this point," Jonas said, "but I have a feeling Barrick isn't prepared to head back into the wilderness. He's looking for a way out, which is going to mean staying as close to the main road as possible and trying to flag down another vehicle.

"We'll work in teams," he continued, turning back toward Madison and Sheriff Hill, "with the two of us splitting up so we're with someone who is familiar with the terrain."

The sheriff handed them each a radio. "We'll keep in contact with these."

"If they're still on foot, we can estimate that they're no more than two miles ahead of us," Jonas said. "Barrick is going to stick to the main roads, so that will hopefully limit the direction."

"If he manages to flag someone down, though, we'll lose him," Simon said.

"That's where the roadblocks come in," Madison said. "We make sure he can't leave the area, and that anyone coming through is aware of what's going on."

"What about my son's phone?" he asked. "Isn't there a way to track it?"

"We've already been running a search, but it's off, so there's no way we can track it."

"What about the phone Barrick stole from the couple on the trail?" Madison asked.

"We haven't been able to pick up a signal from that either, though we are working to get the phone records. It's still possible he made a call at some point."

"Any word on the couple?" Jonas asked.

"We had one of our officers pick them up. They're taking the man to the hospital as a precaution, but they should be fine."

"Good."

"We'll head out now. Johnson, you're with Deputy US Marshal Quinn. I'll go with Deputy US Marshal James. Stay in radio contact."

Beads of perspiration formed across Jonas's forehead as he headed out with the deputy. There were a lot of variables at play in this search, but at least it was still daylight. Once darkness hit, finding someone out here was going to be nearly impossible. And Will—while the evidence showed that the young man was smart, so was his adversary. In the meantime, they'd driven four miles ahead and now were doubling back on foot, with teams searching parallel to the road.

Jonas let out a sharp huff of air as he and his partner combed the ground for clues.

"What do you think his plan is?" the deputy asked him.

"It's hard to even guess. We know this wasn't a planned escape. Everything he's doing is spur of the moment."

"Which makes it harder to anticipate his next step."

"Exactly," said Jonas. "Running from the law is complicated."

"Especially, I would think, if the convict's hoping to leave the country for some tropical isle where no one would find him."

The deputy was right. Reality was rarely that simple.

Jonas scanned the tree line, looking for movement. Listening for anything that sounded out of place in the thick forest surrounding them.

Will would want the authorities to hear him, and yet if he was hiding from Barrick, he'd have to bide his time. Barrick, on the other hand, didn't want to be discovered. His main goal would be getting as far away from here as possible, as fast as possible. What bothered Jonas the most was that Barrick was desperate, and desperation made men even more lethal.

"A US Marshal. Sounds like an exciting job."

Deputy Johnson's comment pulled Jonas out of his thoughts.

"Yeah. Sometimes it's a bit too exciting."

"A plane crash and now a fugitive chase." The deputy shook his head. "We don't have a lot of action like that around here. Definitely not many fugitives. More missing hikers."

"Hmm, well, where would you go if you were Barrick?"

The deputy rubbed the back of his neck. "What kinds of supplies does he have?"

Jonas smiled. The man was asking the right questions.

"A backpack from my partner and two from a couple of hikers."

"What about a gun?"

"Yes."

"And in the packs?"

"The hikers had your typical supplies for a day trip. Food and water. A map and compass, a gear repair kit, and a first aid kit. On top of that were basics like sunscreen, matches, and an emergency blanket."

Even for those who knew this land, this search was going to be a challenge. "Even if we bring in air support," the deputy said, "most of this wilderness foliage is so thick, it makes the infrared sensors useless."

"But he doesn't know these woods, and even with a map I'd think it would be hard to navigate," Jonas said. "What can you tell me about this area?"

"There's close to two and a half million acres of backcountry. And it's full of secluded habitats for mountain lions and gray wolves."

"And this is your backyard," Jonas said.

"Born and raised here. You're looking at everything from mountain ranges to steep canyons to whitewater rapids—and of course forest covering most of the area."

Jonas stopped and held up his hand. A flash of color to the right caught his eye.

"What was Will wearing?" Jonas asked.

"According to the information I received, jeans, and a red hoodie, and boots."

"There's something at two o'clock," Jonas said.

He saw it again. A slight flash of color that didn't match the brush. Will might want to be found, but if he was out here and alone and hiding from Barrick, he couldn't risk being found by the wrong person.

They crept forward quietly until they spotted it. A red shirt was stuck beneath the brush.

"What do you think happened?" Johnson asked.

"Looks like he shed his bright hoodie so he could blend in better."

"Which will make it harder for us to find him."

Jonas scanned the surrounding area. "But it goes with the assumption that he's still out here on his own."

"Jonas." The deputy stopped and pointed at the hoodie. There was blood on the sleeve.

"It could be from the accident. There was a lot of glass. And we saw blood at the scene."

It didn't mean the injury was serious.

His radio crackled and Jonas grabbed it out of his pocket.

It was Madison. "We just found Will."

THIRTEEN

It had already been forty-five minutes since they brought Will back to the sheriff's office in town, hoping to get some information from him that would help them find Barrick. But so far, the young man wasn't talking. Instead he was sitting in the middle of the large office, staring at the desk.

Madison stopped in front of Jonas and Simon. "Anything?"

Jonas shook his head. "We still can't get anything out of him."

"I've updated Michaels on what's happening," Madison said. "He's not happy that Barrick slipped away again."

"Trust me. Neither am I." Jonas folded his hands across his chest. "Will's pretty shaken. He's barely said a dozen words to his father, and I think I intimidate him."

"He gets this way when he's stressed," Will's father said. "He shuts down."

"Can you tell me what helps get him through it?" Madison asked.

"His mother always can reach him, and she's on her way, but it's going to be at least an hour."

They didn't have an hour.

"I think we're going about this all wrong," she said. "I have a friend whose daughter is autistic, and I spend a lot of time with her. Will needs to be somewhere quiet in a situation like this. With your permission, Simon, I could try talking to him one-on-one, out of all this chaos. He's been bombarded with too many people trying to get information from him. That would rattle anyone."

"You're right," Simon said. "That might help. I wasn't thinking about that, I was so focused on getting him to help. But that's why he likes the ranch. If there's ever too many people around, he can walk outside and get away from it all." Simon glanced back at his son. "And you definitely might come across as less intimidating to him than a bunch of officers."

"Is there anywhere outside we could go that's quiet?" she asked the sheriff.

"There's a bench along a trail behind this building that has some beautiful views of the mountains."

She nodded. "Sounds perfect."

Pastureland spread out in front of them as Madison sat down next to Will on the metal bench behind the sheriff's office. In the distance, snow-capped mountains rose up, making a spectacular view. She wasn't sure their plan was going

136

to work, but at least Will had agreed to come with her—though it was probably more to get away from the chaos inside than a desire to talk to her.

"This is better, isn't it?"

Will simply shrugged.

From her pocket she pulled a chocolate bar that she'd gotten out of a vending machine and handed it to him, looking for any way she could to connect with the young man.

"It's not exactly on the food pyramid, but I thought you might be hungry."

"Thank you," he said, taking the chocolate.

"I spoke with your mother earlier today."

Will looked up at her. "Is she okay?"

"She's fine. She seemed really proud of you. She said you love to fix things and that you love music. I played the violin in junior high and high school. Sometimes I wish I hadn't stopped practicing, though to be honest, I didn't have a lot of talent."

"Instruments take a lot of practice."

"She also said you love working the land with your father. That's quite a gift. A hundred-plus years ago, if people lived out here and didn't have some of the skills you have, they wouldn't have made it through their first winter."

She waited for him to respond, not wanting to push him, but needing to make progress. "What are you thinking?"

"I don't want to get in trouble."

His statement surprised her. "Why would you be in trouble?"

"I was supposed to help catch the bad guys."

"Will, that man lied to you. He wasn't a US Marshal."

"Yeah, I figured that out."

"He is an escaped fugitive from prison."

"He's killed people?" Will asked.

"He has."

A long silence hung between them, but she decided to wait.

"I've never felt so scared in my life."

"I know, but you were very brave."

"He tried to kill me. He pulled out a gun, but I pulled on the steering wheel to stop him. He crashed the truck and I . . . I ran."

"Will, I know what you've just gone through is terrifying, but you did the right thing. I need to talk with you about what happened. Would that be okay?"

Will hesitated, then nodded. "Is my family okay?"

"They're all fine."

"Is he going to come back and hurt my family?"

"No. He's far away from here, but we need to find him."

"Can I go home?"

"We're going to get you and your father home as soon as possible. I promise. I just need to see if there's anything you can remember. And I promise you're safe right now."

His leg shook beside her as he slowly unwrapped the paper from the candy bar. "The only time I get a candy bar is when we come to town. You should try my mom's chocolate cake though. It's better than a hundred candy bars."

"I'm sure you're right." Madison glanced at her watch. Barrick could be halfway to the state line by now. "Can you tell me what happened after you left the ranch?"

"My mother didn't want me to go, but I convinced her I'd be fine. I wanted to help."

"From what your mother told me about you, I'm not surprised."

"But once we got about a mile down the road, he wasn't nice anymore." He stared straight ahead for a few moments before continuing. "I noticed red marks across his wrists, and he'd hurt his leg. He said he'd been in a plane crash, so I started asking questions. He didn't like that."

"What kinds of questions?"

"What it was like being a marshal. How many bad guys he'd caught. If he'd ever been shot. If he'd been scared when the plane crashed."

"And his reaction?"

"He told me to shut up and pulled out a gun. Said if I tried anything stupid, he would kill me."

"And when you got to the main road?" Madison asked.

"I believed what he said, that he would kill me, so I knew I had to do something. As soon as we got onto the main road, I grabbed the wheel and pulled it as hard as I could toward me. When we stopped, I jumped out of the truck and ran as fast as I could."

"Did he hurt you at any point?"

"No. I was just banged up from when the truck smashed into a tree. I hit my head against the window."

"What about Barrick? Was he injured?"

"I think he hit his shoulder and maybe broke his nose, because it was bleeding." Will shrugged. "And he looked like his arm was injured as well."

"Like a gunshot wound?" Madison asked.

"Maybe."

Both could explain the blood in the car.

"Do you know where he went after the crash?"

"He came after me, tried to track me through the trees, but eventually he gave up."

"Do you know what he did next?"

Will nodded. "I decided to track him, so I doubled back and was able to pick up his trail as he headed out of the woods and toward the road."

A couple with a Jack Russell passed by on the trail.

"You like to hunt?" Madison asked Will.

"I've spent my entire life hunting, so I knew how to stay quiet and hidden."

"What did you see?"

"He walked down the road and flagged down another car." This time Will turned to her. "I saw the license plate."

Madison worked to keep her excitement in check. "Do you remember the numbers?"

He nodded, then recited them. "It was a Ford—an SUV—and it was gray."

Madison radioed the information to Jonas.

"I know this has been hard, but you've been a huge help, Will. Is there anything else you can think of that might help us track him down?"

"He took my phone. Made a call, then threw it out the window."

"That's why we couldn't trace it. Do you have any idea who he might have been calling?"

"He didn't say much. Just that they should wait for him."

"Not bad, kid. If you ever think about going into law enforcement one day, give me a call."

Will laughed, then shook his head. "I think I'll stick to working on the ranch."

Back inside the station, Jonas had already come up with a name.

"It's a rental car," he said. "Rented to a Ryan Phelps. The rental place gave a local address where he is staying."

"Who is he?"

"A tourist, up here in a cabin with his family

for a week. We've tried calling his cell several times, but no one answers."

"We need to go see if he's there, or if his family has heard from him."

Jonas nodded. "I already have a car arranged for us. We're also working to get his phone records, in case Barrick used his phone to make a call."

In most cases, they were able to have records released from phone companies if they had evidence that the owner was in danger. And as far as she was concerned, Ryan Phelps's life was in danger.

Fifteen minutes later, they'd pulled into the driveway of a quaint log cabin that was set back off the road and nestled among the trees.

"I'm not usually the jealous type," Madison said, as they walked toward the front door, "but if I ever happen to get stranded in the woods again, I wouldn't mind something like this."

Madison held up her badge when the door opened, then introduced herself and Jonas to the woman standing there. "Are you Katy Phelps?"

The woman nodded, a look of worry crossing her face.

"We're sorry to bother you," Jonas said, "but we're trying to locate your husband. Ryan Phelps."

She tugged at the end of her ponytail. "Is something wrong?"

"We're not sure at this point. That's why we're here."

The squeals of kids playing got louder as one of the children ran through the entryway, flying a LEGO plane.

She glanced back into the house. "Can we talk out on the porch?"

"Of course."

Madison took a step back, making room for the woman, who shut the front door behind her.

"Something's wrong, isn't it?" she asked.

Madison glanced at Jonas. "Why do you say that?"

"My husband was supposed to be back two hours ago. He's never late like this. And now two marshals show up on my doorstep. What am I supposed to think?"

"We honestly don't know where your husband is at this time, but we do need to ask you a couple questions."

The front door flung open, and a girl around fourteen stumbled out with a scowl on her face. "Mom, the twins are driving me crazy. Will you please make them stop?"

"I'll be there in just a minute, Krissy."

The young woman stopped short. "What's going on?"

"Nothing. But if you'll get the twins washed up, we'll eat in a minute."

"Mom—"

"Just do as you're told." Mrs. Phelps waited for the door to shut, then turned back to the marshals. "Sorry about that."

"It's fine."

"What do you need to know?"

"Was your husband driving a gray Ford rental car?"

"Yes."

"Ma'am." Jonas hesitated for moment. "We have reason to believe that your husband's life is in danger."

Color drained from Katy's face. "What do you mean?"

Madison let out a sharp breath, hating this part of the job. "We're searching for an escaped felon, and we think it's possible your husband picked him up."

"No. That's not possible. My husband doesn't pick up hitchhikers. He never has."

"We aren't sure what compelled your husband to pick him up this time, but we do have a witness who says he did."

"No." The woman shook her head. "There must be some mistake. You're telling me my husband picked up a felon and is now missing?" She pulled her phone from her pocket, swiped it on, then placed a call. "Pick up . . . pick up . . ." Katy's eyes widened in fear. "He's not answering. Why would he not answer?"

"That's what we're trying to find out," Madison said.

"Can you track his phone?"

"We're working on that right now as well, but his phone has been off."

"What am I supposed to tell my kids? That their father might not come home?"

"We don't know that anything has happened to your husband. We just want to make sure he makes it home safe."

"So what do I do now?"

"Go eat lunch with your kids, and we promise we'll be in touch as soon as we know something."

Madison headed back to the car with Jonas, praying that the next time she saw Mrs. Phelps, it wasn't to tell her that her husband wasn't coming home.

FOURTEEN

Pizza boxes lay spread out across a desk inside the sheriff's office as they worked through their next move. They'd updated the BOLO issued to law enforcement officers across the state with photos and background information. On top of that, they were working with other law enforcement agencies who had dealings with Barrick in the past to ensure the information they had was complete. An extensive dossier was a first step in figuring out where he would go for help.

"His mother lives in Denver," Jonas said, writing the name of the woman on the whiteboard along the far wall of the room. "She works as a receptionist for a local dentist office."

"He's going to need cash," Madison said, "but he knows we'll go to her first."

"Along with everyone else on this list," he said as he added to it.

She pulled out information on the last place he'd rented and double-checked the landlord information. It was the tedious part of working a manhunt. They talked to family members and neighbors. Checked credit card activity, phone activity, and bank records.

"We need to have the top five names brought in for questioning by local law enforcement and find out if he's contacted them," Jonas said. "But my gut tells me he's going to try and go to someone he thinks we don't know."

"Or strangers like he's already done." Madison tapped her fingers on the table.

The prepaid phone she'd bought in town vibrated in her back pocket. Madison pulled it out and checked the call log. There were three missed calls from her sister. A twinge of guilt surfaced. She tried to make it a priority that family always came first, but it wasn't always easy when she had no idea when she'd be gone and for how long.

Like today.

"I need to make a phone call," she said.

"Sure." Jonas glanced up from the desk. "Is everything okay?"

"My sister called. I left her a message telling her I was fine, and that I'd call when I could. I just need to smooth things over with her so she doesn't worry, then I'll be back."

"Take as long as you need. Seriously."

Madison went back to the bench where she'd sat with Will and called her sister, surprised—not for the first time—by Jonas's softer side.

"Danielle," she said once she answered. "It's me. Are you okay?"

"I don't know." There was a long pause on the

line. "Listen, I probably shouldn't have called you, and I apologize for not leaving a voice mail, but I got your message, then I couldn't get through. I was worried."

"It's fine. I have a few minutes. I would have called sooner, but things have been a bit crazy."

"I got your message about the plane crash and now it's all over the news. Are you sure you're okay? I have to say, I'm a little freaked out over all of this."

Madison let out a sharp sigh. At least it sounded like everything was okay on her sister's end, and she couldn't blame her for being upset. Leaving a message that you'd been in a plane crash wasn't something that happened every day.

"I'll be honest, it's been a rough twenty-four hours," Madison said, "but I really am okay. You don't have to worry. I'll let you know as soon as the case is closed and I'm on my way home, though it might be a few days. You'll need to tell Lilly how sorry I am to miss her birthday dinner. I'll take her somewhere special once I'm back."

"That's fine. She'll understand. Daddy's here for Lilly's party, which is a good distraction for her. I'll tell her we're going to have a second party later on."

"I really am sorry, Danielle. I never should have left a message like that, but I was so worried about you finding out something on the news."

"It's fine, though to be honest, sometimes I hate

your job and wish you were—I don't know—a cafeteria worker or something, so I didn't have to worry so much."

"I promise I'll be home soon, and we'll all go out and do something normal with the kids. I've been wanting to take them to the aquarium or the zoo."

"I'd like that, but there's something else."

Madison felt the worry surface again. She got up and started pacing. "What is it, Danielle?"

"I found a note on my front porch today. Slipped into my mailbox."

Immediately Madison felt her guard go up. "What does it say?"

Danielle paused. "It says, 'Consider your next move. I have more reach than you think. I know what would hurt you most.'"

Madison felt a wave of panic strike. "Is that all of it?"

"Yes, but it probably just scared me because Ethan's gone, and I was watching this creepy movie last night. But then after your message, I started wondering if they were somehow connected to your work." Danielle let out a sharp breath. "You know. Someone using me to get to you."

Madison's mind was racing. There couldn't be a connection to Barrick. Could there? Had he found a way to threaten her family in order to get them to let him go?

"Is there a way to tell where it came from?" she asked.

"It wasn't signed, but there were two initials. DB."

The ground began to spin beneath her. Madison walked across the grass and sat down on the bench.

DB.

Damon Barrick.

How had he been able to get to her sister?

"What are you thinking, Madison?"

She hesitated. Her mind raced through the options, unwilling to take any chances of putting her sister or her family's life at risk. "Those are the initials of the fugitive we're after."

"So someone is using me to get to you?"

"I don't know how, but yes. When did you say Ethan gets home?"

"He flies in Saturday night."

Two more days.

And she had no idea when she'd be able to get back. Even if she tried to get a flight out now, they were miles from the nearest airport.

"I want you to listen. Don't panic but pack your bags. I'm going to call my boss. You've met him once—Chief Deputy Carl Michaels. You can trust him. I want you and the kids and Daddy to go to your in-laws' for a few days. At least until we catch the fugitive we're after."

"Madison—"

"Promise me you'll do what I said."

There was a long pause on the line. "Fine, but—"

"No buts, just promise."

"I promise."

"Good. I'll be in touch."

She hung up and began dialing Michaels but stopped when Jonas approached her.

He stepped in front of her. "You look upset. What happened?"

She hesitated, not wanting to tell him the truth. She didn't want him to ever believe she wasn't capable of doing her job objectively. Hated that the last twenty-four hours had left her feeling vulnerable and out of control.

"You look like you just saw a ghost." He sat down next to her.

She drew in a breath and told him about the threat. "I'm worried my sister and her family might be in danger."

"Wow. I'm struggling to understand how and why he did that, but I certainly don't blame you. If you feel like you need to leave—"

"I will if I feel like I have to, but I talked to her about going to her in-laws' for a few days."

"I think that's a great plan. Ask Michaels to put a detachment on them until we can figure out what's going on."

She nodded, pulling her phone back out. She set things up with the deputy director, but her mind refused to stop running through all the worst-case scenarios.

Jonas gave her a look. "What are you thinking?"

"How would Barrick arrange something like this, and if he did, what does he really believe he'll accomplish getting my sister involved?"

"I don't know," Jonas said. "But Michaels will be able to get to the bottom of this."

She stared out across the pastureland and let the mountain air fill her lungs. "What happens when no matter what you do, you can't fix things?"

"Are you talking about the case, or something else?" Jonas asked.

"I don't know. Both maybe. People count on us. Expect us to bring these guys in so it doesn't happen to someone else. But sometimes every-thing goes wrong. Luke died. My sister's being threatened—"

"I promise we'll do everything we can to keep your sister and her family safe no matter who's behind that note."

"I know that. On one level, anyway. But I keep thinking of Katy Phelps and wondering what will happen if she finds out she lost the father of her children because he tried to do something good? Because I know what that is like. How are we supposed to stop things that are simply so unfair?"

"Is this about Katy Phelps or is it about not saving Luke?"

She shrugged at the question as she tried to put things into words. "It's about stopping it from happening to someone else. It's about hating lying to her to make her feel better."

His gaze narrowed. "You told her what she needed to hear. Besides, you could be right. We don't know what happened to him. There's a chance he's just stranded on the side of the road where Barrick dumped him."

"You know as well as I do that the chance of that father never coming home is pretty high." She stepped around him and started to leave, then turned back. "I'm sorry. I don't usually ramble like this."

"You have nothing to be sorry for. This isn't a normal situation and on top of that, we've been through a lot the past twenty-four hours."

"I still shouldn't let it get so personal."

"But it is. There's no way around it. We were in a plane crash. You were attacked, shot at, then held at gunpoint by a bunch of ranch hands, and now your sister's life has been threatened. If you ask me, that's pretty personal."

She shot him a half smile. "Well, when you put it that way . . ."

"And all of this while you're grieving the loss of your husband. Give yourself some grace, Madison. You might be a marshal, but you don't have to be Superwoman 24/7. It's okay."

She studied his face and shook her head. "You're not like most men I know."

His cheeks turned a bit pink before he smiled. "It's why you became a marshal, isn't it? You lost your husband and decided you don't want it to happen to someone else."

She let out a low chuckle. "You make my decision sound so valiant."

"Isn't it? Why else do you do what you do?"

"I don't know. It's just always been a calling. Wanting to defend justice. Wanting to make a difference somehow in this world."

"I remember we talked briefly about our faith during our training. Do you feel that God called you to do this?"

"I do."

"And we do what we do because this world is full of sin and evil that needs to be stopped. Because we want to see good thrive and justice reign."

"Yes," Madison said. "But sometimes the darkness seems so much stronger than the light."

"Maybe, but God is so much bigger than the darkness. You have to keep remembering that."

"I know. Sometimes I need something tangible, you know? Like now, when my sister's being threatened. What if I can't keep her safe?"

"I'm here. I'm listening. The battle is fierce, but we know who wins in the end. And in the meantime, we're going to go out there and find Barrick and put an end to this."

She sucked in a breath at the reminder, but he was right. "Thank you."

"For what?"

"For listening."

"That's what partners do."

She nodded as Sheriff Hill walked up to them, a frown on his face.

"Sheriff?" Jonas said. "Is everything okay?"

"I've got some news, but you're not going to like it. We found a body. It's Ryan Phelps."

FIFTEEN

The sick feeling that had taken root in her gut deepened. Ryan Phelps was dead.

"You're sure it's him?" Madison asked.

The sheriff nodded. "We double-checked with his DMV photo, but yeah, we're sure."

Jonas cupped her elbow with his hand. "Madison?"

She allowed herself to lean on him. A man was dead, and someone was going to have to tell Katy Phelps her husband wasn't coming home.

"Where did you find the body?" Jonas asked.

"A local hiker and his dog stumbled across it. I assume that your felon thought he could bury the body in a shallow grave, and no one would discover him until he was long gone, but he chose the wrong spot. Buried him too close to a favorite local hiking spot."

The weight of their decisions pressed against her chest. She'd told Katy Phelps there was no reason to believe anything had happened to her husband, and yet somehow she'd known. Known Barrick wouldn't hesitate to kill the man if he came between him and his freedom.

"How did he die?" Jonas asked.

"The coroner will do a full autopsy, but because of some defensive wounds on the body, it looks as if they got into some kind of altercation and then Barrick shot him."

"He could have just taken the car and left him alive on the side of the road," Madison said.

But instead darkness had won again.

"There's more," the sheriff said. "We also just got Phelps's phone records and found something interesting there you're going to want to see." The sheriff held up a piece of paper. "According to phone records, the last call made on Phelps's phone lasted three minutes. Because of the time stamp, I'm pretty sure we can assume that Barrick made the call."

"Which makes sense," Jonas said. "He didn't expect anyone to connect him to Phelps, or for us to find his body anytime soon, so he thinks he's in the clear for now."

"Exactly." Madison nodded, knowing she needed to channel her anger into action. Barrick might have won the round, but they were going to take him down. "So he thought he was safe and used the man's phone. Who did he call?"

"A woman by the name of Mary Margaret Parker in Stanley, Wyoming."

"Where is that?"

"About fifty miles from Casper."

"Do you know anything about her or the town?" Jonas asked.

"A quick search didn't come up with anything."

"I don't remember seeing her name in any of the files," Jonas said.

"I don't either." Madison turned to Jonas. "We need to go there ourselves. Like you said, Barrick has no idea Will saw the car he stole, or that we can connect him to Ryan Phelps. This gives us a small advantage. And if he doesn't think we can connect him to Mary Margaret, he thinks he's going to someone totally off the grid."

Jonas didn't look convinced. "All we know is that he called. We can notify local authorities, but there's already a BOLO out on him."

She hesitated, understanding where he was coming from, but she was still convinced this was the right next move. "What do we have to lose? An hour if we fly? In the meantime, we keep following up with everyone he knows and might go to. One thing we do know is that he's long gone from here, and this is our best lead at the moment."

"Okay." Jonas shoved his hands into his pockets. "I trust your instincts, and you do have a point. In the meantime, we don't want to tip anyone off that we're looking there."

"Agreed." Madison turned to the sheriff. "We need to keep the discovery of Ryan Phelps off the news cycle for as long as possible. If Barrick gets even a hint that we're on his trail, he'll change course and we'll lose him again. And if we don't hurry, he'll find a way to disappear for good."

This had become a game of cat and mouse. Chasing the fugitive who had managed to stay a step ahead of them so far. Anticipating his next move was the only way of winning. And something told her that Mary Margaret was the key.

"The quickest way out of here is a chartered plane." Sheriff Hill pulled out his phone. "If you'd like, I can try to arrange a flight with one of the locals, but it will probably be hard to get out before morning. You can fly into Casper and rent a car. If Barrick's driving there, it will take him a good nine or ten hours, so you wouldn't be far behind him."

Madison nodded. "Let's do it."

At seven in the morning, they were at the airstrip ready to go. She and Jonas had stayed up late, poring over the information they had on Barrick, until he'd insisted they both needed a good night's sleep. He'd been right. Six hours of sleep and a double espresso from a local coffee shop this morning, and she was ready to go.

She stared out the window as they flew over tens of thousands of acres of forested land. She'd visited Wyoming once with her family as a child and still remembered visiting Devil's Tower National Monument and the Grand Tetons. The scenery below them, with the Rocky Mountains to the west and the High Plains to the east and a sprinkling of ranches in between, almost made her want to leave Seattle's traffic and crowds and settle down on a piece of land out here. But the remote location of much of the area also made it the perfect place to hide.

By nine thirty, they were driving their rented car into Stanley. Wood-planked sidewalks reminded her of the history of the hundred-plus-year-old town and made her feel as if she'd stepped back in time. But if Barrick had come here, he wasn't going to sightsee and wouldn't be found here in the middle of town. There would be too many possible witnesses. No. More than likely he'd have set up a place to meet Mary Margaret outside of town. What they would have to find out was where.

The sheriff's office sat on the edge of Main Street, invoking memories of episodes of *Longmire* she used to watch with her father, with its old-fashioned brick façade and frosted windows. They introduced themselves to Sheriff Fischer, who was sitting behind the desk, giving out strong vibes of reservations at their arrival.

"We don't get a lot of law enforcement around here from out of state, though from your earlier call, I understand you're not here to visit our gorgeous scenery."

"Unfortunately, no. Like we said on the phone, we're looking for our fugitive, Damon Barrick,

160

and we believe he might have come here to visit Mary Margaret Parker."

"Now, that's where we might have a problem." The man scratched his beard and stood up. "I saw the name on the information you sent, and I have to say I think you're chasing the wrong person. I can personally vouch for her."

"We're not here to stir up any trouble," Madison said. "But we do need to talk with her. Can you tell me where we might find her?"

"She works at one of the town's local diners as a waitress, but I'm telling you, Mary Margaret's a decent kid. I say kid, but she's twenty-nine. Honestly, though, I can't imagine her getting hooked up with someone like Damon Barrick."

"Unfortunately, you can't always judge a murderer by his looks," Madison said. "Barrick's charming and persuasive from what we've learned, but he's also on the run. He's killed at least four people now, and we think there's a good chance that he's already here. Phone records say he called Mary Margaret, and the only explanation is that he needed her help."

"What can you tell us about her?" Jonas asked.

"She's lived here her whole life. Married a local, Tom Parker. She volunteers at our local food bank and runs a reading program at the library in the summer. All I'm saying is, she isn't exactly the kind I can see having an extramarital fling."

"Has she had any problems with her husband?" Madison asked, still not convinced.

"What couple doesn't have problems?" he said.

"We'll need to keep this quiet, but she'll have to come in for questioning," Jonas said.

The sheriff looked back and forth between the marshals, then sighed. "Then let me bring her in."

Jonas glanced at him. "That's fine, but if you see any sign of Barrick around, call us in before you do anything. The man's armed and dangerous."

"Nothing I haven't dealt with before."

Madison ignored the comment. "In the meantime, if you'd have one of your deputies check local stores and find out if she bought a burner phone here in town in the past twenty-four hours, we'd appreciate it. They're going to need a way to communicate."

Sheriff Fischer grabbed his hat off a hook on the wall, then headed for the door. "Can't say that I'm happy about this, but who am I to argue with a US Marshal."

Mary Margaret didn't look a day over twenty-one with her platinum-blonde hair and pink diner uniform. She sat down across from them in one of the back offices of the sheriff's department, clearly wanting to be anywhere else but there.

"Mary Margaret, I'm Deputy US Marshal Jonas

Quinn and this is my partner, Deputy US Marshal Madison James."

"I don't understand what's going on. The sheriff wouldn't tell me anything."

Madison slipped a photo across the table. "We're looking for this man. His name is Damon Barrick, and we believe you've spoken with him recently."

She sat back in her chair and folded her arms across her chest. "I've never seen him before."

"We have information that says otherwise. Phone records that say he called you yesterday."

"Then you must be mistaken. I don't know him. Maybe it was a wrong number."

"Except it wasn't," Jonas said. "He called you yesterday afternoon, and you spoke for three minutes. That's not a wrong number."

Mary Margaret shrugged. "I'm sorry, but I can't help you. And I really need to get back to work."

"Here's the thing. You're protecting a murderer, Mary Margaret." Madison leaned forward. "And that isn't going to end well. Damon Barrick has been in prison the last nine months in connection with two murders. He murdered a fellow inmate while incarcerated. And two days ago, he escaped from a prisoner transport and now another man is dead."

"I don't know what you want me to say."

"How about the truth." Madison slid a second photo across the table. "Look at this photo. This is Ryan Phelps. It was his phone that Barrick used to call you. Ryan had three kids. A teenage daughter and twin boys. They were on vacation for a week, and Barrick killed him because he needed his car to leave Idaho. We need to know where he is and what his plans are before he kills someone else."

Mary Margaret turned her head away from the photo.

"What did he ask you for?" Jonas asked.

Tears welled in the woman's eyes as she shoved the photo back across the table. Maybe they were getting somewhere. "I told you I don't know who he is."

Jonas stayed silent, looking directly at her. Finally he spoke. "The law is very clear on what happens to someone who helps a felon evade detection or even escape. Charges can be brought against you. The only way out of this for you at this point is if you help us find him."

Mary Margaret stared at a chip on her fingernail.

"We can protect you," Madison said, "but you're going to have to tell the truth."

A clock on the wall clicked by the seconds. Ryan Phelps's vacant stare seemed to fill the room. They were right. Madison knew it. At the very least, the woman had spoken with Barrick. More than likely had seen him as well, which meant he was here.

Mary Margaret shifted in her seat. "I had completely severed ties with him, but then he called me yesterday."

"What did he say to you?"

"That he was in trouble. That he'd been framed. He didn't want me to believe what I was going to see on the news. Said that the couple they say he killed—he didn't do it. He was set up."

"Say you are right and he's innocent. Protecting him won't help either of you. He won't be able to keep running. We need to know where he is right now."

"I don't know where he is. He didn't tell me. He wanted to protect me."

Madison leaned forward. "That isn't true, is it?"

The woman's jaw tightened as she avoided looking at them. Whatever Barrick had told her, she clearly believed.

Jonas signaled Madison to step into the hallway with him.

"She's stonewalling us," Jonas said the moment they were out of earshot.

"She's trying to protect him."

"And herself. What's her husband going to think when he finds out what she's been doing?" Jonas sighed. "She's our best lead right now, but if she won't talk, we're back at square one."

"She could be telling us the truth. Maybe she really doesn't know," Madison said.

"Either way, he called her for a reason. He needed something from her, and we need to find out what that was."

Madison leaned against the wall. She almost felt for the girl who'd clearly been conned by a man who probably didn't care what happened to her.

"Let me talk to her again," she said. "Alone. She's in love with him. Maybe as a woman I can get through to her the importance of telling us everything."

Jonas nodded. "You were pretty good with Will. Go talk to her, and I'll see if I can get on the sheriff's good side."

A minute later, Madison set a coffee down in front of Mary Margaret. "Can I get you anything to eat?"

"I'm not hungry."

"I know this has to be hard on you, and I'm sorry."

"I've never had to talk with the police before. Never seen a dead body . . . Damon didn't kill those people. I know he didn't and one day, the truth will come out."

"I hope you're right."

"Do you?"

Madison nodded, then sat back down across from her. "Can you tell me where you met him?"

"At the diner, actually. He loves this part of the country and does a lot of hunting up here.

At least he did before he got arrested. There was something different about him. Something about the way he talked to me and looked at me. It was always like I was the only one in the world."

"How long ago did you meet?"

"A couple years."

"And you had an affair."

She let out a sharp breath, then nodded. "Damon showed up at a time when Tom and I were first having problems in our marriage. He came up here to go hunting, and I don't know. We had a lot in common and hit it off right away. We'd slip away to a cabin for a few hours. I know it was wrong, but I don't want my husband to find out."

"Then why did you do it?" Madison asked.

"I don't know. Sometimes I felt—feel—so empty. I've lived my entire life here. I love this town and the people, but I've always felt like I'm missing something. Damon seemed to be that missing piece." She fingered the edges of the photo that still sat on the table in front of her. "He was handsome, charming. Made me feel beautiful and smart. I'd never really felt that way before."

"And when he was arrested?"

"He swore to me that he didn't do it. That he'd been in the wrong place at the wrong time. I wanted to help him, but I didn't know what to do. He didn't want the police to know I knew him."

"I know you want to help him," Madison said. "And I understand you're wanting to do that now, but in the end, you're only hurting him."

Mary Margaret looked up at her, eyes wide. "How can I be hurting him? You want to send him back to prison, but he's innocent. He doesn't deserve to be there."

"Then that's all the more reason he needs to come in. What we want is the truth, but the evidence—"

Mary Margaret cut her off. "The evidence is tainted. Don't you get it? And besides that, do you really think they're going to just let him go? They needed someone to take the fall for those murders."

"If he's really innocent, like you believe, then he'll be acquitted."

"But you don't think he's innocent."

"His innocence isn't up to me to decide. My job is simply to ensure he's brought in and gets a proper trial. The alternative is that he has to run the rest of his life, and that can't be what either of you want." Madison met the woman's gaze. "Not if you really care for him."

"He's running because he doesn't think anyone will believe him."

The tension in Madison's shoulders and neck tightened. They were going in circles. Maybe talking to her was futile.

"At least tell me what he wanted from you."

168

Mary Margaret chewed on the chipped finger-nail before answering the question. "He asked me to get him some money."

"How much?"

"Three thousand dollars and my grandmother's ring. He promised he'd pay me back."

"Where are you supposed to meet him?"

She avoided Madison's gaze.

"Mary Margaret, please. Trust me. If you really want to help him, you'll tell me where you were planning to meet him."

"There's a cabin about fifty miles from here near Hickory Lake. He used to stay in it when he went hunting up here. We'd go there sometimes. I'm supposed to meet him there at noon."

"Thank you." Madison patted her hand. "You did the right thing."

"Did I?"

"Yes. You did."

Mary Margaret looked up at Madison, clearly not convinced. "Can I come with you?"

"You'll need to stay here."

"Can I see him when you bring him back?"

"I'm sorry, but I can't make any promises."

Madison left her in the room and went to talk with Jonas and Sheriff Fischer. "She was planning on meeting him in a cabin near Hickory Lake. She was going to take him cash and her grandmother's ring."

"You were right." Jonas turned to the sheriff.

"Can we borrow a couple of your deputies?"

"You can have whatever you need." He glanced at the back office where Mary Margaret was still waiting for them. "I guess I was wrong."

Jonas nodded. "She completely believes he's innocent, but we don't know what kind of lines he's feeding her. Based on what she's already done, she'll do whatever he asks."

"And based on what he's done," Madison said, "he'll kill anyone who gets in his way."

SIXTEEN

Five minutes later, they were headed toward their vehicles with the sheriff and four deputies.

Sheriff Fischer stopped beside their rental car. "I had one of my men talk to the owner of the cabin before we left, like you asked, and he just called me. He said that the cabin was a last-minute rental for a week by Mary Margaret. The owners know her and didn't think anything about it. She said she was arranging the stay for some friends who were coming in from out of town."

"I guess she failed to mention that her friend had recently escaped from prison and was currently on the run." Jonas laughed.

The sheriff smiled. "That probably didn't come into the conversation."

"What can you tell us about the cabin?"

"There are dozens of them scattered around the area. Most of them are short-term rentals for vacationers, and others are used exclusively by the owners. This one in particular is pretty isolated. According to the GPS it's the last cabin on a dead-end gravel road, so you're not going to get people just wandering by. Basically, it's off the grid. There's no cell or Wi-Fi service. Sounds like a landline is the only way to communicate. We've got roadblocks set up both directions leading out of town in case he decides to run, though it sounds like he's gotten past them before."

"Sounds good," Jonas said, unlocking their vehicle with the key fob. The last thing he wanted was someone else getting hurt, but they'd done everything they could at the moment. Now it was just a matter of catching Barrick off guard and bringing him in.

Madison was quiet as Jonas pulled out of the parking lot and turned down Main Street behind the sheriff and his deputies. "What are you thinking?" he asked her.

"There's something still bothering me."

"What's that?"

Madison drew quiet for a moment. "We're assuming he's either going to try and disappear, which isn't easy. Or leave the country, which also isn't easy, but would make more sense long term. Instead, he decides to go into hiding in a place where there is no cell service or internet. Only a landline, which is going to make it very difficult for him to plan anything."

"Maybe he thought coming here would give him a few days off the grid to make a plan. Either option would need to be thought out."

"And he'll need help."

"Someone besides Mary Margaret?" he asked.

"If he's looking to change his identity, he'll need someone else who can get him new IDs while he waits here."

"Agreed, but who would he go to?"

"I don't know. Someone he was in prison with or someone he knew before prison?"

"Which narrows it down to what . . . a few dozen people, maybe more?"

All he knew was that this cabin was their best shot at the moment.

"It's beautiful out here, isn't it?" she said, staring out the window as if trying to soak up some of the beauty of the place.

"Extremely."

"Makes it tempting to forget why we're here. My father used to make trips out to southern Wyoming or Colorado to go hunting with his brother every other year or two. He loved the Northwest, but always said some of the best hunting he'd done was out here."

"What did he like to hunt?"

"Typically elk," Madison said.

"What about you?" Jonas enjoyed the momentary distraction. "You said you did some hunting with your dad growing up. Did you ever come out here with him?"

"He never took me on one of those trips. I think my uncle didn't want a kid hanging around. And now that my dad doesn't hunt anymore, I lost my partner."

"Sounds like he was quite a man."

"He was." She paused. "He is. It's tough watching him forget."

"You should bring him back here. No matter how much he's forgotten, I bet it would make him happy."

She smiled. "I don't know why I didn't think of that before. I have been thinking a week's vacation in the wilderness sounds like a bit of heaven. But I'm not talking about hunting. I'm talking about a roaring fire, snow falling outside while I'm cuddled up in a thick blanket, reading a good book. Hot chocolate and takeout."

A picture of her snuggled next to him in front of a fire in one of these cabins surfaced unexpectedly. Legs pulled up beneath her. Hair down around her shoulders. He'd always been impressed with her work ethic, but he'd only seen her on the go. She'd always been professional and focused, but today he'd seen another side of her. The side that didn't see her job as a simple checklist but truly cared about the lives that had gotten tangled up in the situation. And it had left him realizing that she was the kind of person he simply enjoyed being around.

He shoved away the image. There was nothing personal about his relationship with Madison, nor did he ever intend there to be. They were too similar—too driven and too focused on their careers—and would end up driving each other crazy. And he knew the danger of falling for people he worked with. That was something he wasn't going to let happen again.

"Michaels said we'd make a good team," he said.

"Really?"

"With my experience and your ability to read people. He was right." He shifted his thoughts, trying to keep them professional only, but realized he was failing. "I saw you with Mary Margaret. You had both the patience and insight to finally get her to talk."

"Did you just give me a compliment?"

"Just say thank you."

"Thank you." She smiled. "I have to say, it's hard not to feel sorry for the girl. She clearly made some really bad decisions. She seems so lost and empty and for whatever reason thought Barrick was going to be able to fill that void."

"That seems to happen a lot. But on the other hand, she chose to lie to us. You can't blame that on being naive. She wasn't thinking about what was right, only about saving him."

"I know, but she just seemed so vulnerable. He used her, and even she has to know that this isn't going to have a happy ending. Either he goes back to prison, or he spends the rest of his life on the run. Neither is something she should be involved in."

"I've never understood it either, but these

men become a project that women want to fix."

"It's just sad. I have a feeling Barrick will use anyone he can to make sure he doesn't get caught."

Which was exactly what had him worried. As far as he was concerned, Mary Margaret was nothing more than a pawn in Barrick's game. He'd have no problem using her and then disposing of her. And from what he'd seen, the girl had no idea just how dangerous a situation she'd wound up in the middle of.

"We're here," Jonas said, pulling up behind the sheriff's vehicle.

Any talk of hot chocolate and roaring fires vanished. The cabin sat off of a windy dirt road on the top of a slight rise, giving whoever was inside the house the advantage. They parked the car in a heavily forested area and made their way single file along the edge of the house, wearing bulletproof vests, their weapons ready.

The key element in any raid was surprise. Being prepared was crucial. They were already geared up and ready to move in as Jonas stepped up onto the wraparound porch while the other officers surrounded the cabin. One of the deputies kicked at the door, and they rushed inside, swiftly moving from the open living room to the rest of the two-story cabin in a matter of seconds.

Soon all the rooms were cleared. The cabin was empty.

Frustration ate at Jonas.

There was no sign of Barrick.

But he had to be here somewhere.

Jonas met Madison and Sheriff Fischer back downstairs.

"There were a couple shirts hanging up in the master bedroom and a toothbrush in the bathroom along with some deodorant," Madison said.

"Maybe he went for a walk," he said.

She frowned. "He doesn't really seem like a nature lover."

"True." He turned in a slow circle in the middle of the living room. Mary Margaret was still at the station without access to a phone, so she couldn't have warned him. But then where was he?

Jonas turned to the sheriff. "Have an officer guard the cabin until you can get a forensic team in here to see if you can find anything Barrick might have left behind."

The sheriff nodded. "I'm on it."

Madison headed toward the door, then stopped.

"What is it?" he asked.

"He was here. He is here."

"How do you know that?"

She picked something up off the floor and held it in the palm of her hand. "This was in my backpack."

He walked across the room to where she was

standing, trying to read her expression. Something had shaken her. "What is it?"

"It's the challenge coin Luke got me when I made it onto the police force."

His mind reached for an explanation. "Maybe it's not yours. It could belong to someone who stayed here—"

"No. It's mine. There's a prayer on the back, the police officer's prayer." She turned it over and held it up. "He had his initials engraved as well. Wanted to remind me that while God was always at my side, so was he. I always keep it in the front pocket of my backpack."

The one Barrick had taken from her.

Jonas looked around the small room, then opened the closet in the entryway. "Here's your backpack."

He set it on the table. "Looks like we have confirmation that Barrick was here. We need to spread out and search the surrounding grounds. This road is a dead end, and we didn't run into any cars, which means he has to be out there."

"Mary Margaret couldn't have warned him," Madison said.

"Maybe he heard us coming and got spooked."

"It's possible he got spooked and ran, but the sheriff said the nearest town is forty miles away. There isn't even any phone service here, so we're going to have to assume he saw us coming and is hiding out somewhere. We still don't know what kind of resources he has. There's a good chance Mary Margaret's not the only person helping him."

Jonas signaled for the sheriff and his deputies. "Our search radius is spreading as we speak, which means time is against us," he told them. "We need to contain the area which, in turn, will limit the area that needs to be searched. The sheriff has officers stationed at roadblocks on the bridge going out of town, and the south main road."

Madison stepped up beside him. "Six of us will do a grid search fanning out from here. We need to move as quickly as possible. Carter, I want you to stay here in case he comes back. We need to move out. Now."

SEVENTEEN

Madison moved forward as they fanned out from the cabin, each step intentional as she paid attention to every sound and movement around her. She could see Jonas to her left through the trees and Deputy Camelia Ferrer to her right. She reached into her pocket and ran the coin between her fingers, irritated at how this case had gotten under her skin. Maybe that was exactly how Barrick wanted her to feel. The threats to her sister's family, finding the coin at the cabin—he wanted her off balance.

No matter what she wanted to think, the past forty-eight hours had become very personal. But she wasn't going to let Barrick get into her head, or steal her focus. He was out there, and they were going to find him.

While it was still several hours before sunset, the heavy tree cover looming above left deep shadows around them. A shiver slid through her, but it wasn't from the dropping temperatures. It felt more like déjà vu, knowing Barrick was out here. Knowing he'd do anything to stop them from finding him.

The terrain they were covering was thick with

trees and sprinkled with a few narrow trails, but for the most part was left wild, leaving a feeling of isolation and being almost completely off the grid. But something still seemed wrong about the whole situation. She'd seen Barrick's profile as she read through his files. Holing up in a cabin and waiting didn't sound like something he would do. So what was his plan?

If she were Barrick, she would never rely on someone like Mary Margaret to arrange his escape beyond the cash she'd offered him. He was going to need someone who could get him what he needed and quick.

Someone let out a yell to her right. Weapon in hand, Madison hurried through the shadows toward Officer Ferrer, who had been walking parallel to her.

She pulled out her radio. "We've got a distress signal from Officer Ferrer. I'm on my way to the location now."

"Stay alert."

"Roger that."

Madison hurried through the thick underbrush. Ferrer had been in her sights only moments before. Now there was no sign of her.

"Officer Ferrer, what's your status?"

"Do you see her?" Jonas asked over the radio.

"Negative."

She heard twigs snapping behind her and turned to see Jonas approaching.

"She was there just a few seconds ago, walking parallel to me."

They found Ferrer a minute later under a tree, holding her ankle.

"I'm sorry." The officer's jaw tensed. "I fell, twisted my leg, and now I'm not sure where my radio is, but someone's out there."

"Our suspect?"

She nodded. "I didn't get a good visual, but from what I did see—from his height and build—it very likely is Barrick."

Madison clicked on her radio. "We've got a possible sighting of our suspect, heading north-northeast. We found Officer Ferrer, but she's injured from a fall."

Jonas helped Ferrer to her feet. "Do you know if he was armed?"

"No. I'm sorry."

"That's okay. We're going to assume he was."

"Leave me here. You need to go after him, and I think I can get back."

Jonas nodded. "Stay here while we go after him. We'll radio and have someone help you back."

Madison glanced up at the rain clouds hovering above them and started praying for both wisdom and direction. If a storm came or darkness fell, it was going to be a lot harder to find the man out here.

They converged on the trail and headed in

the direction that Ferrer had seen their suspect traveling on foot. So far, Barrick had been ahead of them every step of the way, but all it would take was one misstep by him, and this would be over.

The image of Ryan Phelps's wife and kids pushed its way to the forefront of her mind, along with the sick feeling she'd had for days. Their job was to get guys like Barrick off the street so things like this didn't happen. It was too late for Phelps, but she wasn't going to let Damon Barrick destroy another life.

"Sheriff," Madison spoke into her radio, "we're heading in the direction he was moving. Where's he going?"

"You're not as isolated as it seems. Two miles in that direction leads to the main road. To the south is a back road, but that's heading away from any towns. I don't know how well he knows the area, but if I were him and had the authorities after me, I'd head to the main road and try to flag down a car."

"What about the roadblocks?"

"If he keeps going east on foot, it's possible he could miss them, but we could move them farther out a mile or two."

"Do it." Madison pocketed her radio and followed along behind her partner.

"Madison," Jonas said, "fifty feet ahead of us."

She saw movement, then clicked on her radio.

They had him. "Suspect is in view. Still heading toward the main road."

They picked up their pace and ran across the uneven ground. Once they were close enough, she held up her gun and yelled. "US Marshals. Put your hands where we can see them and turn around now."

The man paused, then turned around slowly. Her heart sank. It wasn't Barrick.

"Drop to your knees!"

The man hesitated again, then obeyed, raising his hands in the air and dropping to the ground. "I don't know who you're looking for, but I'm just here on holiday. I'm looking for my dog."

Jonas searched the man for weapons, then took a step back.

"He's clean."

"Of course I am. Let me see your badges, then tell me what in the world is going on."

"What's your name?" Jonas asked, holding up his badge.

"Mike. Mike Wells. I'm renting a cabin not far from here."

"Do you have any ID on you?"

"I'm on holiday in the middle of the woods, so no, I don't have any ID on me."

Madison met the man's gaze. "Where are you from?"

"Fort Collins."

"What are you doing out here?"

"I'm a writer, working on a book. I noticed my dog was missing, so I came out to look for him."

"We're looking for a fugitive who escaped a prison transfer. We have reason to believe he's in the area." Jonas held up a photo of Barrick on his phone. "Have you seen this man?"

"Wait a minute—an escaped fugitive? Are you kidding?"

"Have you seen him?" Jonas repeated.

"No. I haven't seen anyone around here for days. Trying to find a little peace and quiet. What did he do?"

"We're going to escort you back to your cabin," Madison said without answering his question. She returned her gun to its holster. "It's not safe out here right now."

"Hold on. I get the whole 'it's not safe out here' thing, because I'm assuming the two of you wouldn't be freaking out if this guy wasn't dangerous. And I'm even fine with going back to my cabin. But what about my dog?"

"With a little luck," Jonas said, "he'll be waiting for you back at your cabin."

Madison hurried ahead a few yards and radioed the sheriff. "I need you to do a background check on a Mike Wells. He says he lives in Fort Collins and has rented a cabin nearby."

"Roger that," the sheriff said. "The second team is almost to the main road and there is no sign of Barrick."

"Go ahead and send them back once they're at the road," she said.

Twenty minutes later, they were at the cabin where Mike had been staying. It was directly beside the cabin Mary Margaret had rented for Barrick. The rest of the deputies had met them there, but there was no sign of the convict.

"Here's my ID," Mike said, dropping it onto the kitchen table. "And feel free to run a background check on me because you won't find anything. All I've done is write twelve hours a day for the past five days. I was just out looking for my dog, like I said."

Madison stepped away with the sheriff.

"So his story checks out," Fischer said. "The cabin owner says he came to work on a book."

"Any criminal background?"

"Nothing more than a couple speeding tickets. He's got several books out." The sheriff checked his notes. "A murder-for-hire series."

"Sounds like a relaxing read."

Madison stared out the window toward the house where supposedly Barrick had been staying. Family and friends often lied because they didn't want their loved one going back to jail. What were they missing?

"We're going to need to canvass the neighboring cabins. He's got to be hiding somewhere," Jonas said as he walked up to them. He turned toward

Mike. "Does your dog normally wander off like this?"

"He never has before."

"He must have run pretty far from your cabin."

"Which is why he's lost."

"What kind of dog do you have?"

"Henry's a white terrier. Perfect for me because he's not too needy. But I've heard there are cougars around here. That's one of the reasons I didn't want to just let him out, but today I was tired, got lazy, and didn't put him on his leash."

"Before you start looking again," Madison said, "we need to ask you some questions. Are you sure you haven't seen this man while you were here?" She held up Barrick's picture again.

Mike stared at the photo, then shook his head. "Should I know him?"

"He was staying in a cabin next door, " Jonas said.

"Wait, is he the felon?"

"You're sure you haven't seen him?" Madison repeated her question.

"I don't know. I've been in my cabin most of the time. I didn't exactly come out here to socialize. I have a deadline in a week."

"So you've been planning this trip for a while?"

"I made the reservations, I don't know, about two months ago. I write under the name Garrick George. You might have heard about me."

"Sorry."

"You're with the US Marshals, right?"

"Yes."

"I'm only asking because I've been playing around with this new series in the back of my head about this tough marshal from Chicago, and to be honest, you look a lot like her. You know, how I picture her in my head."

Madison shifted uncomfortably, clueless about how to respond to the man.

"I'd love to do an interview with you," he rushed on. "Ask you some questions about the nitty-gritty day-to-day. You know. Get some insight into what it's like tracking down a felon and putting your life at risk while hunting the worst of the worst."

Jonas took a step forward. "Mr. Wells, perhaps we can table the soliciting for help with your book series for now."

"I'm sorry." Mike held up his hands. "I didn't mean to overstep. I just thought—"

One of the deputies stepped inside the house. "I think we found your dog."

"Henry?"

The deputy held open the door and the dog rushed to his owner, jumping up on him and licking him.

"We're going to leave now," Madison said. "Please call the sheriff immediately if you see the man from the photo."

"Are you sure I'm safe? I mean if he's out there somewhere."

"We're not done looking," Jonas said. "We're going to canvass the surrounding cabins and have a couple deputies watching the place. In the meantime, keep your doors locked and think of all of this as fodder for your book."

"Thanks, but I'd prefer not to live my stories."

"I think Mike the author has a bit of a crush on you," Jonas said as they walked down the sidewalk to where the sheriff was waiting for them.

"Very funny."

"I don't know. You might have ended up as inspiration for his next series."

"I have no desire to be anyone's inspiration for a book."

"Sounds kind of cool to me."

"Yeah, and Richard Castle already did a great job with it."

"Marshals."

Jonas and Madison turned around.

Mike hurried down the sidewalk toward them with Henry nipping at his heels. "You know, I didn't think about this until now, but I did run into someone out here this morning."

"Who was that?"

"An old classmate, and it's crazy, because I haven't seen the guy for at least ten years. He acted as if he didn't recognize me—not that we were ever great friends—but we were in the same class."

"What was his name?"

"Charlie Gibbons."

The sheriff walked up to them, his boots crunching on the gravel driveway. "Charlie Gibbons is Mary Margaret's brother."

EIGHTEEN

W ait a minute." Jonas turned toward the sheriff. "You know the name?"

"Charlie Gibbons has been in and out of trouble for years. He's usually unemployed and makes money doing odd jobs around town."

"So Mary Margaret's brother just happened to be out here at the cabin where Barrick is supposed to be," Jonas said.

Madison leaned against the side of the car. "It makes sense that Barrick would need extra help."

"Charlie could have picked him up and brought him here."

"I think we should still keep searching," Jonas said.

"Agreed," Madison said. "I want to talk to Mary Margaret again, but I want to talk to Charlie first."

"That's not a problem." The sheriff jiggled his keys. "Try at the Bull's Bar & Grill on Main Street. When he's not working, he hangs out there."

"We'll head back to town and talk to him," Jonas said. "Can you stay here and keep searching the area for Barrick?"

"And make sure Mary Margaret still has no access to her cell phone," Madison said. "We need to keep her isolated for the time being."

"I'll remind my deputy," Sheriff Fischer said. "And we'll check in if we find anything."

Jonas took the driver's seat again and he and Madison made their way back toward town on the winding, narrow road that cut through the trees. There was a question nagging at him. "Do you think Barrick has something on her?"

"You mean is he blackmailing her?"

"It's something to consider. He could have threatened to tell her husband if she didn't do what he said."

"It's possible, but love can have just as strong a hold on a person. Something tells me that she honestly believes he'll take her with him wherever he runs to. Especially if she had no intentions of turning him in. But I think you're right in at least considering blackmail. We're talking about a small town where she's lived her entire life. Something like that would be devastating. We might even need to talk to her husband. See if he knows anything." Madison looked out the window. "They say love is blind, but there's a good chance he at least has suspicions his wife hasn't been faithful."

He was impressed with her insight. Her ability to look at a situation from more than one angle. It was their job in tracking down criminals—to get into the heads of whoever they were after, never giving up until they were found.

Once they were close to town, Madison glanced at the GPS on her phone. "Take a left at the next street. That will get us onto Main Street. The restaurant is two blocks ahead on the right."

Bull's Bar & Grill was old and run-down, but the parking lot was packed. Inside was just as rustic, though the smell of garlic and seared beef made Jonas remember he'd missed lunch. If they managed to get through before the place closed, he wouldn't mind coming back for a burger and fries.

He walked up to the bartender and raised his voice above the music. "We're looking for Charlie Gibbons. We heard he comes here after work."

"Who's asking?"

Jonas held up his badge.

The bartender frowned, then nodded across the room. "He's over in the corner. Black T-shirt and a white beanie."

"Thanks."

They walked across the room, ignoring the stares from a couple of the patrons, then stopped across the table from him, blocking his exit. "Charlie Gibbons, I'm Marshal Jonas Quinn and this is my partner, Marshal Madison James."

Charlie pushed his chair back, but there was nowhere for him to go. "What do you want?"

"We need to talk."

Charlie hesitated, then shoved the entire table forward, knocking it over before running past them and heading outside.

"Seriously?" Madison threw up her hands.

"I'm always surprised at how often they run," Jonas said as they chased after him. "Where does he think he's going? We know his name, where he lives, where he works."

Charlie jumped into his pickup and peeled out of the parking lot, but they were right behind him.

Madison pulled out her cell phone and put the call on speaker. "Sheriff, Charlie Gibbons got spooked and decided to run. He's heading northeast out of town toward the highway, driving a red pickup truck."

"I know the truck. I'll send a deputy your way for backup, but he won't get past the roadblock."

"Copy that. And tell the officers there that we're coming right at them and to hold all cars coming in our direction."

Madison grasped the armrest as Jonas flew down the two-lane road headed out of town.

Jonas jerked the steering wheel to the left, matching the erratic turns of the pickup as it darted around the corner. He followed as close as he could. Things were starting to add up. This had been nothing more than a wild-goose chase so Barrick could run. Which meant he could be anywhere.

"Where does he think he's going?" Madison asked.

"I don't know, but the sheriff's right. He'll never make it past the roadblock."

Jonas pressed on the accelerator, knowing what she was thinking. Car chases with the authorities rarely ended well and should be avoided. There were too many chances of involving civilians. But the one running rarely thought of that.

A mile later, Charlie was still in front of them, but now they could see the roadblock up ahead. Two patrol vehicles had blocked the two-lane road where the tree line hugged the road, giving drivers no real choice but to stop.

Charlie had to see it as well, but at the speed he was going, his options were limited to running the roadblock or trying to skirt around it. Neither was a good option.

"He's not slowing down. He's going to ram right through it."

Jonas's hands clenched the steering wheel. He'd never make it.

Tires squealed as Charlie tried to stop at the last second. Too late. The truck flipped three times, then landed upside down, skidding across the road before smashing into a tree.

Jonas parked a couple dozen feet from the accident and hurried out of the vehicle. A second later flames erupted at the back of the pickup.

He ran toward the wrecked vehicle. "We need to get him out of there now. The fuel tank must have ruptured."

Charlie was hanging upside down from his seat belt. Both deputies who'd been working the roadblock ran toward the truck with fire extinguishers.

"Madison—"

"I'm right behind you. I've got the fire department and ambulance coming."

Jonas held his hand up across his face as they approached the truck. So far the fire was behind the cab, which would hopefully give them the precious extra seconds to get Charlie out. He tapped the handle of the door, thankful it wasn't hot yet. But the man wasn't moving.

"Charlie . . . Charlie, can you hear me?" Jonas tugged on the door, but it was stuck. He kicked at the bent frame, but it wasn't going to open. A plume of smoke gushed out of the cab. A tire exploded in the back with a loud pop. They were running out of time.

"We're going to need to get him out through the window."

"Let me see if I can get a fireproof blanket," Madison said.

One of the officers shouted at her to grab one out of the trunk of his car. "There's a seat belt cutter in there if you need it."

Jonas aimed his boot at the glass and kicked. His lungs were burning. The fire was getting closer. They just needed a few more seconds. Madison ran back and laid the blanket down across the shattered glass, then stepped back. Jonas tried to undo the seat belt, but Charlie still wasn't moving, and the seat belt wouldn't budge. He grabbed the cutter from Madison. Getting him down that way was going to be a problem if he was injured, but with the fire spreading, they had no choice.

He sliced through the thick fabric, then tried to lessen the impact as the man fell. Charlie groaned as they pulled him out and set him on his side a few dozen feet from the accident.

"He's breathing," Jonas said. "Pulse is fast, but steady." Jonas put a hand on the man's shoulder as he tried to sit up. "Take it slow and just breathe."

Charlie nodded.

Madison handed him a bottle of water. "Take a sip."

"We've got an ambulance coming. Can you tell me what you're feeling?" Jonas asked after he'd taken a couple sips.

"I don't know." Charlie pulled his knees toward his chest and coughed. "My lungs are burning, and my ribs hurt."

"Do you remember what happened?" Jonas asked, noticing the raised bump on his forehead and hoping he didn't have a concussion on top of everything else.

"I was trying to avoid that roadblock."

"Not your smartest move," Madison said. "And not easy to do when you're driving too fast."

"You spooked me."

"What did you think we wanted?"

"I don't know. The sheriff was out at my place last week, asking me about something that happened in town."

"We're US Marshals. We don't investigate crimes. We go after people," Madison said. "And sometimes, like right now, we track down felons."

"I'm not a felon or a convict."

"We know," Jonas said. "We need to talk to you about your sister."

"Why?" Charlie held his wrist and groaned. "I think it's broken."

Jonas ignored him. He'd get help soon enough. "We're looking for Damon Barrick, an escaped convict, and we think you know where he is."

"Who's that?"

Madison pulled a photo up on her phone and held it out to him. "Recognize this man?"

Jonas didn't miss the slight shift in his eyes.

"I've never seen him."

"Are you sure?" Jonas asked. "Because we believe you've not only met him but that you are also involved in helping him escape."

"Why would I do that?" Charlie asked.

"Maybe as a favor to your sister?"

"You think my sister's involved in helping a felon escape? Because if you do, you don't know her very well. My sister's totally by the book. Ask anyone in town. She doesn't even have a parking ticket. She'd never get involved with a felon."

"Everyone has their secrets," Madison said.

"Not Mary Margaret."

"Then what were you doing out at the cabins near Hickory Lake this morning?"

Charlie managed to sit up, then rested his arms against his knees. "I do repairs for the owners sometimes. I was called out there to fix a gas stove."

Jonas could hear the whir of sirens in the background. He glanced at Madison, his frustration rising. "So all of this is just a coincidence and has nothing to do with Damon Barrick?"

"I said I've never seen him."

"Charlie, please. Our only objective is to find Barrick. Assisting a fugitive is a federal crime that will put you in prison."

Charlie's jaw tensed. "I'm not lying."

An ambulance pulled off to the side of the road behind them, and a moment later two paramedics hurried toward them. Jonas stood up and glanced at the truck. The fire was out now. What if there was any evidence that hadn't burned?

"I'll be right back."

Madison nodded, then turned to the paramedics.

The smell of smoke was still strong even though the cab of the truck had only partially burnt. On the inside of the roof were some old fast-food wrappers and a toolbox that had spilled its contents across the dashboard. A piece of paper was jammed into the console and was partly sticking out. Jonas opened the box, careful of the heat where the plastic had melted. He was surprised that the contents hadn't burned in the fire or fallen out when he opened the top, but they were wedged tight. The inside of the console was filled with napkins, packets of condiments from fast-food restaurants, and a stash of receipts. He grabbed the slips, then hesitated as he saw a wallet jammed next to the console. He flipped it open and found five hundred dollar bills stuffed inside.

Madison walked up to him as he crawled away from the burnt vehicle. "What have you got?"

"A bunch of receipts, and a wallet full of cash. Thought it might be interesting to see where he's been, and I'm thinking I was right."

He gave half the pile of receipts to Madison, then sifted through the others. His search came up empty, but he saw her looking closely at one of the slips he'd handed her.

"What do you have?"

"According to this receipt, Charlie was in Salt

Lake last night." She glanced up at him. "What was he doing there?"

"I don't know, but I'm going to find out. Put those in an evidence bag," Jonas said. "I'll be right back."

He hurried toward the ambulance before they shut the back door.

"Hold on." He held up his badge. "I need to talk to your patient before you leave."

He stepped up into the back of the ambulance where Charlie was lying on a gurney, hooked up to oxygen.

"This gas receipt has you outside Salt Lake City just before midnight last night. What were you doing there?"

Charlie pulled off the mask. "I make supply runs for a couple businesses in town on a regular basis."

"Who were you working for last night?"

Charlie hesitated. "A builder in town."

"I need a name."

Charlie looked away.

"You can't give me one, can you? Because you met Barrick last night and gave him money from your sister—keeping some for yourself— then you brought back the backpack to be used as 'proof' he was here."

"That's not how it was."

"Then how was it?" Jonas asked.

"I . . ." Charlie's gaze swept the ceiling. "I was

doing a job for my sister. She never told me the guy was a felon."

"What did she tell you about this job?" Jonas asked.

"Just that she'd pay me to drive to Salt Lake and give a friend a package."

"Damon Barrick."

Charlie nodded. "I didn't know the man's name, but it was the guy in the photo you showed me. She knows I can use the money."

"Do you know what was inside the package?"

"I never asked. Didn't think it was my business."

"So you didn't notice you were taking him cash?"

Charlie avoided his gaze, but Jonas wasn't finished pushing for answers.

"Where did you meet him?"

"At the Perry Rest Area, north of Salt Lake."

"What was he driving?"

"He wasn't. Said he was waiting for a ride."

"And the cabin? What were you doing there?"

Charlie let out a sharp breath. "Mary Margaret asked me to take a few things from Barrick there for a friend who was planning to stay there."

"So Barrick was never here?"

Charlie shook his head.

"One more thing I need to know. Where was Barrick heading?"

"I don't know."

"Charlie—"

"I swear I don't know." The man's jaw tensed as he looked straight at Jonas. "We didn't say more than a dozen words to each other."

Jonas stepped out of the ambulance and headed back toward Madison. "Mary Margaret lied to us."

"What did he say?" she asked.

"You know why it's felt like Barrick's been one step ahead of us this entire time? He was never here. Mary Margaret sent Charlie to set things up. To make us believe Barrick had been here. And giving him time to get away."

Madison rubbed her eyes. "It would explain why my challenge coin was here."

"Charlie planted it in that cabin to make it look like he was here. To keep us running in the wrong direction as long as possible."

Jonas ran his hands through his hair. The longer they spent chasing nothing, the farther away Barrick could run.

"That's when Mike saw him," Madison said. "When he was back at the cabin, planting evidence."

"If your author friend hadn't recognized him, they probably would have gotten away with it, and we'd still be looking," Jonas said, smirking. "You just might owe him that interview now."

"Very funny." Madison rolled her eyes at him.

"But if Charlie is involved, then it looks like Barrick was never headed here, but instead to Salt Lake City."

Jonas's phone rang and he pulled it out of his pocket. "Sheriff?"

"I just heard from my deputy back at the office. Mary Margaret bought a burner phone from a gas station about five miles outside of town yesterday."

"We're on our way back to the sheriff's office now."

Bingo. Damon Barrick had just made what Jonas hoped was a fatal mistake.

NINETEEN

Madison walked into the sheriff's office with Jonas, furious that the last several hours had led them farther from Barrick. But while Barrick might have convinced Mary Margaret to cover for him, they were going to have to convince her that she was playing on the wrong side.

Besides a confession, what they really needed was the burner phone she'd bought. With the number Barrick was using off the call log, assuming he hadn't dumped the phone, they'd be able to pinpoint his location. But she'd been searched when they brought her in and there had been no sign of a second phone, and no communication with Barrick on her personal cell.

"How do you think we should play this?" Madison asked. "Though I'll tell you right off, I'm in the mood to play bad cop."

Jonas grinned at her. "I think I'll let you, though I'm thankful I'm not the one on the other side of that interrogation table."

Sheriff Fischer walked in behind them. "Your best angle is to use her brother against her."

"Meaning?" Jonas asked.

"They're pretty close. She does everything she

can to keep him out of trouble, but he's already been arrested for two felonies. A third one would get him up to fifty years, and she knows that."

"Then that's the leverage we need," Madison said. "We let her know we've arrested Charlie, and that we have proof of him aiding an escaped felon. See if that's enough motivation to get her to tell us what we need to know. Because without some kind of deal, he's going away for a long, long time."

Jonas nodded. "She just needs to know that the only way to help her brother is to cooperate."

"That's what we'll count on."

"How is Charlie?" the sheriff asked.

"He's pretty banged up. Broken rib, fractured wrist, and a bunch of bumps and bruises, but he's lucky. It could have been a whole lot worse," Madison said. "I do have one more question before we go in there. When you went to the diner to bring her in, did Mary Margaret ever have any time alone?"

"You mean time alone to ditch a phone?" the sheriff asked.

Madison nodded.

He tilted his head. "I had to wait for her to grab her stuff in the back."

"How long was she gone?"

"I don't know. A couple minutes. I didn't think it was a problem at the time. It's not like she was under arrest."

"I want you to go back to the diner," Jonas said. "See if you can find a burner phone she might have ditched. Inside the restaurant, the back dumpster, her car . . . I don't know where it is, but I need you to find it."

"Will do." He headed out the door.

A minute later, Madison was watching Mary Margaret through the one-way glass. She could see the fear in the woman's eyes as her fingers drummed against the desk in the interrogation room. Madison had felt sorry for her at one point, but her frustration had grown as they learned more about the case. Barrick had never been in that cabin. That was clear now. But they still needed Mary Margaret to tell them where he was going.

"You ready to go in?" Jonas asked. He held up a Coke and a candy bar from the vending machine. "I figured if I'm supposed to be the good cop, and the candy bar worked with Will . . ."

Madison chuckled. "That's not a bad idea, though I might be the one who needs chocolate right now."

"My grandmother used to say if she was going to die of something, it might as well be from eating too much chocolate," Jonas said as they approached the room. "She always insisted Belgian chocolate was the best, but she'd eat anything dunked or covered in chocolate."

"I think I would have liked your grandmother."

Once inside, Jonas set the drink and candy bar in front of Mary Margaret, then sat down. Madison took the chair next to him.

"How are you doing?" he asked.

Mary Margaret frowned. "I'm tired and don't understand why I'm still sitting here. I've told you everything I know."

"That's because you haven't told us the truth," Madison said.

"What do you mean?"

Madison tried to keep the anger out of her voice. Playing the part of bad cop wasn't hard, but she had to remember that this wasn't personal. Mary Margaret hadn't exactly been honest, but their main job was to find Damon Barrick. "You lied to us. In fact, you've been lying to us this whole time."

"No. I haven't—"

"It's over, Mary Margaret." Madison leaned forward. "Your brother was involved in an accident this afternoon."

"What?" Her face paled.

"His truck flipped while he was trying to evade us. And in the process of finally questioning him, we learned that Barrick was never here. We know you played us—keeping us distracted—so he'd have a chance to get as far away from here as possible. Lying about the cabin—"

"No, wait"—she ran her hands through her hair—"you said Charlie was in an accident."

"It looks like he has a broken rib and a broken wrist, but he'll live," Jonas said. "The problem right now is that he's in a lot of trouble. Both of you are."

Madison continued. "He already has two felonies on his record, which unfortunately for him means that this could put him in prison for up to fifty years—"

"Fifty years? No. You don't understand." Mary Margaret clinched her fists together. "He didn't even know what was in that package, or who he was meeting!"

"So you admit to helping Barrick."

"Yes . . . no—"

"Which is it? We have evidence Charlie was in Salt Lake, and on top of that, we have a confession from him. He recognized the man he met with as Damon Barrick, and by the way, he also helped himself to some of the cash you sent with him."

"I didn't think he'd get in trouble."

"I'm not sure what you thought might happen, but there's another problem. We also know that you've been communicating with Barrick. We know you recently bought a burner phone at a gas station up the road."

"There's no crime in that."

"No, but it is—as we've made clear to you before—a crime to help an escaped prisoner," Madison said.

"He told me he was innocent." Mary Margaret sat back in her chair, her resolve to protect Barrick clearly slipping. "He said he needed my help. My marriage is falling apart. It seemed like an option."

"Does your husband know about any of this yet?"

"No. Not that he would care. He's out of town for a couple days for his job. Like always."

"I don't know about your marriage, but do you really think it will be that easy to start over? Barrick's either going to be running or he's going to get caught. That is his life from now on." Madison caught her gaze. "Tell us where he is."

"I don't know."

"Stop lying, Mary Margaret."

"I'm not. He really didn't tell me. Just that he would get in touch when he was ready for me."

"Do you have a passport?"

She nodded. "I got one last year when I went to Mexico with my husband."

"So you're just supposed to wait for him."

She was afraid. Madison could see it in her eyes. She could also tell she was beginning to waver. But there was also a chance that she really didn't know where he was.

"Always on the run from the authorities is no life, Mary Margaret. You have to know that."

She just shrugged. "Can't be any worse than a loveless marriage."

Madison felt some of her anger melt. The woman was so unhappy she actually thought living on the run would be better than the life she had. But whatever she was thinking was nothing more than a fairy-tale dream that could never have a happy-ever-after ending.

"I know you don't believe us," Jonas said, "but he used you. He needed someone who would keep us busy while he runs. Nothing more."

"You're wrong." Mary Margaret's voice sounded almost faint. "He told me I just had to be patient and wait for him."

"And while you wait, the DA is going to come in and charge you as an accessory to murder." Madison shoved a picture of Phelps in front of her. "Remember this photo? We know Barrick killed him. He had a wife and three children."

"No, I never meant—"

"It's too late for what you did or didn't mean to happen," Madison said. "Where was Barrick heading?"

"I don't know. I've told you everything I know."

There was a knock on the door.

Madison stood up. "We'll be back in a minute."

Out in the hallway, the sheriff stood waiting for them.

"I'm not sure we're going to get any more out of her," Madison said.

"Maybe it doesn't matter." The sheriff held a

phone in a clear evidence bag. "We found this in a dumpster behind the diner. We got Barrick's number off it."

"You're sure it's hers?"

The sheriff nodded. "Thought you might want to look at it, though it doesn't give us much to go on."

Madison scanned through the texts while Jonas read over her shoulder.

> The police are here.
> Somehow they know.

Don't panic. Remember what we talked about if something goes wrong.

> The cabin.

It will give me time to get away.

> Where are you going?
> I could meet you somewhere.

Too risky. I'll be in touch.

"Maybe she really doesn't know where he is," Madison said, turning to face Jonas.

"It's looking like that," he said.

The sheriff glanced up. "That's the end of their

conversation. Looks like she dumped the phone, then hurried back into the diner."

"What about a trace on the phone?" Madison asked.

"I'm already on it," the sheriff said. "You guys have some pretty sophisticated ways of tracking people. I spoke with your boss and he was able to accomplish in a matter of minutes what would take me days."

"And?" she said, trying to hurry the man along.

"Unfortunately, Barrick's long gone. He dumped the phone. But we can confirm he was outside Salt Lake City."

"With Charlie." Madison frowned. "We need more."

"His options are limited," Jonas said. "He'll never get on a plane without ID. Or rent a car, for that matter. Denver would be his best option. He lived there. Knows the area. Would probably know who to go to."

"So his options?" Madison asked.

"He could steal another car, but if I were him, I'd be wary of any attention if something goes wrong," Jonas said.

"Agreed."

"There's an Amtrak station, along with a bus station, that both have routes to Denver," the sheriff said. "But how easy would it be for him to buy a ticket?"

"With Amtrak he'd have to use a ticket counter

if he didn't buy one online," Madison said. "But again, he'd still need to use an ID."

Jonas shoved his hands into his front pockets. "We've already got a BOLO out on him. I think the next step has to be going through security footage of both the train and bus stations in Salt Lake and searching through his file for contacts that might help him."

Madison nodded. "If he doesn't want to spend the rest of his life looking over his shoulder, he's going to have to disappear."

TWENTY

Jonas managed to get a few hours of sleep before they met back at the sheriff's department early the next morning. They'd discussed the option of heading for Salt Lake the previous night, but they knew Barrick wasn't planning to stay. By the time they could get there, he was more than likely going to be long gone.

But *where,* was the question.

Jonas stared at the US map hanging on the back wall of the office they were using. They had to move quickly, but he had no desire to spend another day on a wild-goose chase. They needed something concrete. Disappearing in the US might be doable, but it wouldn't be easy. Avoiding leaving a digital footprint was almost impossible, and he would need cash—far more than the three grand Mary Margaret had given him.

If he was planning to leave the country, Barrick was going to need someone who could get him across the border with a passport that would pass the inspection of border patrol. No doubt he could have made connections while in prison.

Jonas glanced at Madison, who was wading

215

back into the files they had on Barrick. She was both determined and focused, but he was still worried about her. There was a fatigue in her eyes that the past few days had brought on. Normal for what they did, but that didn't make it easier.

He had a feeling she'd argue with him, but he couldn't help but wonder if he should order her to go home. He was impressed with her focus despite the situation, but not worrying about her family was impossible. She'd called her sister again last night, wanting to make sure that the plan to move to a safer space had been implemented, but she wasn't able to get through. He knew it had her worried.

She'd told him she felt like she had to stay, but he wondered if she wasn't regretting her decision not to get on the next flight back to Seattle. If anything happened to Danielle or her family because of her work, he knew she'd blame herself, no matter what the circumstances. But the truth was, sometimes, even if you were right, there was nothing you could do.

He pushed away the thoughts and focused back on their work. The most likely place Barrick would go was back to Denver where he had friends and contacts—and right where they wanted him.

Jonas stood up, needing to stretch his legs, and walked across the room to where there was a pot of coffee. He poured the thick sludge from the bottom of the pot into a Styrofoam cup.

"Reminds me of our training," Madison said, stepping up next to him. "I never understood who put Rob in charge of the coffee, but it looks like he might be working here."

He took a sip. "It does have the same bitter, metallic, stale taste."

Madison laughed. "I think I'll avoid the risk and try the tea instead of a second cup."

"That's probably not a bad idea, though I could go for a double shot of caffeine," Jonas said, grimacing as he took another sip. "Find anything?"

"I did, actually. Two things."

"I'm listening."

"I've been going through Mary Margaret's phone records."

"And?"

"A couple hours before we picked her up, she made a call to an area code in Salt Lake City. I traced the number and it belongs to a Chris Matthews—who just happens to have a criminal record. I contacted the marshals out that way and they're going to bring him in. They'll let us know what they find out."

"So Barrick might have been on his way there to try and pick up a new passport."

"That's what I'm thinking." She dunked her tea bag in the hot water. "I've also been tracking

Barrick's mother's cell phone, and a few minutes ago, she got a call from a burner phone. Call lasted three minutes."

"That has to be him."

"Agreed. He's taking a risk, but if he's headed to Denver, he has to reach out to someone."

"Maybe he simply called to say goodbye."

"Maybe, but we need someone to talk with her. To see what was said." She yawned, then took a sip of her tea. "I'm also putting a track on the number that called her, though based on his past actions, he's going to use it and dump it."

Jonas set his coffee on the counter, then studied her face. "Did you get any sleep?"

"Probably about as much as you did." She shrugged. "To be honest, I'm worried about my sister."

"Did you get ahold of her?"

A shadow crossed her face. "Not yet. But I know Michaels would tell me if something was wrong. Still, it's hard not to be there."

He couldn't blame her for worrying. Having someone you love threatened or hurt was always personal. He'd learned that firsthand with Felicia.

"Michaels will make sure they're okay until we can figure out what's going on," he said, not sure his reassurances were enough. "And in the meantime, you'll just have to leave it in God's hands."

"I know."

He took another sip of his coffee, then added a second spoonful of sugar, hoping it would mask the taste. "I could order you to take the next flight back to Seattle."

"You could, but I need to stay here. If Barrick is the one behind this, they won't be safe until he's behind bars."

Officer Carter walked in with a couple drinks and held one out to each deputy. "First thing I learned working here was never drink the coffee. This is how coffee should taste."

Jonas took Madison's tea and dumped both their Styrofoam cups into the trash before accepting Carter's offering. "You're a lifesaver! We definitely owe you one for this."

Carter laughed. "I'll remember that if I ever need a favor from the US Marshals."

Jonas's phone rang, and he pulled it out of his pocket and moved aside to answer it.

"I'm calling for Deputy US Marshal Jonas Quinn."

"This is he."

"This is Blake Peters calling from the US Marshal offices in Salt Lake City. Your partner called me about a person of interest in our jurisdiction."

"Chris Matthews?" Jonas asked.

"Yes. He turned out to be a dead end. He's currently in New York, but I think we might have found your man."

"Great. What have you got?" Jonas asked.

"I'm sending you security footage now. It's a possible sighting of Barrick at the Amtrak station in Salt Lake City about three hours ago. He managed to miss all the cameras except for one. Check your email."

Jonas signaled for Madison, then headed to the computer he was borrowing from the sheriff's office. He opened up the email. "It's downloading now," he said, putting the phone on speaker. He turned to Madison. "One of the marshals from Salt Lake is sending us some security footage. They think they might have seen Barrick at an Amtrak station. They want us to see if we can identify him."

"I still can't see him taking Amtrak."

"Go to the two-minute mark," Peters said.

Jonas ran the video forward, paused the frame, then set the footage to full screen. Dozens of passengers strolled through the busy station, hurrying along the crowded walkways.

"I was wrong," Madison said, pointing to a man with a visible scar on his chin. "That's definitely him."

Barrick had managed to change his appearance somewhat with glasses, a baseball cap, and some baggy clothes that made him look ten pounds heavier, but there was no hiding that scar.

"Can you tell where he's heading?" Jonas asked the marshal on the phone.

"It's a cross-country Amtrak train, the California Zephyr, that runs from San Francisco Bay to Chicago and back."

"Which direction was he going?"

"East. There's a train that left at three in the morning in the direction of Denver."

"He had to have stolen an ID. Can you track what name he's using?"

"We believe he used the ID of a man named Eugene Cahill," said Peters. "We've got a local address on him. I'm sending officers now to check on him."

Madison took a step back. "You have to be right. He's heading to Denver."

"I thought he was smarter, but they always head for the familiar." Jonas stared at the video then turned back to the phone. "Do we have any way to verify that he's on the train and not just throwing us off again?"

"I'm trying to get ahold of a passenger list," Peters said. "I'll also see if any other tickets were bought under that name."

"Keep us updated," Jonas said, then ended the call.

"So how do we want this to play out?" she asked. "Do we want to have local LEOs pick him up at one of the stops?"

"I think we need to be there to coordinate. We can't let this go south. He's an armed fugitive, so we'll have to handle things carefully."

Madison nodded. "I agree."

He pulled the information Peters had sent about the train along with the video. There were seven stops between Salt Lake City and Denver. Provo, Helper, and Green River in Utah, then Grand Junction, Glenwood Springs, Granby, and Fraser-Winter Park in Colorado.

He took a long drink of the coffee the deputy had brought him. "Once he gets to Denver he'll disappear. What are our options?"

Madison drummed her fingers on the desk. "We could evacuate the train. Stop at one of the stations and have everyone get off. Arrest him as he exits."

"Too risky," Jonas said. "He'd know something was up. We have to avoid turning this into a hostage situation. If we start marching people off the train, he'll get spooked."

Deputy Nelson walked back over to their station.

Madison took a sip of her drink. "It's normal to have officers walk through the trains, and delays are inevitable, which could play to our advantage."

"Agreed, but boarding the train will be just as risky. We'll have to search every compartment with passengers on board. If he sees a bunch of officers—"

"We go in undercover," she said. "No uniforms. Just as passengers. We identify him, then we just keep our eye on him until he gets off the train."

"It might work," Deputy Nelson said. "But I thought the two of you were in the transport plane with him. He'll recognize you both."

"We could do something to change our appearances," Madison said. "He'll try to blend in. We have to as well. And I think it's worth the risk. We can recognize him faster than someone who only saw a photograph."

"You're right. Our best bet may be to get to one of the stops before the train arrives with a few undercover officers. Then we can keep our eye on him until he gets off."

Madison glanced at the map. "The train goes through Glenwood Springs just after twelve. That would give us time to plan and get everything in place."

Jonas nodded. "We'll coordinate with the Amtrak police as well as local police. We need to make sure that we don't spook him. Nelson, we're going to need detailed schematics of the entire train. Sleeping cars, restrooms, showers, luggage compartments, café—everything. Could you get that for us?"

"I'm on it."

Jonas glanced at his watch. "I'll get us a flight out, and in the meantime, we'll work out the details."

Because one wrong move and he'd disappear for good.

TWENTY-ONE

Madison studied the timetable they'd come up with, wanting to ensure they hadn't missed anything. The frustration that Barrick had managed to evade them this long had yet to dissipate, but even more frustrating was the fact that her family had been threatened. Putting her life in danger was one thing, but her family? No, that wasn't acceptable. And even though she trusted Michaels with their safety, until Barrick was back behind bars, she wasn't going to be able to rest.

Jonas walked up to the desk where she was sitting and set down a to-go bag. "Michaels is arranging our flight. Said we can be out of here within the hour. In the meantime, I grabbed us breakfast from one of the local cafés. You need to eat. We both do."

She opened up the bag and breathed in the smell of bacon and sausage. She'd always told her sister she could be a vegetarian if it weren't for bacon and sausage.

"They're breakfast burritos," Jonas said. "Something I remember you liking from our training. There's also orange juice. I hope that's okay."

"It's perfect." She pulled out one of the burritos, handed it to him, then pulled out a second one for herself. "I didn't realize how hungry I was, but this smells delicious."

He sat down across from her, hesitating before unwrapping his. "You've been quiet since we decided to go. Are you okay with the plan?"

"Considering the circumstances, yes. I think this will work. It has to."

"I've said it before, but if you want to fly back to Seattle to be with your family instead, no one would question your decision."

"No." She took a sip of her orange juice. She'd been tempted to tell him she had to leave, but she didn't feel at peace about that decision. And if she stayed, she needed to be one hundred percent on board. "The best thing I can do for my sister is find Barrick and stop him. And that's what I plan to do. Michaels will make sure they're safe until then."

"Okay, I just wanted to make sure you're good with how things are moving forward, because I know this is tough. I know you're worried about your family."

"I am."

She'd always known she'd end up working in law enforcement. Between her grandfather's and father's examples of serving their country, it had always seemed inevitable. But up until this point, she'd always been able to keep her work and family separate. This time, things were hitting far too close to home.

"Madison?"

"Sorry. You're right though. It's hard not to want to be in both places at the same time. Because my sister just had a baby, she tends to be overly emotional, though I can't blame her. She has every reason to be worried, but my dad's going to be the biggest struggle. He hates anything out of his schedule. Danielle will definitely have her hands full with all of them cooped up together."

"I know this is hard, but your sister will be with him, and she won't be alone. He'll be okay. Especially if he's as stubborn and feisty as his daughter."

"Funny."

She glanced up at him and caught his goofy smile as he looked back at her. Something unexpected flipped inside her. Surely he wasn't flirting with her. She shoved away the thought as quickly as it surfaced. That was ridiculous. Jonas had made it very clear that he was not looking for a relationship, and she certainly wasn't. She liked him. As a friend. Respected him even more as a colleague, but anything beyond that couldn't be in the picture.

It had to be the fact that she needed a good night's sleep in her own bed without the heaviness of the case keeping her up. But until she got that . . . just because she'd let herself become vulnerable with him didn't mean anything.

"Consider that a compliment," he said, before biting into his burrito. "We make a good team."

She couldn't deny that. "Yes, we do."

"Why don't you take a few minutes to call your sister before we leave and make sure she's okay. We'll head for the airstrip in about thirty minutes."

"I'll be ready."

She finished her breakfast then, deciding that the noisy sheriff's office wasn't the place to make a call, and headed outside. She pulled her phone out of her pocket, hesitating before placing the call. The sun felt good on her face. She'd been so cold since that night in the forest. She took in the view of the picturesque Wyoming wilderness. Mountains rose up in the distance, and the air felt invigorating. After living in Seattle for so long, she felt drawn to the rugged yet small-town feel. And being here was almost as if she'd stepped back into another century.

The US Marshals had been established over two hundred years ago by George Washington and were known for their posses and manhunts on the frontier. It had been different back then when men like Wyatt Earp and Bat Masterson worked to keep law and order where there was no local government. They had taken down infamous gangs and arrested criminals, becoming heroes during a lawless time in the country's history. And now she was a part of that history by apprehending fugitives and transporting prisoners. It had always been something she was proud to be a part of. But this situation had thrown her.

Maybe it was simply the timing of everything. The black rose in her bedroom. The threat to her sister. She missed Luke and wished he were here to talk to her and tell her what to do.

In the five years since his death, she tried dating half a dozen times, but it had never seemed right. Or at least she'd never really connected with any of the men who'd asked her out. Maybe her problem was that she was always comparing her date with Luke. Which wasn't fair. Luke hadn't been perfect—even he would have agreed—but with him she became a better person. He helped her grow in her faith and pushed her to do things even she'd never imagined doing.

Like becoming a US Marshal. He never felt threatened by what she did, and if he were still alive, he would have encouraged her to make the career move. That was what she missed. The trust and companionship. It's why she wouldn't compromise even if she did decide to open up her heart again.

If.

She wasn't sure if she'd ever be ready to go there again, and for now she was as content as she could be with life. And it wasn't as if coming home to an empty house at times wasn't lonely. She was the one who had to fix the broken washing machine and the leaky faucet in the kitchen. But with work, family, and friends, life was full. She wasn't sure there was room in her heart even if someone as handsome as Jonas one day decided to try to walk in and win it.

She shoved the ridiculous thought away and called her sister.

"Danielle."

"Maddie, hey, are you okay?"

"I'm fine. You're the one I'm worried about."

Danielle let out a sharp breath of air. "The baby is crying and Daddy's upset, but it's not like we have a choice, I guess. And really, we're fine here, but I can't help but wonder if we're all overreacting."

"I'm sorry you have to do this, but we can't take any chances."

"I know. And I feel like I should be a whole lot braver. I mean, you risk your life every day, but this has shaken me up some. I just don't know how you do this, because honestly, Maddie, I'm spooked."

"I know, and I'm sorry. But Michaels will take care of you. I can promise you that. When does Ethan get in?"

"About seven. We've decided to treat it like a vacation. At least with the kids. Not that this is the kind of vacation I would ever want, but we're fine. I've promised them that they can watch as much TV as they want—something that never happens—and Ethan's dad brought home pizza and popcorn, so they think this is almost as good as Disneyland. One of the deputies even brought a dozen cupcakes for Lilly's birthday."

Madison smiled at the image, feeling better. "It will all be over soon, but in the meantime, you need to be careful. Please. I can't have anything happen to any of you."

"We will, but you're the one who's risking your life."

"I'll be careful. We have a lead and are getting ready to fly out of here, but I'll be in touch as soon as I can. If all goes well, this will all be over in the next twenty-four hours. We'll find this guy."

"I hope you're right."

"Once I'm back home, I'll keep the kids for a night and let you and Ethan get some real time off."

"That would be nice, but right now all I want is everyone home safe."

After yet another flight, they were on their way to the train station in Glenwood Springs, Colorado. Their plan was simple. They'd already arranged to have local officers waiting at each stop, in case Barrick decided to get off the train at any point on the line, but so far there had been no sign of him. Once the train arrived, they'd have about ten minutes to search their assigned section. Assuming Barrick was on board, they didn't want to spook him.

Madison glanced at her watch. The train was due to arrive soon, but an announcement revealed that it would be ten minutes late. She sighed. There had been no sign of Barrick at any of the other stops. Unless he'd somehow slipped past the officers that were in place.

She'd been here once before, the resort city nestled in the Rocky Mountains and surrounded by the White River National Forest. Mountains hovered behind the brick station with the red tile roof, and a handful of people stood ready to get on the train with their luggage. She could hear the Colorado River running below them and the sound of cars passing behind the station.

"Ever ridden a train?" she asked, moving next to Jonas.

"When I was seven, we took a train trip to see my cousins. I just have a few vague memories of miles and miles of cornfields and fighting with my brother."

Madison laughed. "We never went on a train but took plenty of long car trips. I'm not sure how my sister and I made it without killing each other."

Small talk passed the time, until finally the train pulled into the station. Adrenaline pulsed through her. She was ready to get this over with.

They boarded the train separately, leaving two plainclothes officers on the platform in case Barrick slipped out. No one paid attention as she stepped onto the train. To the rest of the passengers, she was just another stranger, heading in the same direction. She'd opted to dress down from what she normally wore. To blend in with the other passengers, she'd come up with a pair of jeans, a T-shirt with a jean jacket, a knit cap, and no makeup. A quick glance in the mirror on the plane to Colorado had confirmed that unless Barrick looked closely, he wouldn't recognize her.

There were five other undercover officers who'd memorized Barrick's photo and were now moving through the train that was made up of sections, including three sleepers, three coaches, and a diner and lounge. She'd been assigned to the glass-framed lounge, trying to look like another passenger who'd just gotten on and was looking for a place to sit. A couple was reading in front of the large picture windows lining the car. A family was busy trying to get their children settled in for the ride, and a couple backpackers had already marked their spots.

She tugged on the strap of the backpack she was carrying. Everything seemed normal. And there was no sign of Barrick.

A voice came over her earpiece. "Diner's cleared."

"So are the engines."

Madison kept walking. Her gut told her that Barrick was going to hide out in the open. A sleeper car would leave him trapped. He would want a way out if he needed to run.

She finished searching her section as the rest of the team continued to clear the train. Jonas came toward her after clearing his section. Every officer had radioed in, and no one had spotted Barrick.

"We missed him, Madison."

Her brain spun with the implications. "What if we didn't."

"What do you mean?"

"Who are we looking for?"

"Again, what do you mean?"

"White male, early thirties, glasses and baggy clothes, possible baseball cap, traveling alone," she said. "He's not going to make it easy on us. He's probably changed again, just in case he was spotted on camera. He's probably dressed like everyone around him. What if he's not on the train alone? What if he changed his appearance? What if he's with someone?"

He nodded. "You and I need to sweep the train again. Head toward the front and I'll take the back. We'll have the officers on standby on the platform. We just can't spook him."

She started at the back of the compartment, heading down the narrow passageway, thankful they'd studied the schematics of the train. She was careful to make sure they didn't miss anything.

"Jonas, do you have anything?"

"Not yet."

She walked down the aisle, then stopped and turned around. Barrick was sitting next to a woman. At first glance, they appeared as a couple, making him easy to overlook, especially with the slight alterations he'd managed to make with his appearance. He'd dumped the baggy clothes and was now wearing a button-down shirt with a jean jacket and a red ball cap, and he had added a goatee.

Madison turned around and kept walking, certain she hadn't been made yet. "I've got him. Red ball cap. Left-side aisle. But he's sitting with a woman."

"A hostage?"

"I don't think so. More of a decoy."

"Take a seat where you can keep an eye on him," Jonas said. "I'll do the same thing."

Madison set her backpack in a seat like she was getting ready to settle in. She pretended to check her hair in her phone's camera while keeping an eye on his movements.

Barrick stood up.

"Wait," she whispered into her radio, "he's spooked. I think he's going to run."

Barrick jumped up and grabbed a toddler who

had been playing on the other side of the aisle, then backed up. The little boy squirmed as Barrick pushed a gun into his side.

The mother screamed and Barrick told her to shut up.

Madison spoke into her radio. "He's got a gun and a hostage."

She moved closer to him. "Don't do this, Barrick. It's over. Walk off this train with me so no one else gets hurt."

"That's not gonna happen."

Jonas moved forward behind him. "It's over, Barrick."

The man looked back and forth between the two marshals. "Here's what's going to happen. I'm going to walk off this train and no one is going to try to stop me. If you don't cooperate, this mom won't see her kid again."

"Please don't hurt my baby, please—"

"I said shut up." Barrick caught Madison's gaze. "You know I will. Don't test me."

"Get the platform cleared now," she yelled, as the kid hollered louder. "He's coming off the train. Give him space."

Barrick backed off the train slowly. Madison was less than a dozen feet behind him as he jumped onto the platform, still holding the boy.

He fired a shot into the air. The situation was quickly spiraling out of control. Which was exactly what they'd wanted to avoid.

Barrick shoved into a group of tourists, let go of the boy, then took off running.

Jonas shouted from behind her. "Where's he going?"

"He's heading away from the tracks."

She frowned as Barrick headed around the train station. What was he thinking? There were two dozen cops surrounding the station.

"Where is he?" Jonas asked.

Madison caught a glimpse of him in the distance as she worked to bridge the gap. "Twenty yards ahead of me, heading west."

"Someone cut him off, now."

"He's headed for one of the bridges."

"I want backup on the other side so we can block off his exit now."

"Copy that," an officer radioed in.

"Keep all pedestrians off the bridge and surrounding areas." Lungs burning, she ran after him. "We have to avoid another hostage situation."

TWENTY-TWO

Jonas sprinted across the bridge, the Colorado River rushing beneath him, while he yelled at people to get out of his way. This time of year, there were plenty of locals and tourists filling up the popular town. They had to stop Barrick now, before someone else got hurt. He started shouting out orders to block off the bridge to ensure no other civilians got involved.

A man in his late fifties rushed up to him. "That's my wife. He's got my wife." The man pointed to where Barrick stood with a woman by his side, their backs to the bridge's railing.

"Sir, I need you to stop right there."

"I said he's got my wife."

Jonas held up his badge. "I know, and we're going to do everything we can to ensure your wife's safety. What's her name?"

"Karen. Karen Sutherland."

Jonas signaled to one of the officers who had been sealing off the perimeter. "I want you to wait back here with him." He turned to the man. "I promise we will do everything in our power to make sure your wife is okay, but I need you to stay back for me right now."

Jonas pivoted to face Barrick, then headed back toward the center of the bridge, where Madison was directing pedestrians out of the way.

"What do you propose?" The local police chief stepped up beside Jonas, matching his pace.

"We need to think before we rush in there. He's already killed at least four people. He's got a weapon. If he thinks using it will give him a way out, he'll do it again. But for the moment he needs her alive, so let's keep the advantage in our favor."

"You need to be the one in charge of the negotiations." Madison came running up beside them.

"I've seen you in the interrogation room."

"Not this time." She shook her head. "We know enough about Barrick to know that you can relate to him better than I will. He had the advantage over me once already, and we don't want him to think he has it again."

"Fair enough."

He knew the risks of a negotiation, especially in a situation like this. It was too easy to let emotions lead, but the bottom line was he was never going to convince Barrick to simply walk away. They were way past that. Their goal for the moment had to be saving the hostage's life.

"Get us a perimeter set up," Madison said to the police chief. "But give the guy some space."

The officer nodded. "I'll get my best man on it."

"What about a sniper?" Jonas asked.

He glanced at Madison and knew they were thinking the same thing. They always wanted to take felons alive, but this time they might not have a choice.

"Taking him out will be our last resort," Jonas reminded the police chief. "But I want to be ready."

"Yes, sir," the police chief said before being pulled away by another officer.

"And, Madison, signal me when the sniper's ready, in case it comes to that. I'll keep him talking in the meantime."

She brushed her hand down his arm. "Just be careful. He has nothing to lose. If he has to take down a hostage or any law enforcement standing in his way, he won't hesitate to do whatever it takes."

"I know. I will."

With his hands up, Jonas started across the bridge to where Barrick stood with his back to the rail and his hostage standing in front of him.

"That's close enough." Barrick pressed the gun against the woman's head.

"Okay. I'm stopping now. We need to talk, Barrick. I know you want this to be over as much as we do." He took a half step forward.

"Just let me go," Karen said. "Please . . . let me go."

"Shut up!"

"Karen, I'm US Marshal Jonas Quinn. I know you're scared, but we're doing everything we can to keep both of you safe and put an end to this as soon as possible." Jonas took another step forward and kept his hands up in the air. "I know you've had a rough few days, Barrick, but we need to find a solution to this without anyone else getting hurt."

"This is far from over," Barrick said.

"Then tell me what you're thinking. How can we compromise?"

"What am I thinking? I'll tell you what I'm thinking. For starters, I'm not going back to prison. I don't belong in prison."

Jonas tried to put himself in the other man's shoes. Tried to imagine what it was like for him. He'd been facing life in prison and the plane crash had suddenly become his winning lottery ticket. A chance to run and disappear. But even if he shot his hostage, Barrick had to know he'd be taken down. But the desperation in the man's eyes had him worried.

"I know this has to be overwhelming, but I'm here to help," Jonas said.

"Don't act like you care about what happens. Besides, what do you know about my case beyond maybe what you read in some file?"

"You're right. I read your file, and that's all I know." Jonas paused for a moment. "Why don't you tell me your side? What brought you here?"

Barrick let out a low laugh. "Like you care. Your job is to track down people like me."

"Yes, but I'm listening."

"You really want to know what happened? What wasn't in that report of yours? I was framed, and I'm not going back to prison."

"I might not be able to guarantee what a judge will say, but I can help you today. And if there are issues in your case, it's possible to file an appeal. But hurting Karen won't look good for you. If you surrender now, it will make things so much easier. All you have to do is put the gun down."

"I know how this works. You'll say anything, do anything to get what you want. You'll promise me things will be okay. That if I'm innocent, justice will always win, and I'll go free. Except you know that isn't true. You know what will happen. It doesn't matter if I'm innocent. All I'm trying to do is get my life back, which at this point might never be possible again."

"What will it take to end this?"

"You don't get it. I have nothing to lose. That plane crash was a second chance at freedom. My way out."

"I understand that, but running is never the way. It will put you in a situation where there is no out. You need to understand that. You're surrounded by people ready to ensure Karen isn't hurt and you're arrested. That is their one goal right now. To do that without anyone getting hurt. And if you come in, I guarantee I'll listen to you."

"That's not true and you know it." Barrick shifted his feet so he was slightly closer to the railing. "They'll put me away for the rest of my life, if I don't get the death penalty. So for me there's only one way out. And she's my ticket."

Jonas knew that reaching for a quick resolution would only get someone else hurt. And he couldn't let that happen. The man had lost every sense of control in his life.

Barrick tightened his grip on Karen. "They wanted a fall guy. That's what all of this has been about."

"I'll be the first to admit that our system isn't perfect, but can you tell me why you think that?"

"Why does it even matter? No one has ever listened to me before. All the evidence against me was circumstantial, because I happened to be in the area."

"The report said you killed two people, then resisted arrest."

"What would you have done? I was on a business trip in Seattle and suddenly at five in the morning, someone's beating on my hotel door and screaming at me to get out of bed. I'm thrown onto the ground, handcuffed, then dragged out of there. I have a feeling you'd resist being arrested too."

"I can't imagine what that would have felt like."

"That's because you're always the one on the other side of the arrest. They questioned me for hours, threatened me with the death penalty. Then the next thing I know my face is on every news channel across the country as some crazed killer. They say they have evidence that I'm connected to some European mob. My lawyer told me he believed me, but the evidence against me made it hard for a judge to get an acquittal. Now they're dragging me back to Denver for my trial."

"If you were innocent, you shouldn't have run."

"What would you suggest? I stay in my seat and wait for the two of you to send me back? Do you think that would have made a judge suddenly drop the charges? No. That was my one chance at freedom, and there's no way I was going to waste it."

"Maybe you didn't kill that couple. Maybe you were innocent, and someone messed up. But what about the guy you killed in prison? Or the man in Idaho who picked you up? You didn't have to kill him."

"The guy I killed in prison had been harassing me for weeks. It was him or me. The same with the guy I caught a ride with. He must have seen my gun and panicked. He pulled a gun on me. I thought he was going to kill me. I can't prove it, but it's the truth."

Jonas inched forward. "I can't change what a judge or jury says, but there are appeals that can be made. I can also help keep you from making things worse from this point on."

"Like things could get worse than this? My life is already ruined. I've lost my job, my home—everything that ever mattered to me is gone. And you can tell me that if I'm innocent I'll eventually be fine. But you're wrong."

"Here's the thing. Everything you've done—including this right now—is only making things worse for you. If you'd just put your gun down—"

"And then what? You arrest me again?" Barrick kept his weapon pressed against Karen's head. "Sorry, but that's not going to happen. I'm not going back."

"Jonas." Madison's voice came through his earpiece. "We've got a sniper in place."

Jonas spoke out of the corner of his mouth. "Give me a second." He turned back to Barrick. "I might have a solution."

"What's that?" Barrick was shifting a lot now.

"I'm a deputy US Marshal, which gives me a bit of clout over everyone else here."

"So?"

"I can get someone on the line right now. A friend who's high up in the Department of Justice who I believe can help you. But only if you end things right now. And that means letting Karen go. You do that and it will be my sign of trust that you're telling the truth."

"He's on the line with you?"

"He can be. What do you say? Will you let her go?"

"Why would anyone want to help me? I think you're just like everyone else who saw me as guilty before they even heard my story."

"The bottom line is that I'm your one chance out of here, Barrick."

"No, you're not." Barrick hugged Karen against him, then managed to pull her over the railing and into the Colorado River below.

TWENTY-THREE

Madison was already heading down the steep riverbank when she saw Barrick pull the woman over the edge and jump. She watched as the two hit the water and went under. Madison scrambled toward the shoreline, scanning the currents for them to emerge.

"I need backup now!" she shouted into her earpiece. "We need to get them both out of the water."

She searched the fast-moving current and spotted the woman bobbing as two more officers came up behind her.

"There she is." Madison ran along the edge of the water another dozen yards, trying to get ahead of the woman, before stepping into the chilly river.

Karen flailed her arms above her as she tried to get to shore. Madison grabbed for her hand and just missed. The woman slipped back into the water. Madison scurried farther down to the water's edge, trying to keep her own balance and not get swept into the current.

Together with the officers, they managed to help pull her out. Someone handed Madison a blanket, and she slipped it around Karen's shoulders. She crouched beside the woman as she tried to catch her breath, then glanced out across the fast-moving water. Barrick had to be close by, but where?

She turned her attention back to the woman. "Karen, I'm Deputy US Marshal Madison James. Your husband's on his way down here right now. Are you okay?"

"I think so. I just cut my leg, and I can't . . . I can't breathe."

"I want you to take some slow, deep breaths. You probably had the wind knocked out of you. You're going to be okay."

Madison turned to one of the officers who helped rescue Karen. "See if you can get some paramedics down here."

The officer nodded and stepped away.

"Karen, are you okay?"

Her husband wrapped his arms around her as she broke down sobbing.

"She has a cut on her leg, but she should be fine. Give the paramedics a few minutes to check her out. They'll probably want to take her to a hospital just as a precaution, but you can stay with her."

Madison moved aside in order to let the paramedics treat her, then had one of the officers take down the woman's contact information.

She climbed back up the embankment, then ran

across the bridge to the other side where officers had spread out in a search for Barrick. She found Jonas barking out orders at someone on the phone. "Where is he?" she asked after he hung up.

"We don't know. He disappeared."

"How is that possible? We all saw him jump. He has to be down here."

"We need to get everyone over here now." Jonas called over the incident officer. "I want him found. Set up a fifty-mile perimeter with roadblocks. I want his photo up on local news stations across the state."

"Yes, sir."

Madison felt her heart sink. How had they finally caught up with him, only to lose him again?

"He's gone, Madison," Jonas said. "He somehow managed to slip away in the chaos. But it's not over. We'll find him."

Madison glanced upriver, trying to go through what his limited escape options had been.

Jonas met her gaze as she turned back to face him. "We assume he went downstream with the current, but what if he swam upriver while we were busy in the confusion, making sure the hostage was okay."

"Giving him a few seconds to swim upstream underwater and disappear into the crowd," Madison said.

"There is another option," Jonas said. "He could have hit his head and gotten dragged under the water."

Madison grimaced at the thought.

The police chief ran up to them. "One of my officers just called in. He spotted Barrick at the farmers market a few blocks south of here."

"Tell him to follow, but don't engage, and that we're on our way. In the meantime, make sure your officer keeps him in his sights."

The street music got louder as they approached the farmers market a few minutes later. Tented booths displayed farm-fresh fruits and vegetables and an assortment of other local products for sale. The crowds were heavy this time of day, with both locals and tourists, so this could be nothing but another foolish quest.

Where was he?

A red hat bobbed ahead of her. She looked closer. Same build as Barrick. It had to be him. Madison pressed through the crowd, making sure she kept her eyes on the moving figure.

"I might have him," she said into her radio. "He needs to be surrounded before he's approached."

"I see you," Jonas said. "I'm coming up to your right. Wait for my signal."

She quickened her pace, worried about the possibility of another hostage situation. They were going to have one chance of taking him down, and they didn't know if he was still armed or if he'd lost his weapon during the jump. They couldn't assume anything. Jonas came up next to her, while the other three officers fanned out in front of them, surrounding the man.

Jonas signaled for them to move in. "Police! Put your hands in the air now!"

"Get down on the ground!" one of the officers yelled.

The man dodged to the left, crashing through a display of candles, knocking them to the ground. Madison followed close behind, but she slammed her shoulder into a metal pole. She fought to catch her balance, then took off after him.

"Stop now! Police!"

Her heart quickened when he didn't obey. She picked up her pace, bridging the gap between them, while Jonas kept up with her. The man knocked over another display, then took off across the parking lot. A car turned in front of them, then slammed on the brakes, barely missing him. The momentary confusion gave them just enough time to catch up. Jonas wrestled him to the ground while the rest of them covered him, then quickly handcuffed the man and turned him around.

Unfamiliar eyes stared back at them.

Madison glanced around. "Why'd you run?" she asked the stranger, trying to keep the disappointment out of her voice.

"Because you were chasing me."

She caught the panic in the man's eyes. What had just happened?

"I didn't do anything."

"Then once again, why did you run?"

"I don't know."

"Let's start over. Where did you get this hat?"

"Some guy offered me fifty bucks to wear it. I gave him my Broncos sweatshirt and hat."

Jonas radioed the description into the station.

"Did he say anything else to you?" Madison asked.

"No. I thought he was crazy—you know, since he was soaking wet and all—but I thought why not. I could use the fifty bucks."

Jonas kicked at the asphalt with his boot, the irritation on his face as strong as hers.

"He couldn't have gone that far," she said in an effort to calm her partner, but frustration dug through her at another missed opportunity. How did he keep vanishing into thin air? With the mountains surrounding them, there were limited ways out of Glenwood Springs, but Barrick had grown up around here. That tipped the advantage once again in his favor.

The police chief drove up in the parking lot while someone took their imposter down to the station. He'd be questioned again, but more than likely would be let go.

• • •

At the police station, Madison and Jonas stood before a map of the city with the police chief.

"If you were trying to get out of here and knew the area well," Jonas said, "where would you go?"

The chief stared at the map. "There aren't a lot of options. He'll probably assume we've set up roadblocks, so he'll want to stay off the main roads."

"What about the water?" Madison glanced at him. "He could rent a boat and head south on the Roaring Fork River, or east on the Colorado." She moved in front of the map and studied the routes. "Where's the roadblock on 82?"

"We have it set up right here," he said, pointing to a pin. "Just south of town."

"So it's possible he follows the river and misses the roadblock altogether. If Denver is his destination, he could find transportation then head south and east toward the city."

Jonas shook his head and took a step back. "Or he could be heading to Albuquerque or Phoenix, for that matter. Without any concrete evidence, there's just no way to know."

Madison frowned. He was right. Barrick's original plan had been to take the train to Denver. With contacts and friends there, it made sense that he wouldn't change his original plans. But they didn't have time to head off on another wild-goose chase.

"I think our best move at this point would be to continue on to Denver," she said.

"Agreed."

"We can give the marshals there a heads-up that we're on our way and coordinate from there."

She started walking, stopping when Jonas called her name.

He stepped up in front of her. "Are you okay? You're holding your shoulder."

"It's fine. I think I slammed it into something while I was chasing the decoy." She hadn't even felt the pain until now.

"Let me see," Jonas said.

She pulled down her sleeve. Her arm was already turning a deep blue.

"You need an ice pack on that."

She nodded, knowing if she tried to argue with him, he'd just insist even more. She shot him a smile. "I'll get one on my way out. I promise. We need to get to Denver."

Three hours later, the city skyline came into view. She'd sat quiet for most of the trip, enjoying the views of the mountains while Barrick and her sister filled her thoughts.

"It's beautiful, isn't it?" Madison stared out the window, finally breaking the silence that had fallen between them. "I've always loved this part of the country."

"Ever gone skiing here?" he asked.

"Once as a kid. Our family did spend a lot of

winters skiing at Mt. Baker though. What about you?"

"My father enjoyed it and used to take me, though one winter I lost control of one of my skis and broke my leg."

"Ouch."

"It wasn't so bad. When I got home, my mother felt so bad for me, she let me hole up on the couch and watch TV for a week, so I never complained very much." He glanced at her. "Speaking of injuries, how's your shoulder?"

"A bit sore, but the ice pack did help."

"I have some good advice every now and then."

"Every now and then."

Jonas's phone rang, and he put it on speaker.

"Michaels," he said, "what's happening?"

"I just got a report from the tail we put on Barrick's mother. They lost track of her about thirty minutes ago at a shopping mall near her house."

Madison frowned. "For how long?"

"About five minutes."

"He's got to be there." Madison tried to push back the irritation. That was plenty of time for Barrick to make contact with her. "Have them check all the surveillance footage."

"Already done, but that's not all of it. She just showed up at our offices in Denver. She's asking to speak with the marshals on the case."

TWENTY-FOUR

The noose might be slowly closing in around him, but Barrick was still one step ahead of them. Madison stepped inside the US Marshals Service building in downtown Denver. It was like a chess game. Learning to think like a fugitive and calculate their next move.

While they didn't know why Barrick's mother had come in, they were going to have to convince the woman that for Barrick, returning to prison was better than running. Because in the end they would find him, and there was no guarantee he'd make it out alive.

They were quickly escorted into a small conference room with nothing more than a table and chairs inside. Damon Barrick's mother was waiting for them with a Styrofoam cup of coffee sitting in front of her. Eyes puffy and cheeks red, she'd clearly been crying. Something had compelled the woman to come in and talk to them about her son, and they needed to find out what.

"Mrs. Barrick?" Madison and Jonas took a seat across from the woman. "I'm Madison James and this is my partner Jonas Quinn. We're both with the US Marshal service. We understand you'd like to talk with us."

"I don't know." She set her hands on the table in front of her, shaking. "I'm not sure I should be here. If he knew I'd come . . ."

"You love your son, don't you?" Madison said.

Mrs. Barrick nodded her head. "Yes, and he's innocent. That's why I'm here. I saw that the US Marshals were tracking him down, and I knew if I didn't at least try to stop him from running away I'd never see him again. I can't let that happen."

"I can't imagine how hard this is for you, but if you're right, we need to find him. Otherwise, it's only going to get worse for him."

Madison waited, not wanting to push the woman, but needing the information she had come to give.

"He wrote me letters from prison," Barrick's mother said. "Told me about his cellmates and the food. Promised me he had a lawyer that would get him out. Asked me to pray for him until he did. I've heard what they are saying he did, but it's not true. I know him."

"Ma'am, we know this has got to be difficult," Jonas said, "but our job isn't to determine whether he's guilty or not. Our only job is to find him. And the sooner he comes in, the better it will be for him, especially if you're right and he's innocent."

"You did the right thing by coming here," Madison said.

"I don't know how we got to this place." She pulled a weathered photo out of her purse and handed it to Madison. "I keep this with me. It was taken at a Boy Scout camping trip when Damon was thirteen. His father died a few months after that. He had no siblings, so it was just the two of us. He always loved the outdoors, but even more so, he was a charmer. Could convince me of just about anything, but murder? I know my son and the things he's capable of, and murder isn't one of them."

Except unfortunately, sometimes those closest to us were the ones who couldn't see the truth.

Madison handed the photo back to her. "We understand you saw your son earlier today. Can you tell us what happened?"

"I'd gone to the mall. I just had to get out of the house. And suddenly he was there. He slipped me a note—told me I was being watched—then waited for me inside one of the dressing rooms. You'll probably think I'm naive, but I didn't know the police were watching me. And whenever I did think someone was following me, I thought it was reporters. They were always wanting to talk with me. Wanting to know why he did the things he did. I don't have answers for them, so I just keep to myself and try to stay busy."

"What did you talk about?" Jonas asked.

"At first all I could think about was that someone would burst into that dressing room and arrest him."

Madison leaned forward. The woman had her attention now. "What did he say?"

"He said he could only see me for a few minutes, but he needed to say goodbye. That he was sorry but running was his only option."

"Did he say where he was going?"

She shook her head. "He wouldn't tell me. He said it would put my life at risk if he did. I told him I didn't care, but he just said he was sorry. Told me he wouldn't be able to see me again."

Mrs. Barrick's shoulders heaved. She grabbed a tissue from her purse.

"Take your time," Madison said.

"I'm sorry," she said finally. "I'm so scared. I sat in the dressing room after he left me, not knowing what to do. If he's innocent I have to help him, because living as a fugitive . . . What kind of life is that? He doesn't know this, but I'm going to hire a lawyer so we can fight the charges. But in order to do that, he has to turn himself in."

"Has he ever talked about leaving the country?" Jonas asked.

"He once told me if he ever went to prison, he would try to escape across the border. At the time,

I didn't take him seriously. I just never imagined it would really happen."

"Did he say anything else? Like where specifically he would go?"

She hesitated again, before pulling something else out of her purse. "I don't know if this will help, but he sent this to me a few months ago."

"What is it?"

"A letter he wrote. I didn't think anything about it. I was simply happy to hear from him. He wrote about the Zookeeper."

"Who's the Zookeeper?"

"I'm not sure. I thought it was someone he was in prison with. Maybe a cellmate. But I think it's someone he knew here in Denver."

Madison took the letter and scanned through it. "Some kind of contact who could help him get out of prison?"

"Possibly. He told me not to worry today. That he had resources. That the Zookeeper would help."

"Did he say anything else?" Jonas asked.

"No. Just that he had to say goodbye. All I could think about was that I'd never see my boy again. And there was nothing I could do. But I can't go the rest of my life without seeing him. I can't do that."

"I'd like to keep the letter," Madison said.

The woman dabbed at her eyes with the damp tissue. "Of course."

Madison pushed her chair back. "We're going to have someone take an official statement from you, but I want you to know that as hard as this was, you did the right thing coming to us."

Jonas and Madison walked out of the room, then told one of the marshals they'd be back after dinner before heading down the hallway toward the elevator with the letter Barrick's mom had given them.

"She's convinced about her son's innocence," Madison said.

"And you're not?"

Madison let out a low laugh. "Damon Barrick might be charming, but after the past few days, I'm convinced the man should spend the rest of his life in prison. Though I can only imagine how hard it must be to believe your child could do something like that. We were right about one thing. He's planning to leave the country."

They just needed to figure out how.

"His name is already on the no-fly list, which means he'll never get out of the country using his own ID," Jonas said.

Madison stepped into the elevator and punched the lobby button. "What about the Zookeeper? Do you think whoever that is fits into the equation somehow?"

"I really don't know, but we do know three things." Jonas ticked them off on his fingers. "Barrick is desperate, he has money, and if he's going to get out of the country like his mother now believes, he needs a passport."

"So the questions are where will he go and what does he have to do to get there?"

Jonas nodded. "We know he's here in Denver. At least for the moment."

"You used to live here," she said. "Do you know anything about getting your hands on a forged passport in this city?"

"I know it's possible, because both forged and doctored travel documents are huge all over the world. I was involved in a case a couple years ago where we arrested a group that was making forged IDs, mainly licenses. Passports aren't nearly as easy, so we didn't run into that as often, but it's out there."

"What did you run into?"

"We found that a lot of them are made overseas and are often sold to terrorists, arms traffickers, and human traffickers. It's such a lucrative business that people often either fly out to get them or send a courier. If you're willing to pay, you can buy anything you want. A fake driver's license, passport, birth certificate."

The elevator doors opened, and they stepped out. "And for someone right here in the States? Where would they go?"

"I don't know, but I do have a CI who might."

"And you trust this guy?"

"His intel has always been spot-on."

"Then I say go ahead and set up a meet," she said. "It can't hurt to see what he might know."

"I will, but while we're waiting," Jonas said, "I know of a little restaurant near here I think you'll like."

"Do they serve chowder?" she asked.

"Very funny."

Madison's phone rang as they crossed the lobby. She answered it as Jonas filed the letter from Barrick's mom with the evidence team.

"This is Detective Paul Randall from the Denver PD. I'm looking for Deputy US Marshal Madison James."

"This is she."

"I just saw the BOLO you have out on Damon Barrick. I have some information that might help you."

"I'm going to put my phone on speaker so my partner can hear what you have to say as well." Madison signaled at Jonas. "What exactly do you have, Detective?"

"We need to speak in person, but I spent eighteen months trying to get that man behind bars. I think I might know how to find him."

TWENTY-FIVE

Detective Randall agreed to meet them at a small bistro in downtown Denver. Jonas hoped that they'd get something out of talking to the man, but after all the time he'd spent scouring Barrick's files, he wasn't counting on gaining any information that would actually lead them to the fugitive.

Barrick's mom had confirmed his theory that her son was trying to get out of the country instead of trying to disappear within the US, but they still needed something more specific. Ideally, they'd find a way to capture him before he left the country, but even if they missed him, their search wouldn't be over. Not by a long shot. As US Marshals, their jurisdiction wasn't limited to the fifty states. It wouldn't be the first time that Jonas had worked with the law enforcement community abroad to bring a fugitive back to US soil.

"I used to eat here at least once a week." Jonas sat across from Madison at one of the quiet restaurant's back tables while they pored over the menus and waited for Detective Randall to show up. "Think of it as upscale street food."

"Well if the smell is any indication of the taste,

it's going to be fantastic." She set her menu down. "What do you recommend?"

"They have the best toasted ham and cheese sandwich you've ever tasted. And their fries are also delicious."

"Sounds good." She took a sip of her iced tea. "That's what I'll have."

"That was easy."

"I'm hungry and it all sounds good. You saved me from having to decide."

"I think I'll take the same then."

He signaled the waiter and placed their orders before turning back to her.

"How are you feeling?" he asked once they were alone again.

"Shoulder's better. I won't have to sleep in the middle of the wilderness tonight, and I'm about to try the best ham and cheese sandwich I've ever tasted."

"Not a bad day if you look at it that way."

"The day's going to end even better if the detective really does have a way to find Barrick."

"I hope he does." He hesitated before continuing. "Speaking of the detective, before he gets here, there is something else I wanted to ask you. I've been thinking about the anniversary of your husband's death a few days ago. I guess I want you to know if you need to talk about it, I'm here. I might not have any answers, but I'm a pretty good listener."

"I'm sure you are, and I appreciate it. I really do. I usually have my sister to talk to about things like this. She's great at putting up with me no matter what my mood. All of this has been a distraction."

"But doesn't help with closure. You probably should have taken the day off."

"I usually do. But I wouldn't be right here right now."

"What was different this year?"

"I don't know. I guess I thought I should be to the point where I can get through the day without letting his death consume me."

"Would it be so bad if that day didn't ever come? If you let yourself feel instead of running."

"Wait a minute." She took another sip of her tea. "Am I talking to the same Jonas Quinn who pushed me through my training until I thought I was going to crack? The same Jonas Quinn students call Terminator behind his back?"

"Hold on." He set down his Dr Pepper. "They call me Terminator?"

"I think most would see that as a compliment. I always did. I knew you were tough and would push me harder than I thought I could go. It's what I wanted."

Jonas shook his head as the waiter arrived with their food. "We're going to have to talk about this Terminator thing, but I do try to show my soft side every now and then."

As the waiter was walking away, Detective Randall showed up, carrying a briefcase and looking like he hadn't slept. "Sorry it took so long for me to get here."

"No problem. We just got our food. Would you like anything?"

"I had an early dinner," he said, taking one of the empty chairs at their table. "But, please, go ahead and eat."

"Jonas Quinn and Madison James," Jonas said, shaking the man's hand. "We appreciate your calling us."

"Of course. Like I said on the phone, I'd been after this guy for eighteen months before he was arrested."

"So you were one of the detectives working his murder case?"

"Tracked him from here in Denver to Seattle where he was arrested. The man should be in for life, and instead he's managed to disappear."

Jonas locked eyes with the detective. "That will happen when we find him."

"*If* you find him, which very likely you may never do." Detective Randall shook his head. "You don't know Barrick like I do. The man's not only a charmer, I'm convinced he's killed more than the couple he was arrested for shooting. I was just never able to prove it. And now he's escaped, meaning he could get away with this."

Madison grabbed the saltshaker and sprinkled

it over her fries. "Not if we have anything to do with it."

"That's why I wanted to talk with you. Everyone has that one case that never got solved that you can't let go of, you know? That one that despite the evidence or lack thereof, you know who did it. You just can't prove it. Barrick was that case for me."

A memory rose to the surface as Jonas bit into his sandwich. He knew. He'd been a beat cop at the time. The hardest part of his job had been handling domestic violence disputes. He'd never forget her name. Angel Sanchez. He and his partner had answered three 911 calls from neighbors to her apartment, but every time she promised them she was fine. That there had been a misunderstanding. But he knew the truth. Saw the bruises. But without her cooperation and no real evidence, there was nothing else he could do. Two weeks after the last call, they found her dead in her apartment. It was eventually ruled that a mixture of sleeping pills and allergy pills had slowed her reaction time and she'd fallen down the stairs in the middle of the night.

He knew it wasn't true. And her boyfriend had gotten away with murder.

It was the constant motivation that made him determined to bring guys like Barrick down.

"I went ahead and brought you copies of my files." Randall pulled a thick folder from his briefcase, bringing Jonas back to the present. "Trust me, I'll do anything to catch this guy."

"You said you were after him for more murders?"

"The cases are officially closed, but I know he's killed more than he's charged with. I just haven't yet been able to conclusively prove it."

Madison tapped her finger against the red folder. "None of that was included in the brief we received."

"I'm not surprised. No matter how hard I tried, I couldn't get the DA to move ahead. And now, from what I understand, someone else is dead."

"And you're still working the case?" Jonas asked.

"I am. Unofficially." Randall flipped open the file. "Barrick is a con man. A grifter who has swindled hundreds of thousands of dollars from at least three women, probably more. And I'm convinced he killed at least two of these women on top of the couple he was arrested for killing."

"Is there any chance he's as innocent as he claims?"

"None. He's good at what he does. That's why I want him brought in as much as you do. Before this happens again."

"If he's behind other murders," Madison said, "why are the cases closed?"

"Because he's that good. I told you, we could never find enough evidence for the DA. But

I've interviewed the families of these women extensively. Stephanie Phillips, who supposedly committed suicide, wasn't depressed." Randall pulled out a photo of the woman smiling up at the camera from what looked like a hiking trail. "She'd just finished running the Boston Marathon, was on the board of several nonprofits, and helped run her family's NGO."

Madison scooted to the edge of her chair. "Families never want to believe someone they loved killed themselves."

"I know, but there were no signs of depression or anxiety. She was looking forward to her best friend's wedding and a trip to Switzerland in the fall."

"Madison's right," Jonas said. "People are good at hiding those things from people they love."

Randall's frown deepened. "Maybe, but I'm telling you, Stephanie didn't kill herself."

Madison leaned forward. "And you believe Damon Barrick did."

"I know he did."

"How?"

"The evidence I do have suggests he conned these women until they got wind of his plan and more than likely would have gone to the authorities and turned him in, something he couldn't let happen. Murders were staged. Clearly premeditated."

Jonas glanced at Madison, then back at Randall.

"What else do you know about these women?"

Randall pulled out a photo of a second woman and slid it toward them. "Daisy Porter. Forty-two years old and heir to the estate of her late husband, who was worth ten million dollars. Died five years ago. She met Barrick at a fundraiser for one of the local hospitals. They dated for six months. When interviewed, close friends said they started noticing that she was giving Barrick expensive gifts, but he made her happy, so they dropped it. Then one night she was killed during a home invasion. There was over two million dollars in jewelry and artwork stolen. The perpetrator knew not only where the safe was but also the code."

"So his motivation for killing the women?"

"My guess is to silence them once they discovered he was just after their money." Randall shook his head. "Here's my advice. Take the next couple hours to go through my files and see if what's here convinces you. Barrick's going to need a source of money in order to disappear completely."

"So you think he'll go to someone he knows so he can get enough cash to disappear."

Randall nodded.

Jonas leaned forward. "Something tells me you have someone in mind."

"I do." Randall flipped over another photo. "A few months before he was arrested, he started seeing a woman by the name of Bianca Carleton. She has a luxury condo in downtown Denver and a large home up toward Aspen."

"Tell us about her."

"Like the other women, she's wealthy. Her father owned a line of jewelry stores, though she's stepped out of the business side of the company, leaving her brother to run them. She spends most of her time volunteering for various organizations. Her husband died a little over a year ago, and she met Barrick through a mutual friend. She never made any public statements after his arrest but did talk exclusively to the police."

"And?"

"She's convinced he's innocent, for starters, but told us that she broke things off with him shortly before he was arrested. At least that's her story."

"But you don't believe her?"

"There's really no way to know if she was telling the truth. I was told that he sent her letters from prison, but that he never received any from her. I always felt, though, that she was still in love with him."

"So if Barrick was to come to town, what are the odds that he approaches her? Or maybe the more important question, would she actually help him if he did?"

"I believe she would," the detective said. "There's a good chance that he's already contacted her for money, and trust me, he'll say whatever he needs to in order to get what he wants."

"Have you ever heard of the Zookeeper in connection with Barrick?"

"The Zookeeper?" Randall seemed to search his memory. "No. Where did you hear that?"

"Barrick's mother."

"Sorry, but I don't know."

Jonas wiped his hands on his napkin, his dinner still mostly untouched, then caught Madison's gaze. "We can go through these files tonight, then we need to pay Bianca Carleton a visit in the morning."

TWENTY-SIX

Bianca Carleton owned a condo in downtown Denver between Larimer Square and Coors Field. With twenty-four-hour concierge staff, a valet, and a fitness center, it was a place for the wealthy to enjoy living in the city without having to deal with any of its inconveniences.

Bianca was the perfect mark for Barrick.

Madison had gone over the extensive file Detective Randall had given them with Jonas until well after midnight. But before they'd finally called it a night, she'd come to a conclusion. Randall was right. There might not have been enough concrete evidence to bring charges against Barrick for the murders, but she was now—like Randall—convinced he was guilty. From what they'd uncovered in the files, there was a definite pattern to Barrick's behavior, and Bianca Carleton was the key to executing his escape.

Jonas pulled into a parking spot beneath the building, then turned off the engine. "You didn't talk much on the way here."

"Sorry. I've just been thinking. And honestly, that hotel coffee didn't quite give me the jolt of energy I was hoping for."

"Four nights of interrupted sleep. Why am I not surprised? I'm already thinking about taking a couple days off when this is over. I'm going to find myself a little place to rent over-looking Puget Sound, where all I have to do is fish and read."

"A couple days?" She let out a low laugh as she slid out of the car. "I'm putting in for at least a week."

But until they found Barrick, she was going to have to put aside any thoughts of time off.

Jonas held the door for her and they walked across the large lobby before flashing their badges at the concierge, who was busy with something on her computer.

"Jamie," she said, reading the woman's badge. "We're US Marshals."

Jamie's eyes lit up. "Like Matt Dillon?"

Jonas cleared his throat. "Yes, but he was . . . um . . . he was a fictional character."

"My father used to love *Gunsmoke*. I watched it with him sometimes before he died. We've had FBI officials stop by, but I've never met a marshal."

"We're actually here to see Bianca Carleton. She's expecting us."

"Bianca. Of course. She called down a few minutes ago. Said to feel free to take the elevator up to the fifth floor and that she's waiting for you."

"Thanks. We do have one other question before we go up." Madison held up a photo of Barrick. "Have you seen this man here before? Possibly visiting her as well?"

"I'm not sure." Jamie leaned forward. "We're really not supposed to discuss the comings and goings with anyone."

"She's not in any trouble. We're here to make sure she's safe, actually."

"What is he?" Jamie asked. "Some kind of stalker?"

"Not exactly, but it is very important."

She bit the edge of her lip. "He was a guest of Mrs. Carleton, but it's been a while. And he was always the perfect gentleman. At least from what I saw. She seemed genuinely happy with him, but if he's dangerous . . ."

Madison handed her a business card. "He is wanted by law enforcement, so if he happens to show up, please call me."

"Of course. He just seemed so . . . so nice." Jamie's gaze flicked toward the elevators. "And please, don't tell her I said anything to you about him."

"Of course not."

A minute later, Madison stepped into the fifth-floor hallway with Jonas, then searched the door numbers to find the woman's upscale residence. Mary Margaret had been willing to do anything for this man. The question now was if she was the only one, or if Bianca had succumbed to his charms as well.

"Mrs. Carleton," Madison said once the woman had opened the door. "Thank you for seeing us."

"Of course. Please, call me Bianca."

Bianca Carleton was fifty-three, according to the information they had, and from what Madison could see, her youthful look was expensive— bleached-blonde hair, a few rounds of plastic surgery, and perfectly manicured nails to finish off the image.

She followed Bianca through the entryway with Jonas right behind her.

"Come on in and sit down. Can I get you anything to drink?"

"We're fine. Thank you."

Madison stopped at the window before sitting down on the couch, pausing for a few seconds to take in the one hundred and eighty–degree view of the city. "This is beautiful."

"I know. My late husband and I bought this condo for the view, though it can't quite compare to the property up in Aspen."

"You own a condo there as well?" Jonas asked.

"A house on top of Red Mountain."

"Wow," Jonas said. "Those views have to be stunning."

"They are, and I love the place. It's just a bit too big when you're there alone. I find myself spending more and more time here in the city, something Jim and I didn't do when he was alive. He always wanted to be outdoors, away from the city. It just starts to feel so isolated."

"I can imagine." Madison sat down next to Jonas on the couch, facing the wall of windows. According to the bio they had on the woman, she also had a home in Florida and a condo in Belize. "We'll get right to the point. As I said on the phone, we need to talk to you about Damon Barrick."

"You're here because you think he's after my money."

"Yes, actually." Madison was surprised at the woman's statement.

"Well, as I'm sure you know, he's in prison, so it's not as if he could hurt me at this point, even if that were true."

"Mrs. Carleton—"

"Bianca, please."

"Bianca," Madison continued, "I don't know if you've been watching the news, but he recently escaped from a prison transport, and we're looking for him."

Bianca's eyes widened. "I heard he was scheduled to come back to Denver for trial at some point, but no, I didn't know he'd escaped."

Madison leaned forward. "We know he has a way of convincing women, wealthy women, for a piece of their checkbook."

"I'm sorry, but I find that completely insulting." Bianca stood up and faced the window for a few seconds before turning around. "I admit, I had a relationship with the man, but he's been in prison. Do you really think I have any desire to affiliate myself with a man like that? I might be lonely, but trust me, I'm not that lonely."

"I'm sorry to upset you. Our only goal is to bring him in and make sure no one gets hurt in the process."

"With that you have my full support."

"When is the last time you saw him?"

Bianca's manicured fingers tapped her leg. "About a week before he was arrested, so about nine months ago."

"And have you had any contact with him while he's been in prison?"

She walked over to an antique desk, opened a drawer, then pulled out a stack of envelopes. "He wrote me letters. You can have them if you want, but you won't find anything in them. Everything he wrote was read by the prison staff, so secret messages are out. And no, I never responded." She gave them a hardened look. "Like I said, that relationship is one I'd like to forget. Damon is someone I completely severed ties with a long time ago."

Completely severed ties.

Madison glanced at Jonas. Maybe it was nothing more than a coincidence, but she'd heard that same wording from Mary Margaret. Almost as if they'd both been . . . scripted.

"I would like to take the letters, if you're sure you don't mind," Madison said. "We'll get them back to you."

"You can keep them. I'm not sure why I did, except he was a bit of a romantic. And I suppose that because of the twenty-odd years between us, he made me feel young again."

"What did you know about him?"

"Damon? He was raised by a single mom after his dad died. Ended up going to college and getting a degree in accounting, of all things. He was charming, funny, spontaneous, and knew how to make a woman feel as if she was the only one in the room." Bianca gazed out at the city. "After my husband died, I admit I was a bit lost. Damon swooped in and seemed to fill in the empty spaces of my heart. Something I wouldn't have thought possible. But then the police came around asking questions. I told them there was no way Damon was involved, but they arrested him."

"That must have been hard," she said. "We appreciate your candidness."

"I know there were rumors circulating that he was nothing more than a con man, and I wasn't his first victim. I spoke to Detective Randall and I know what he thinks, but whatever my thoughts are about the man, I know he didn't do it."

Madison tried to judge the woman's expression and whether or not she was telling the truth. Something told her she wasn't. "Would you mind if I use your restroom?"

"Of course not. There's one down the hall to the right."

"Thank you. I'll be right back."

"I just have a couple more questions while she steps out," Jonas said.

Madison walked down the hallway, then closed the door to the bathroom from the outside. Across the hallway was an office. She stepped inside. Two walls were lined with bookshelves, and a third was another wall of windows overlooking the city. A desk faced the windows. They needed to know what the woman was planning. If Madison's hunch was right, Bianca had been in contact with Barrick while he was in prison.

She lifted the edge of a short stack of papers, looking for a planner or a note the woman might have left. If she'd been in contact with Barrick, like Madison was convinced she had, there had to be some kind of evidence. She could hear Jonas's voice but couldn't make out what either of them was saying.

She sifted through another pile of papers and found a planner. Dentist on Friday. Lunch with Carol on Saturday. No indication that his escape had changed her plans. But Barrick's actions had been spur of the moment.

She moved on to the computer and opened it up, surprised there was no password. She quickly checked Bianca's browser history.

Search underway for escaped inmate Damon Barrick.

So she had lied. And if she'd lied about not knowing of Barrick's escape, what else was she lying about?

Madison moved on to the trash, looking for something—anything—that might be a clue that she'd been in contact with him. A white-and-yellow envelope caught her eye. The return address was a company that expedited government documents and visas.

Like a passport.

So Bianca had renewed her passport and expedited it, because . . . because she was getting ready to leave the country with Barrick?

Jonas's voice rose from the other room. Madison stepped back into the hallway, opened the bathroom door, then stepped forward as Bianca rounded the corner.

The woman's hands fisted at her sides. "I guess you found the restroom?"

"I did. Thank you." They walked back toward the sitting room.

"Did you have any other questions?" she asked.

"I think we're done here," Jonas said. "We appreciate your time."

"Of course. Anytime. I hope you find him."

"Actually, I do have one more question." Madison stopped in the entryway. "Though this one is purely personal. Are you planning to take any trips soon? I couldn't help but see some of your photos on the walls. They're stunning. I'm sure your travel log must be incredible."

"No. I . . . I used to travel more when my husband was alive, but I don't make as many trips now. I do some volunteer work here in the city, and sometimes spend my weekends up in Aspen. That's about it, anymore."

They thanked Bianca for her time and said goodbye.

Madison and Jonas stepped out into the hallway, then waited for the elevator door to shut before talking.

"She's the perfect mark," Jonas said, as the elevator began its descent. "He convinced Mary Margaret to mislead the authorities. Who's to say he hasn't done the same thing here? We know he needs a passport, but he also needs money. And if he wants to disappear, he's going to need lots of it. Here's someone who has it."

"She's planning to go with him," Madison said.

His brow narrowed. "You found something on your trip to the bathroom?"

"For starters, she lied." Madison crossed her arms. "She knew about Barrick's escape. I checked the browser history on her computer and there was an article about it."

"You were busy. "

"I'm pretty sure she's talked with him and didn't want us to know."

"You're good."

"Thought I'd try to be worth my keep."

He shot her a smile. "Funny. What else?"

"There was an envelope from a company that expedites passports," she said, serious again.

"How quick can you get them?"

"I'm pretty sure it's possible to get them in twenty-four hours if you're willing to pay."

"So it's definitely possible that she heard from him after the crash and then ordered herself a new passport."

"Definitely." Madison shifted to rest her hands on her hips. "And something else. Did you notice the way she answered our questions?"

"I did. It was like they'd been . . . rehearsed."

"Exactly. She even used the same wording as Mary Margaret. 'I completely severed ties with him.' Maybe it's just me, but it seems a bit formal, and for them both to use that phrase . . ."

"I thought the same thing. And she was nervous. Especially when you stepped out. She kept glancing at the hallway. It threw her off."

"She was probably worried I was searching her office."

"Which you were. My guess is that she tried to make it seem like she had nothing to hide. Invite us in, offer us something to drink, admit a relationship with Barrick, but claim she now had nothing to do with him since he was arrested."

"Which was all nothing but a lie. Now we just need to get her to lead us to Barrick."

TWENTY-SEVEN

Back at the US Marshals' offices, they started putting together a plan to see how they could use Bianca to get to Barrick. The evidence Madison had found in the woman's office pointed to the fact that not only was she aware Barrick had escaped, she was also planning to leave the country with him.

What they didn't know was Barrick's plan.

When they'd talked to Mary Margaret in Wyoming, she'd been sure that Barrick was going to send for her, something Jonas was now convinced was a pipe dream. In fact, he was certain that anything Barrick had told her was a lie. He'd gotten the money he'd needed and never looked back. The only positive outcome for Mary Margaret was that, unlike some of the other women Barrick had had relationships with, she was still alive.

Bianca, though, was different. The woman had money. Enough to set Barrick up comfortably for the rest of his life. What he wasn't sure about was if Barrick actually intended for her to come with him, or if she was just his bankroll out of the country.

Jonas glanced down at the banking information he'd just been sent, verifying that Bianca had made both a hefty transfer of funds to a location they were still trying to trace, as well as a large withdrawal over the past twenty-four hours. If Detective Randall was right, and Barrick had killed Stephanie Phillips and Daisy Porter, it was very likely he had no intention of taking Bianca with him. And no matter what he'd told her, he could very well be planning to get rid of her as well.

"I know we've been tracking her phone." Madison looked up from the other side of the table where she and two deputy marshals had joined them. They were currently reading Detective Randall's files, in particular the information they had on Bianca Carleton. "But I think we need to get a detail on her as well. From everything we have on her, it's definitely looking as if she's in contact with Barrick. We need to guarantee we don't miss him if he shows up."

Deputy US Marshal Lance Patterson scooted his chair back. "I can arrange that."

Jonas nodded. "I agree. She's definitely our best lead at this point, and we can't let him slip out of our hands again."

Jonas's phone beeped. He pulled it out of his pocket, then stepped away from the table to take the call. "Biggie?"

The familiar sound of his longtime informant's

voice came on the line. "Hey, Boss. It's been a long time."

"Thanks for calling me back."

"Are you back in town?"

"For a few days. I need a favor."

"I thought you might."

"Can we meet?"

There was a pause on the line. Jonas waited for an answer, worried Biggie would say no. "Biggie?"

"Do you remember that old café we used to meet at?"

"Yes."

"It closed down, but there's an empty warehouse not far from it. I'll text you the address and meet you in the back by the loading dock at three. There shouldn't be anyone around today."

The warehouse was deserted when Jonas drove behind it. He parked the car, then shut off the engine.

"How long have you known this guy?" Madison asked.

"I met him when I was a detective years ago. He's the best CI I ever had."

Madison glanced at her watch. "You think he's still coming? He's already ten minutes late."

"You're not nervous, are you?" he asked.

"Just antsy, I guess. I'm ready for this to be

over. We're so close to Barrick and yet he's always a step ahead."

"Give Biggie time. He'll be here."

Five minutes later, an old beat-up Mustang pulled around the corner and stopped at the other side of the dock. Biggie climbed out and headed over to them. At six three and two hundred fifty-plus pounds, Biggie hadn't changed at all from the last time Jonas had seen him.

"It's good to see you again," he said, introducing Madison. "We appreciate your meeting with us. How have you been?"

"Staying out of trouble."

"That's good. Did you hear about the plane crash in Idaho?"

"I heard something about a prison transport that went down. One dead and the other escaped."

"We need to find the escapee, and we believe he's here in Denver."

Biggie tugged on the edge of his shirt. "So what do you need from me?"

"He's trying to leave the country, but he needs a passport," Madison said. "We need to know where he's planning to get it."

"There's more than one option in a city this big."

"True," Jonas said. "We have a list of suspected forgers, but this person would have to be fast. Say a twenty-four- or forty-eight-hour turn-around, and good enough to ensure a passport would make it through security. Someone who takes cash."

"Which means they'd probably be using a stolen passport and not forging the entire thing," Biggie said.

"For that kind of turnaround, exactly."

Biggie folded his arms across his chest and frowned. "And when the cops come arresting him and word gets out that I was behind it, then what happens?"

"All we need is a name. No one will ever know it came from you," Madison said.

"No one will know, Biggie. I've worked with you for years and I've never betrayed you."

"I know, but you can't guarantee that. It's hard out there."

"In all the time I've worked with you, you've always come through for me, and I've always been fair to you."

"True."

"Then why are you so jumpy tonight?"

Biggie shoved his hands into his front pockets. "I had this guy come up to me at the bar yesterday. He threatened me and my family. Accused me of being a snitch."

"You're still doling out information."

"Every once in a while. But it made me reconsider if it's worth it."

"I understand, but this man might kill someone else. We need to stop him."

"It's always urgent, but if anyone finds out I'm here, I'll be the one you're carrying out in a body bag."

Jonas held up a photo of Ryan Phelps on his phone. "This man is dead because of Barrick. He had a wife and three kids. And he's not the only one our guy has killed. We believe he's waiting for new IDs, then will head across the border. Once he's out of the country, it will be a lot harder to find him."

"All we need from you is a name of who he might approach to get a new passport," Madison said. "You can help us stop a murderer, Biggie."

Jonas handed him a wad of bills.

Biggie shoved the money in his pocket. "I can think of a few people. But nobody—and I mean nobody—can know I gave them to you."

"Everything you tell me is confidential, Biggie. I swear."

"Things like driver's licenses are a lot easier to get your hands on, but for passports, there's not a lot of options. At least not for someone who can do the job right and ensure you can get through security without raising any red flags. I've got a couple possible names."

Jonas tried to swallow his frustration. They needed to narrow it down.

"How about we give you a name?"

Biggie shrugged. "Okay."

"What about the name Zookeeper?" Madison asked. "Does that mean anything to you?"

"The Zookeeper." Biggie rubbed the back of his bald head. "It's been a long time since I heard that name."

"Who is he?" Madison asked.

"He dabbles with a whole bunch of things, which is why they call him the Zookeeper. Money laundering, identity theft, forgery, insider trading . . . you name it. I heard it said that whatever you needed, he could supply."

"Even fake passports?" Jonas asked.

Biggie nodded.

"Then that has to be him." Madison glanced at Jonas. "Do you have a name?"

Biggie hesitated again. "I don't know his last name, but his first name is Yuri."

"How do we contact him?" Jonas asked.

Madison turned to Biggie. "You could get me in there, couldn't you? If I needed a new passport?"

"You?"

"If Yuri finds out we're onto him, Barrick will never show up," she said. "We also need some kind of guarantee that we're on the right track. Otherwise, we'll have to set up a handful of stakeouts and we might still end up with nothing."

Biggie shook his head. "This guy will spot a cop a mile away. You'd never pull it off."

"He's right," Jonas said.

"Maybe," she said. "But I've done plenty of undercover work."

"I'm still not convinced—"

"I could go in as a single mom, say, running from an abusive relationship." She turned to Jonas.

He frowned, not surprised she'd come up with a risky plan. "If you had the right cover story, and managed to convince him, it might work."

"This guy has a reputation for handling problems himself," Biggie said.

"Meaning?" Madison asked.

"He's not one you want to cross, and if he were to end up finding out you worked for the government—"

"He won't," she said.

"You can't know that."

"Biggie might be right," Jonas said. "There are just too many things that could go wrong in this scenario."

"Something I think every time I do an early morning raid to bring down a fugitive. The way I see it, this is our only lead right now. It's worth the risk." She turned back to Biggie. "Can you get me in to see him?"

"I could try."

"If we don't find this guy, more people will die," she said. "If we know he has to pick up a passport, that means we'll know where to watch for him."

Biggie sighed. "Fine. I can't make any prom-ises, but I'll try to set up an appointment."

"We'll come up with a background story," Jonas said, "and he needs to know that this is a rush job."

"He'll want cash. Up front."

"Not a problem," Madison said. "Are you good with this, Jonas?"

"It might work."

"You didn't answer my question."

His hesitation had nothing to do with Madison. He had to remember that she was not Felicia.

He nodded. "Actually, despite the risks, I think your idea's spot-on if we want to find Barrick without scaring him off. What do you say, Biggie?"

"I'm in. When do you want to see him?"

"Can you get me in with him tonight, Biggie?" Madison said.

"Works for me."

"Then let's go," Jonas said, and turned on the engine.

TWENTY-EIGHT

At half past four, Madison finished her water in one of the marshals' offices, then dumped the bottle into the recycling bin, trying to channel her nervous energy. A rush of adrenaline was inevitable, but she could never let it affect the role she was playing.

"Madison . . . or should I call you Chrystal?" Jonas leaned back in his chair and folded his arms across his chest. "Before you go, I want you to pretend I'm Yuri and tell me who you are."

"Pretend you're Yuri." Madison sat down across from him. "Are you serious?"

"I'm always serious." His frown deepened, but there was a mischievous glint in his eyes.

"This isn't the first time I've done this."

"I have no doubt in your abilities, but that doesn't mean I don't want to ensure you're ready. Just do it. For me."

She hesitated, but knew he was probably right. They needed the information from Yuri without scaring away Barrick. If she gave Yuri any cause to believe she was there undercover, it would blow everything.

"Fine." Madison took a deep breath and focused

on the backstory they'd created for Chrystal. "I'm a single mom with a three-year-old, trying to get away from an abusive relationship. He's taken my passport and driver's license and birth certificate, which is why I need a new one. I need to leave the country."

"How did you find out about me?"

"I have a friend who has a cousin who's involved with some . . . under the table things. He promised to set me up and gave me your number."

"And the money . . . where did you get the money?"

"I have an aunt across the country who has some stashed away. I didn't tell her what it was for, but she was willing to help."

"Why not just move in with her?"

"Because as long as I'm in the country he won't stop looking for me. I have an old college roommate—someone he doesn't know about—in Calgary who's promised to let us stay with her until I can get back on my feet."

Jonas shook his head. "Don't tell him where you're going. If you're as scared as you should be in your situation, you wouldn't want anyone knowing your destination. If you can find Yuri, so can your ex."

She nodded. He was right. Maybe the practice wasn't such a bad idea after all. "Okay, let's keep going."

"Did you tell your aunt what you're doing?" Jonas asked.

"No. I haven't told anyone, because I don't want anyone else involved. If he finds me, he will kill me."

"What about a best friend, or another family member?"

"No one."

He paused, looking her over. "Good, just don't overplay your hand. More than likely you're not the first person he's dealt with in a situation like this. You want to make sure you don't set off any red flags."

One of the other agents handed Madison a jean jacket to go over her army-green tank top. She tugged it on, then applied a layer of lipstick. She hardly recognized herself in the mirror.

"My job is to find out if Barrick has been there, and what name he's planning to use," she said.

"And if you can't get the information, then get out. We'll go with plan B and raid the place."

"Which will guarantee Barrick doesn't show up."

He nodded slowly. That was the problem they were facing.

"The main thing is you can't look like a cop. You can't look confident and ready to take down anyone who comes after you. You're a mother running for her life, with a child in the mix. You're scared, vulnerable, and terrified of getting caught because you're risking everything and Yuri's going to know that. Remember, if your ex finds you, he will kill you. If the cops find out what you're doing, you'll lose your child."

"I can handle this, Jonas. Quit worrying so much. I was a detective before I was a marshal and I did dozens of undercover jobs."

"I know you're up for the job, it's just that I'm—"

"What? Worried about me?"

"Of course I'm worried. I'm always cautious when a partner does something risky."

"We've been over this before. You'll be there if I need you. All I'm trying to do is find out if Barrick was there."

"Get in and get out as soon as you can."

"There is one other thing," she said.

"What's that?"

"I need a small handgun."

"You can't go in there carrying."

"I'm a single mom, terrified that my ex is going to kill me. A cop would go in there unarmed. A scared single mom wouldn't."

"Where did you get a weapon?"

"My father taught me how to shoot before he died."

"I don't know, Madison—"

"You know, this is exactly what I was afraid would happen." The wave of frustration that had been building up over the last few days surfaced.

"What do you mean?"

"You found out that my husband was killed, that I'm a widow, and now you're treating me with kid gloves."

"No, I'm not. I'm treating you like I would any partner who's about to risk their life."

"Really? Because before you knew about Luke—when we were training together—you didn't treat me differently."

"That was a simulation."

"And this is my job, Jonas. I've been extensively trained and I'm good at what I do. I don't need you to treat me like I'm wounded material. My grief has changed; it still hurts. Every single day. But I made the decision to move on with my life. I know I'm not where I should be, but I'm doing my best to move forward. And one of those areas is my job. I'll never let my personal loss get in the way of my duty to my country. If anything, I'll take that anger over my loss and funnel it into what I'm doing. Never let it compromise who I am."

"You're right." He dropped his hands to his sides. "I'm sorry."

She stared at the floor, her own realization surfacing. "No, I'm sorry. You didn't deserve that reaction. I've allowed myself to get too caught up in this."

"I think we should simply give each other some

slack. I'll trust you moving forward and not worry."

She studied his expression, and felt her defenses crumbling. He was different, and maybe that was what had thrown her. She was a woman living in a male-dominated world, and her expectations were sometimes skewed about how she would be treated.

She readjusted her jean jacket before knocking on the basement door at the address they'd been given. She hadn't been completely honest with Jonas about one thing. Situations like this always kicked her adrenaline into high gear, but her awareness was also what made her good at what she did. Her job was to expect the unexpected, and that was what she was ready for.

"Chrystal?" A man opened the door, then sized her up.

Hesitantly, as if she wasn't one hundred percent certain of her actions, she answered. "Yeah."

"Come in."

She hesitated a couple more seconds before obeying. He was shorter than she'd imagined and unassuming, though maybe that's how he wanted to appear. Someone who could slip into a crowd and vanish without being noticed.

"Don't look so nervous," he said. "People do this every day."

"Well, I don't do stuff like this every day."

"Relax. It will be fine. Though I'm going to have to check your bag."

"Of course." She held it against her for a couple seconds while taking in the space that was sparsely furnished and smelled like carryout. "Sorry, but I . . . I've got a gun."

He took her bag, opened it, then scanned the contents inside. "I can understand. You're on the run from something or someone."

She nodded. "My ex . . . he took all my IDs to keep me here. I need to get out of the country. I have a son. Grayson—"

He motioned for her to sit down. "I don't usually ask for details."

"Sorry."

"And quit saying you're sorry."

"I'm just . . . okay. I'm not used to doing things outside the law." She took a seat across from the desk where he'd sat down.

"People who come to me are usually desperate."

"How fast can you get me something?"

"Depends on what you want. Brand-new IDs can take a few weeks."

She jumped up. "I don't have a few weeks. Why do you think I have a gun in my bag? He's threatened to kill me."

"I understand and there are options. Please. Sit back down. I can match you with a passport and get it to you by tomorrow. I'd just need to take your photo and get some information."

"Wait a minute . . . Someone else's passport?"

"It's the quickest way for me to get you one. I can't make any guarantees of what might happen when you get to the airport, but this isn't the first time I've done this."

She started pacing in front of him, taking in details. He had his desk set up as a place to work, but there were no passports or obvious signs of what he really did for money.

She stopped in front of him. "Do you have a sample of something you've recently done? I just . . . I need to know this is going to work."

"You're having second thoughts?"

"I've been having second thoughts since I got in my car to come here. I can't end up arrested and in prison. What would happen to Grayson?" She raised her voice a pitch. "I can't let anything go wrong."

"I'm working on one right now. Just finished it, in fact."

"Can I see it?"

He hesitated, clearly not pleased with her question.

She picked up her purse. "I don't think I can do this. This was a foolish idea. Maybe I don't have to leave the country. He'll find out. He always does. I don't think I was followed, but he's good. If he finds out I was here . . ."

"Trust me. You're not the first spouse to walk through those doors looking for help."

She let out a nervous laugh. "I see what you're saying, but trust doesn't exactly come easy for me right now. I mean, you forge passports for a living, and you want me to trust you."

Jonas's words of caution about not laying it on too heavy ran through her mind. She had to come across as legitimately vulnerable and scared.

"We all do what we have to do. If you want to escape your ex, you'll have to trust me."

She nodded. "Okay. But can I just look at one? It'll have to pass security."

Yuri looked into her eyes. A few silent seconds passed before he leaned down and unlocked the drawer in front of him. He pulled out a passport, then handed it to her.

She opened it up. There was no photo.

"The next step is to add the client's photo."

"How long will it take you?" she asked.

"This client, for example, came in late yesterday. I plan to have it finished tonight."

"So, what—twenty-four hours?"

"You give me the payment now, and I'll try to push it through and have it ready tomorrow night. But it takes time to ensure it will pass through security. If this were easy, everyone would be doing it."

She opened up the front page and ran her finger across it as she examined the fake ID. "It looks real, but there's no name or photo."

"It looks real because it is. We just make a few

minor changes. Primarily the photo. It takes time to do it right."

"Okay." She closed the passport and dropped it back onto the table. "I was told to bring forty-two hundred for both passports."

"Correct." He grabbed the passport and put it back into his drawer. "Where'd you get the money?"

She offered him a weak smile. "You don't trust me now?"

"We both have to be careful, don't we? That's no small amount of cash, particularly for someone in your position."

"I've been saving and I have an aunt down south who sent the rest. I've got enough to buy plane tickets out of the country. I thought about renting a car, but without a driver's license, I don't think I can."

"I have a passport that will work for you, but you might run into some issues with your son. Traveling overseas without some kind of note giving you permission from his father could throw up some red flags and cause you to be detained."

"We were never married. I do have Grayson's birth certificate. His father's name isn't on the document."

"That should work then. Just make sure you carry the birth certificate with you. I'll also need a photo of both of you."

"I didn't want to bring my son, but I did bring photos of him on my phone. I can text them to you."

"That was smart."

She texted a stock photo from her phone to the number Biggie had given them, then looked up at the man. "Would you mind taking a couple of me and letting me choose? I'm not trying to be vain, but I did a few things, wanting to make sure he can't recognize me." She ran her fingers through her hair and looked up at him, worried she was taking it too far. "I'm being way too paranoid, aren't I? I can hear it in everything I'm saying to you. I'm not usually like this."

"Don't worry. If I were in your place, I'd feel the same way."

She blew out a breath. "Thanks. Do you mind using your phone? My camera isn't very good."

Yuri studied her expression and she did her best to look innocent. It must have worked because he nodded and a moment later, she pressed her back against the wall as Yuri took a few shots.

She was thankful she'd taken the measures to change her appearance, but she still needed a way to prove Barrick had been here.

He handed her the phone. "What do you think?"

She pretended to study the photos he had just taken. She had a couple seconds at most to find Barrick's photo. She scrolled back through the last few photos he'd taken . . . Bingo. Barrick's gruff mug stared back at her. He'd been here. Time stamp said late last night. Which meant he'd pick it up tonight.

"Let's go with the second one." She handed the phone to Yuri after scrolling back to her photo. "Do I meet you here to pick it up?"

"Come after seven tomorrow evening. It'll be done."

She set the cash on the table. "Thank you. I'm finally feeling like I might be able to do this."

"There's no reason why you can't."

She walked out the door and up the steps without turning around. Got in the car she'd driven over. Jonas and a team were waiting in the shadows. Her backup in case anything went wrong. But nothing had and now it was just a matter of time until they found Barrick. She drove to their meeting place, making sure she wasn't followed. She couldn't take any chances that Yuri might be playing her. That he suspected anything.

She slid into the car where Jonas was waiting for her.

"Good job."

She caught the relief in his face in the streetlight.

"You actually saw Barrick's passport?"

"He showed me a passport, and I saw Barrick's photo on his phone, and from what he told me, I think it has to be the one he's working on.

Barrick is supposed to pick it up later tonight."

"So your sob story worked."

She smiled. "The guy did seem to feel sorry for my single mom with a baby act. Dropped his guard some."

"And the gun?" Jonas asked.

"Definitely the right move."

"I'm impressed, though not at all surprised."

"So my idea wasn't so bad after all," she said.

"I just wanted to make sure we did things right, so the guy didn't off you."

She let out a low laugh. "That would have made for a lot of extra paperwork."

"You said it, not me." He turned the key in the ignition. "We could have someone else stake out the place."

"Forget it." She pulled on her seat belt. "I'm in this till the end, and it's time we caught this guy."

TWENTY-NINE

Jonas had always hated stakeouts. He'd take a predawn raid any day to get his blood pumping. A few fugitive arrests by noon, and the adrenaline would keep him going for hours. Sitting in a car drinking coffee to stay awake was mind numbing. On the other hand, being stuck in a car with a beautiful woman wasn't all bad.

They sat in a rented car, kitty-corner from Yuri's place, while Madison talked to her sister. It was almost midnight and there had still been no movement at the house. Hopefully Yuri hadn't somehow gotten spooked and changed his plans, but since there was no way to know, they'd have to stay put for the moment.

Madison ended the call and set her phone in her lap.

"Everything okay?" he asked.

"I think so. My sister just wanted to check up on me."

"It's hard to blame her."

"At least she's okay." She shifted in her seat, turning toward him. "We've talked a lot about Luke, but you never told me much about the woman in your life."

"As I recall, you fell asleep."

"As I recall, you changed the subject, like you're doing right now."

He swallowed hard, not sure he wanted to go in this direction. He couldn't remember the last time he'd talked about Felicia. It was a topic his friends and family had finally stopped asking about.

"Long story short, I almost married her. In fact, I was planning to propose, I just hadn't bought the ring yet."

"What was stopping you?"

"Nothing in particular. We both had busy schedules, and . . . I don't know. For some reason the timing was never right. Before I could propose, she broke things off with me and moved back to her hometown."

"And you didn't follow her?"

Jonas frowned. It wasn't the first time he'd been asked that question, but the answer was always the same. "Sometimes you have to accept it when things are over. And things were over between us."

She looked up at him and studied his face, but he'd learned to keep certain pages of his life closed to others a long time ago. And Madison was no exception to the rule. Besides, it wasn't as though he owed her an explanation. Felicia had been out of his life for a while now and nothing was going to change what had happened between them. What had changed was his ability to open his heart.

"I'm sorry," she said.

"Don't be. It was a long time ago. She was my partner and I trusted her with my life. It was somehow an easy step to trust her with my heart as well. That is, until things unraveled."

"So no one since?" she asked.

"What? Is it hard to believe someone as handsome and dedicated as I am isn't tied down?" He let out a nervous laugh, trying to shift the conversation back to Madison, but he had a feeling she could see right through him.

"You're really good at changing the subject." She took a sip of her coffee and waited for him to explain before continuing, but he didn't. "Can I ask what happened to her?"

He stared out at a large oak tree, its branches swaying in the wind beneath a streetlight, surprised she'd gotten him to say this much. Because Felicia wasn't something he talked about. Instead it was this piece of his past he'd managed to completely bury. It just seemed . . . better that way.

"We had a confrontation with an armed suspect during a raid. She was shot in front of me."

"Oh, Jonas, I'm so sorry. She died?"

"No, actually." His fingers clenched in his lap. "A top-notch surgeon was able to save her life. Just not her leg."

"Wow. That had to be devastating for her."

"It was, but I told her it didn't matter. That I still wanted to marry her because I loved her. I meant it, but she refused to talk with me. Couldn't see herself with me anymore, because we wouldn't be able to do everything we'd planned before the accident."

"So she pushed you away because she was worried if you asked her to marry you it would only be because you felt sorry for her."

He let out a huff of air. "It doesn't matter anymore. It was a long time ago. Taught me firsthand the bad idea of a relationship on the job. There's just too much combined baggage."

"Do you ever see her?"

"No. Nothing I did or said changed her mind. Last I heard, she was living back in Texas and doing well. Or at least I hope she is." His jaw tensed at the memories. "Back then, I thought I could help fix her. I was so sure that if I could convince her I was willing to walk that road with her we'd be okay."

But he'd been wrong. He couldn't fix someone who didn't want to be fixed.

"I'm sorry."

"I've talked to her grandmother a few times, but Felicia never changed her mind. And eventually . . . eventually I had to move on. Anyway, it's nothing like what you went through."

"It still couldn't be easy."

He set his coffee in the console between them. Sitting quietly forced him to think. Maybe that was why he never slowed down. "I guess you never really know how you're going to react to a situation until you're the one facing it head-on. Over the years working as a detective, I met dozens of families whose lives were completely turned upside down because of a crime, but when you're the one facing the crisis, you can't help but look at things differently."

"It changes everything, doesn't it?"

"In an instant."

And for him, it had made him hesitate about falling in love again. Though maybe that was okay. He loved his career, had plenty of friends, and most days didn't have time to feel lonely. But somehow Madison was a reminder of what he'd always assumed he'd have. A wife, kids, and a somewhat normal life.

If someone with his career choice could ever have a normal life.

Not that he was falling for her, but he was surprised at how much they had in common. He stole a glimpse of her profile in the light from the streetlamps. How her hair swept across her brow, the tiny scar on her chin that was barely visible right now, and the splash of freckles across her cheeks. In some ways, she reminded him of Felicia, though physically they were completely different. It was that inner fire and spirit that he'd loved about Felicia. Her determination to make the world a better place when sometimes it seemed like there were more questions than solutions.

"For me, there was something inside me that broke after Luke's death," she said. "I was convinced it would happen again and I'd lose someone else I loved. Convinced that whoever killed Luke was going to strike again. It's like we think we're safe, that those things only happen to other people, but when they happen to us, it makes it hard to love and trust again."

It surprised him that talking to her seemed so . . . therapeutic. The circumstances were different, but she understood what it was like to love and lose someone.

"I can also see why you don't want to date," Madison continued. "I can't tell you how many blind dates my sister has tried to set me up on. She keeps telling me that five years is plenty of time to heal, and that I'd be happier if I found someone else. How Luke wouldn't want me to be alone."

"Except we all have our own schedules of moving through grief," he said. "There's really no right answer. Have you dated since he died?"

He caught her hesitation, wondering why he was asking her such a personal question when he could hardly talk about Felicia. Wondering why her insight really mattered to him.

"Nothing serious. The first date I went on, I felt as if I was betraying Luke. I came home and told my sister that was the last time I was ever going out on a date. And it was another year before I even thought about it. Going there has been hard."

"And now?"

"I'm still making excuses to my sister." She laughed. "I don't let myself slow down enough to get lonely. I figure if I'm working, then I don't have time to think about it."

"I understand."

She took a deep breath. "My sister is right about one thing. I know Luke would want me to move on. It's just that there's more involved than simply taking a step forward. You have to find that right person. The one who understands who you are. I'd rather be alone than settle for someone that wasn't right for me."

He understood the need for resolution. For closure. Always had wondered what would have happened if he'd asked Felicia to marry him before the accident. Maybe Madison was right. Maybe Felicia would never have been able to believe he truly wanted to marry her.

It was something he'd never know.

He let his mind wander back to Madison. She understood what motivated him. But he couldn't shake the idea that the whole mixing work with pleasure and falling for a coworker thing would end poorly. Not to mention his fear of getting another broken heart.

"So you don't ever think about getting married . . . starting a family?" she asked.

"Sometimes." He grabbed for his coffee, suddenly feeling caught by the shift in the conversation. The back of his hand brushed against hers. "Sorry."

"It's fine, I . . ."

His thoughts paused as she looked up at him. Her light brown eyes were barely visible in the darkness of the car, but he could hear her breathing, feel his own heart beating . . . He set down his coffee, caught up in the sudden intensity of the moment.

His body leaned forward automatically as his gaze shifted from her eyes to her lips. They were slightly parted as if she wanted the same thing he did.

She blinked, then turned at the sound of a vehicle.

"Jonas, wait a minute . . . someone just pulled up."

In an instant, the moment was lost.

A car pulled into Yuri's driveway. "It's a pizza delivery."

Jonas radioed the marshal who was helping coordinate the stakeout. "Patterson, I need you to check out the following license plate." He read off the numbers. "See if the car's stolen."

"Give me a minute. I'm on it."

Jonas drummed his fingers on the steering wheel. He wasn't sure they had a minute. If this really was a pizza delivery guy, marching up to the house now would blow their cover. But if they didn't check it out, and this guy was here to pick up Barrick's passport, they could end up missing him.

He was at the front door now. Another fifteen seconds and they'd miss their chance.

"Patterson, I need something now." Jonas glanced questioningly at Madison.

She matched his gaze. "I agree."

He pulled the keys out of the ignition and spoke into his radio. "Have the other team follow the delivery car. We're going in."

They ran across the street, Madison running around back while he stopped at the front and banged on the door.

The sound of rustling came from inside as Jonas continued hitting the door.

"Yuri's car is gone." Madison radioed. "I'm coming around front."

A man opened the door, but Jonas had seen Yuri's mug shot and this definitely wasn't him.

"Where's Yuri?" Jonas asked.

"I don't know."

"What do you mean?"

Madison hustled over from the side yard. "He's the pizza delivery man. They switched places."

"How do you know that?" the man asked.

"It's the only thing that makes sense."

"And Yuri took the passport," Jonas said.

The man shrugged, holding up his hands. "All I know is that Yuri asked me to do him a favor. He had a client who was worried about being followed and Yuri decided to placate him."

"Where is he now?" Jonas asked.

"I don't know. He said the less I knew, the better."

Jonas watched as Madison began questioning the decoy. He touched his earpiece. "Patterson, we need that delivery vehicle."

His radio crackled. "I know, but they just called in. They lost it."

Jonas turned around, his agitation growing. "You can't be serious."

"I wish I wasn't. But I do have some news. I've been going through flight lists like you said, and something just popped up."

"It better be some good news."

"It is. Bianca Carleton just booked a flight for Houston for eight o'clock tomorrow morning."

THIRTY

Early the next morning, Madison sat in a row of chairs against the back wall of the gate in Terminal A, eating a sausage biscuit and studying each passenger as they entered the area. Bianca had taken a chair by the window overlooking the runway and was reading a novel. It was tempting to walk up to her right now, drag her into an interrogation room, and demand answers, but if they did that, the chances of her leading them to Barrick would more than likely evaporate.

Jonas tapped on the armrest between them while scanning the passengers. She enclosed her fingers around his hand to stop him, before realizing what she'd done, then quickly pulled away.

"Sorry." He tugged his ball cap lower on his forehead, then pulled his hands into his lap.

"It's just that you're usually the calm and collected one," Madison said. She turned her attention back to the growing crowd, finding it harder than normal to focus. Something had passed between them during the stakeout last night, and she'd yet to completely figure it out. Not only had he shared about his ex-fiancée but for a moment, she'd actually thought he was going to kiss her. She took the last bite of her biscuit. That, though, was ridiculous. He'd made it quite clear that he had no desire to get involved with someone he worked with, and she had as well.

He rested his elbows against his thighs. "I don't think he's coming."

She took a sip of her orange juice. "She doesn't look like she's waiting for anyone."

"I agree."

"Which wouldn't be a bad idea. If it were me, I'd either meet him in Houston and take a flight together from there or, even better, meet him at my final destination. By then, they'd be out of the country, where it will be a lot easier to disappear."

Jonas nodded. "He's going to need to stay a step ahead of us, and he can now that he has a passport."

A passport meant he was freer to move around. Especially since they still didn't know what name he was using. But if he was here, getting ready to fly with Bianca, they were going to catch him.

"Here's my question," Madison said, leaning back in her chair. "We asked the same thing about Mary Margaret, but what is it about Damon Barrick that would make a woman—and now two women—decide to go on the lam?"

"I keep asking myself the same thing. Randall said Bianca was married to a banker for twenty years."

"So she's looking for adventure?"

"It makes sense," Jonas said. "Her husband worked long hours, spent most of his time at the office. She's traveled some, but without children her days are most likely spent working with non-profit organizations and sitting on their boards. She's lonely and wanting something more with her life but doesn't know what to do."

Madison could see it. "Barrick sweeps in, he's charming and charismatic. And even with a bit of a temper, she brushes it off and finds herself in love."

"But to just walk away from all her friends and her life here . . ." Jonas shook his head. It still didn't really seem to add up. "That would have taken a lot of convincing on his part."

"Maybe not. Maybe the only thing she's giving up is a bunch of superficial relationships. She has a fat bank account, he's her true love, and it's an adventure. They can spend the rest of their lives on some idyllic beach or island. He changes his identity, no one is looking for him . . ."

"And you think she really believes he's innocent?" Jonas asked.

"She believes what she wants to believe."

Jonas gathered their trash from breakfast and dropped it into the paper bag. "I can see the attraction, especially if you're looking for something more. My aunt and uncle retired to Panama and never looked back. They have this ocean-view condo, uncrowded beaches, golf, tennis . . . They keep begging me to visit. Say it's the best decision they've ever made."

"Sounds like a Caribbean paradise."

"I might have to consider it one day."

Madison shot him a smile. "Above selling worms?"

"I love the Northwest, but year-round sun might beat out putting up with half a year of rain in the forecast."

"I don't know. I can't see myself trading it in even for the Caribbean sunshine."

A flight announcement came over the loud-speaker.

"We're up," Madison said.

The usual announcements for families with small children and any active military personnel followed, but there was still no sign of Barrick.

Jonas nodded. "It's getting crowded. Why don't we split up and keep searching? He could show up at the last minute."

She made her way to the back of the line, scanning the crowd of passengers with their rolling carry-ons and backpacks. A little girl screamed on the floor over one of her toys. A couple teens sat absorbed in their phones. Slowly the line of passengers grew until it snaked outside the gate.

Bianca made her way to the priority line. There was still no sign of Barrick. Bianca handed her ticket to the gate agent, then headed to the plane. Patterson had pulled some strings and managed to change her seat, so she was by the requested window but in the last row of first class. Their tickets were for the first row, guaranteeing, they hoped, that she didn't notice their presence on board. If she figured out they were after her, they risked the chance of her signaling Barrick, which they couldn't afford to happen. They needed her to lead them to him. But when they finally boarded the plane and took their seats, there was still no sign of the man.

She clicked on her seat belt, and Jonas nudged her with his elbow. "I don't think I told you, but you're cute as a redhead."

She felt her cheeks flush at the compliment. Not that it really mattered what Jonas thought. "As a child I secretly wanted to be a redhead with freckles. I might have to try something that doesn't just wash out."

"I think this is the first time I've been able to relax."

Madison let out a low laugh. "I never thought about an airplane ride as a time to relax, but you're right."

"You might as well close your eyes," he said. "She's not going anywhere."

"As long as history doesn't repeat itself and we take an unexpected landing."

"Let's not even joke about that."

● ● ●

An in-flight announcement pulled her out of her sleep. Maybe she'd been more tired than she'd thought.

"Ladies and gentlemen, we have just been cleared to land at George Bush Intercontinental Airport. Please make sure your seat belt is securely fastened . . ."

Madison pretended to stretch out her back to turn around without suspicion. She caught sight of Bianca's blue sleeve as she reached to adjust the air flow above her. Their plan seemed to be working so far. Not that she should be surprised. There was nowhere for the woman to go.

She and Jonas were the first to depart the plane as planned. Their strategy depended on keeping tabs on Bianca without the woman recognizing them. The passengers of flight 1184 slowly filed off the jetway and into the gate with their hand luggage.

But there was no sign of Bianca.

"Where is she?" Madison asked.

"I don't know. She should have already deplaned."

Madison searched her mind for probable scenarios. It was always possible that Bianca had waited in her seat for some reason, but why?

A siren wailed as an announcement came over the loudspeaker. "Ladies and gentlemen, we need all passengers to leave the terminal as quickly and calmly as possible. I repeat, all passengers to leave the terminal as quickly and calmly as possible."

"Jonas," she said. "What's happening?"

"I don't know."

Agents started shouting orders at the passengers. Several argued back. The hallway around them filled with people evacuating the terminal as the siren continued to wail. Madison shoved her way through the crowded concourse, back toward the gate agent who was still standing at the podium.

"We need to get back on the plane."

"I'm sorry, but we've got a security issue."

She held up her badge. "What's going on?"

"They're evacuating the terminal." The woman dropped her voice and leaned forward. "There's a possible bomb threat."

"We need on that plane."

The woman nodded, then opened the door to the jetway for them.

"Why don't you have Patterson put a trace on Bianca's phone, while you stay out here and keep looking for her," Jonas said. "I'll search the plane."

Madison made a call to the marshals in Denver who were still acting as their backup.

"She's missing? How is that possible?" Patterson asked.

"We never saw her come off the plane, and now

they're evacuating the terminal, so the place is in complete chaos. She must have slipped through the crowd."

"I'll find her."

Jonas came out a minute later, shaking his head. How had they lost her? Madison felt like a fish swimming upstream as she split off from Jonas toward the end of the terminal. She scanned the crowd, but so far there wasn't anyone matching Bianca's description. Only dozens of unfamiliar travelers, all carrying backpacks or rolling carry-on bags.

Her frustration rose as the announcement continued to repeat over the intercom.

An agent confronted Madison as she searched the crowd. "We're going to have to ask you to leave, ma'am. This terminal is being evacuated."

"I understand." She held up her badge as Jonas jogged back over to join her. "We're US Marshals. My partner and I are looking for a key witness who was on one of the planes."

"What's going on?" Jonas asked.

The woman scanned both of their badges before answering. "An unattended bag was discovered by one of our dogs. We're waiting for the bomb squad as a precaution."

Madison frowned. This couldn't be a coincidence. Flights were going to be delayed as law enforcement investigated the bag. People would panic. Somehow Barrick was behind this.

Her phone rang again. "What have you got, Patterson?"

"She's in the terminal."

"You need to narrow it down. We're looking at dozens of gates and we're running out of time. I also need officers in the international terminal looking for both of them."

"I'm on it. We've got officers stationed at the end of the terminal and have sent out photos of her. Wait a minute . . . I've got a ping on her phone."

"Okay, where?"

"There's a restroom about thirty feet behind you. Looks like it's coming from there or at least nearby."

"I'm on it."

Madison ran through the crowded terminal toward the bathrooms, wondering how they'd missed her. But there were dozens of places she could have hidden if she hadn't evacuated.

The women's bathroom was quiet as she slipped in and checked the stalls one by one.

Nothing.

She checked the counters and the trash. Something caught her eye.

"Patterson, we've got a problem. I found Bianca's phone in the trash, but she's long gone."

He sighed. "All right. I'll do some more searching."

Madison ended the call and hurried out of the

restroom, Bianca's phone in her hand. Irritation ate at her. Jonas was outside, waiting for her. "She's gone."

Jonas frowned. "She can't go far, and it's pretty clear she's left this terminal."

She wished the airport wasn't so big. It made it too easy to miss something. "We're looking at a hundred and fifty thousand people passing through here, and the evacuation is already causing chaos," she said.

"Exactly what they wanted."

"So she knows—or at least she believes we're after her."

Her phone rang and she dug it out of her pocket, standing in the almost empty terminal.

"She's got another flight booked," Patterson said. "United Airlines to Newark, leaving out of terminal E in less than an hour."

"Have backup meet us there, but make sure every TSA agent, airline employee, and law enforcement officer in this airport is still looking for her." She turned to Jonas. "We found her. Terminal E. She's got a flight out of here."

Jonas shook his head. "I don't think she'll be there."

"What do you mean?"

"It's too obvious. She knows we'll find that out."

Madison nodded. "She's going to leave the airport."

THIRTY-ONE

They found her waiting for a rideshare outside Terminal B.

Jonas pulled out his weapon as Bianca looked to run, but there was nowhere left to go. "Put your hands in the air. It's over."

They contacted airport security, then escorted Bianca to a secure office inside the Airport-IAH division of the Houston police department, wondering what had brought her to this point. How could Barrick have been so convincing that she wasn't able to see through his lies?

Soon Madison and Jonas were sitting across from Bianca as she stared at the table, avoiding Jonas's gaze. "How'd you find me?"

"Barrick has proven himself to be the master of misdirection. Something spooked you, and he helped you run. It made sense that you'd try to ditch your next flight."

"You were on the plane with me, weren't you?" Madison nodded.

"It's ironic. Truth is, I never saw you. I just . . . I don't know. I panicked. There was this guy at the gate who kept looking at me. I was convinced he knew who I was. I didn't know what to do."

Madison rested her elbows on the table. "We need to know what the plan is, Bianca. We need to know where Damon is."

She shook her head. "You don't understand. He's innocent and this . . . this is his only chance to live a normal life."

"Running for the rest of his life? That's hardly normal," Jonas said. "But what if everything he's ever told you is a lie? What if he was simply using you to gain access to your money?"

"That's not possible. We were planning to go away together, because that plane crash . . . it was like a second chance for both of us."

"*Was* being the key word. Because you won't be traveling to meet him, I can assure you of that. Your best option right now—your only option—is to cooperate."

"The only thing he's guilty of in all of this is getting a forged passport. But what was he supposed to do? He was stripped of everything that was his. He had no choice. If he wants to stay out of prison, he has to leave the country."

Jonas glanced at the clock on the wall, irritated. Every second that passed was another second Barrick was getting away. How could she be so blinded to who Barrick really was?

"Where is he?" Jonas asked.

Bianca's jaw clenched, but she just stared at the table in front of her.

"So is this how things are going to play out?"

Madison asked. "Because here's the thing. We will find him. And even if he is innocent of murder, which I'm convinced he isn't, the consequences of using a forged passport are pretty stiff. Up to fifteen years imprisonment, a $250,000 fine. On top of that, there's a side dish of felony crimes served up. He will go back to prison."

Bianca shook her head. "He's smart. Smarter than you think."

"And you're willing to go to prison for helping him escape?" Jonas caught her gaze. "Because we can prove what we're saying."

"How?"

"For starters, check your bank accounts. See how much money is left."

Bianca didn't flinch. "He's not after my money. It's a perk. Sure. And it will allow us to do what we want to do, but he loves me—"

"Just check."

Madison slid Bianca's phone across the table, then waited.

"There must be a mistake."

"Why do you say that?" Madison asked.

"Because . . ." Bianca dropped the phone onto the table, her hand shaking. "He wouldn't just take my money."

"How much is missing?"

"There was about a hundred thousand in there." Bianca's face was pale. "But the rest of my money is safe. He had me move six million into an account offshore so we could have easy access. But without my signature"—she struggled to take a breath—"he can't touch it."

"So he still needs you," Jonas said.

"This is a nightmare." Bianca pressed her fingers against her temples. "I thought he was planning ahead. I gave him access to that account so he could arrange our passports and tickets and whatever we'd need once we left the country. I trusted him. No, I don't care what you say, there's an explanation."

"I'm sorry," Madison said. "I know this isn't easy, but we need your help to find him, Bianca. He's done this before to other women. And we now believe that at least two of those women are dead."

"No. You don't understand." Bianca's expression was resolute. "He told me this might happen. He said if I was ever brought in, you would try to confuse me. Get me to say what you want to hear. But you don't know him like I do. This . . . this doesn't change anything." She pushed the phone across the table.

"There's more," Madison said. "Remember Detective Randall? He found some interesting things in his investigation about your husband, Jim, who died fourteen months ago."

"What does he have to do with any of this?"

"There were a few interesting inconsistencies with his death that we found in his case files."

"I don't understand."

"Detective Randall is convinced your husband didn't die of natural causes, and in fact, we've asked to reopen the case."

"That's not possible. My husband died of a heart attack. I was always begging him to lose weight. To eat right and stop drinking, but he never listened to me."

"Did you know he'd filed for divorce?"

Bianca's eyes widened. "What are you talking about?"

"Two days before he died. But you knew that. Because if he divorced you—especially if it was found out you were having an affair—you would have lost everything, wouldn't you?"

"I didn't kill my husband," Bianca said.

"Of course you didn't," Madison said. "We think Damon Barrick did."

"No. This is nothing more than another one of your tricks. You're trying to get me to confess something that didn't happen. I know Damon. He wasn't even around the weekend my husband died. Jim and I had gone to spend a few days in Aspen."

"But you were having an affair with Damon while your husband was still alive."

"No . . . yes . . . it doesn't matter. Any sparks had died out in our marriage years before, but that didn't mean I would kill him. There was no reason to. He left everything to me if he died, yes, but I always had access to what we owned."

"But it was financially advantageous for Damon," Madison said. "And what else did he tell you? That he loved you. That the two of you would find a way to leave the country together."

"This was never about money."

"A hundred thousand gives him enough to get out of the country."

"No. He wanted me to go with him."

"You told us you broke things off with him when he went to prison," Jonas said, "but you didn't, did you?"

"No . . . I . . ." Bianca fidgeted with her ring. "He had this crazy plan that he was going to escape, and I needed to be ready. I transferred money and did everything he told me to do so we'd be ready to run once he escaped."

"So you waited."

"He said I should trust him."

"Maybe you shouldn't have done that." Jonas tried to keep the irritation out of his voice. "How long will it be until he dumps you just like the other women? All he really wants is your money."

"I don't believe you."

"But I think a part of you does believe us," Madison said. "Otherwise you would have given him full access to your offshore account as well. Right?"

Bianca stared at the table. "I know what you're doing. You feel sorry for me. You wonder how

I can still believe he's innocent after everything you've told me."

Madison tilted her head. "It is hard to understand why you risked everything for him."

"Why does any woman put her heart on the line like I did? We do it for love. For adventure. And yes, I still love him."

"And you believe he loves you?"

"You can show me all the evidence you want, but I know Damon. I know he loves me. You don't have to understand, but my first husband . . . he provided for me financially, but ours was more a marriage of convenience. Two people who had a lot in common and whose marriage was, well, convenient. But there wasn't a whole lot of love between us."

"Just tell us where he is," Madison said.

Bianca dismissed the request with a shake of her head. "I don't know. I don't even know what name he's using."

"We have more proof, if what we've given you isn't enough." Jonas pulled up a photo of Stephanie Phillips on his phone. "Recognize her?"

"No."

"This is Stephanie Phillips. We have growing evidence that Damon killed her. He's a con man. A grifter who has swindled millions of dollars from at least three women."

Bianca wiped away a tear off her cheek. "None of this is true."

"Think about it," Madison said. "What do you think he'll do when he gets the rest of your money?"

"You are so wrong." Her voice rose. "Damon would never hurt me. He loves me."

Jonas could see the struggle in the woman's eyes and the hesitation in her voice and knew they were winning. She'd banked everything on one man's promises, and every last one had just shattered into a million pieces.

"It's time to stop playing games, Bianca." Jonas switched photos. "This is Daisy Porter—"

"No. I never saw this as a game. I gave up everything for him." Her shoulders dropped, defeat etching her face. "Left everything. If it was nothing more than a lie . . ."

"I'm sorry," Madison said.

Bianca avoided their gazes. Silence fell between them for a moment before she asked, "What do you want me to do?"

"We need you to help us bring him in. What exactly was the plan?"

She took the tissue Madison offered her and blew her nose before continuing. "After I landed, I—I panicked. Damon had already arrived on a different flight and told me he'd make a distraction. Then he told me he'd arranged a ride for me to meet him. I don't know. If he thinks I've been compromised . . . or I've turned on him . . ."

"Call him and let him know your luggage was late and you're on your way."

She hesitated, then dialed and placed the call on speaker. "Damon—"

"Where are you?" a low voice replied.

"I'm on my way. I'm sorry. My bag was late. I missed my ride."

"We're running out of time. Is anyone following you?"

"No."

There was a slight pause on the other end. "I'll send the driver back for you. His name's Tyler."

"Are you sure that's safe?"

"Do you trust me?"

Bianca hesitated, but only for a brief moment. "You know I do. Where are we meeting?"

"I've got us flights out of the Hobby airport. It's better if we don't leave together." Barrick hung up the call.

Madison signaled at Jonas. "I need to talk to you outside."

He stepped into the hallway behind her, then closed the door. "Patterson's trying to trace Barrick's phone, but in the meantime, we can put a tracking device on her, and she'll lead us right to him."

"Maybe, but we need to be careful."

"You think he's onto us?"

"I don't think he'd risk his life for her," Madison said. "He wants his hands on that money, but he'll get rid of her if he thinks anything is off. He's not going to let anything stop him from getting out of the country."

He tried to read her expression. "Agreed."

"I'll go in her place," Madison said. "The driver doesn't know what she looks like. Then you can follow me, but at least having someone in the car will ensure we don't spook him."

"What happens when you step out of the car and Barrick realizes who you are?"

"You'll be right there surrounding him."

He rubbed the back of his neck. "I don't know. There are too many variables we can't control. Too many things that can go wrong."

"If Patterson can trace his phone, there's a good chance you can take him down before I even get there. But we need insurance that he doesn't change his plan or disappear again." She shot him a smile. "You're not going to talk me out of this, are you?"

"Not unless Michaels pulls the plug on the plan. You're the most capable marshal I know."

She smiled. "Well said."

Michaels turned out to be easy to convince. After hanging up with the chief deputy, Jonas instructed one of the officers to hold Bianca at the station. Then he and Madison headed back through the crowded airport to meet Bianca's ride.

"We're tracking you on both your phone and the tracking device in your shoe," Jonas said.

"Good, because you're not worried or anything, are you?"

"It's always better to be safe than sorry."

"I think your overprotection has to do with that bet we made." She raised her eyebrows. "You're worried he's going to get away and we won't have our chowder celebration dinner."

"This guy isn't getting away, no matter how far he goes. And yes, I'm getting my chowder dinner as well." He stopped beside her, then turned and brushed his hand across her shoulder before catching her gaze. "Just promise me you'll be careful. I don't completely trust Bianca, and I certainly don't trust Barrick."

"I will be. I promise."

They stepped out into the humid Houston air to the pickup area. Jonas moved to the side like he was waiting for a ride, but stayed close enough to see the pickup.

A black sedan pulled up beside Madison and the driver rolled down the window.

"You're Tyler?" Madison asked.

"Yes."

"Thanks for picking me up. Sorry I'm late. I had some baggage issues."

"That's fine. Can I help you with the bags?"

She shook her head, picked up Bianca's suitcase, and opened the back door. "How far is the other airport?"

"A little more than thirty minutes away, depending on traffic. Don't worry. Your boyfriend arranged everything. You're in good hands."

THIRTY-TWO

The plan was simple, in theory. Madison would pose as Bianca, luggage and all, with Bianca's driver. Jonas and one of the officers who worked at the airport, Sergeant O'Conner, would follow her from a distance, with a second unmarked car following close behind. Madison's phone was being tracked along with the additional backup tracker they'd placed in her shoe. On top of that, there were a dozen agents on their way to the Hobby airport who would be there as backup in case Barrick decided to put up a fight. The noose was slowly tightening.

So why did he feel so on edge?

Jonas blew out a sharp breath. He trusted Madison. There was no doubt about that. But he also knew they couldn't trust Bianca. She was being held at the airport so she would have no chance to communicate with Barrick. He might believe the information they'd given her had shaken her, but he wasn't convinced her loyalty didn't outweigh anything new that she learned. And they couldn't take a chance of their plan changing.

He glanced at his watch, knowing time was

running out. In a few short hours, if they didn't find him, there was a good chance that Barrick would be across the border and long gone with or without Bianca's money. Something they couldn't afford to let happen.

They headed down the highway, three cars behind the driver, making sure they stayed far enough back that they weren't made, and yet close enough to keep them in their sights.

"I'm surprised Barrick doesn't just try to cross the border into Mexico," O'Conner said.

"He knows we're after him," Jonas said. "He probably also knows that we have a field office in Mexico. The chances of him getting through are slim to none."

Jonas reached up and tried to rub the knots out of the back of his neck. After nearly a week of hunting Barrick and always being a step behind him, he was ready to put an end to this.

"Stay closer on his tail. I don't want to lose her."

"Relax. If I'm not careful, he's going to spot us following him. Besides, we're tracking her phone and she's got a tracker on her. We've got them."

Jonas frowned, still uncomfortable with the situation. He should have insisted on driving. He might not know Houston like O'Conner did, but sitting in the passenger seat only made him feel less in control. He drummed his fingers against the armrest, keeping his eyes focused on the black sedan ahead of them. One thing he did remember about the handful of times he'd been in Houston was that rush hour wasn't limited to morning and evening hours. Even at midday, the multilane highway felt congested. But O'Conner was right. Even if they lost sight of the car, they could still track her. Worrying was only going to eat him up.

"Are you usually this keyed up during a case?" O'Conner asked.

Jonas pulled his hands into his lap and folded them. "Let's just say it's been a difficult few days."

"I skimmed through the report. You guys have had it rough."

"I guess a few missed nights of sleep will be worth it in the end."

"So what's up between you and your partner?" O'Conner asked.

"What do you mean?"

"I got the impression you were . . . I don't know. Maybe more than friends."

Jonas sighed. The last thing he wanted to do was defend his relationship with Madison. "I met her back in Nashville for some field training and now we're working this case, but just as partners."

"So is she single?"

Jonas frowned at the probing questions. "Widowed."

"Same thing. Does she date?"

"I wouldn't know. You'd have to ask her that."

A wave of overprotectiveness shot through him. Madison wasn't exactly helpless and didn't need him acting in her defense, but still the move rubbed him wrong.

Because you wouldn't mind dating her yourself.

The thought tripped him. He had no desire to date Madison or any other woman he knew at the moment, because he was, in fact, perfectly happy with his life. Moving to Seattle wasn't a sign that he was burnt-out. It was simply that he wanted to move in a different direction. Change didn't have to equal running from something.

He frowned, realizing his focus was off. If he was going to ensure Madison's safety, there was no time for distractions.

His phone rang, and Jonas pulled it out of his pocket. "What have you got, Patterson?"

"Something you might to like to hear. Local PD just found Yuri. And let's say, he had no problem ratting out Barrick if it will keep him out of jail. He gave us the fake name he used for Barrick's passport. Sean Montgomery. He was on a flight from Denver to Houston."

"Anything out of Houston now?"

"He's got a ticket out of Hobby for South America," Patterson said. "Leaves in two hours."

"Good work, Patterson. We'll stick to the plan and pick him up at the airport. Make sure our backup teams are watching for any sign of him at Hobby."

He hung up the phone as a semi pulled in front of them, blocking his view.

Jonas leaned forward. "Pull around the semi in front of us."

The truck finally pulled into the right lane, but Madison's car had disappeared.

"Where is she?" he asked.

"They should be three cars ahead."

Should be, but she wasn't. He drew in a deep breath. Not that he was worried. Not only could they track her, they now had confirmation where she was headed.

Jonas grabbed his phone and sent Madison a text.

Where are you?

Avoiding traffic.
Turned off onto 45.

"Take the 45 exit," Jonas said. "They just took the turnoff."

we're right behind you.

"I'm on it," O'Conner said.

They crossed a few lanes to take the next exit. He caught sight of the vehicle again and blew out a sharp huff of air. O'Conner was right. He was too on edge. Too jumpy. This was exactly why he refused to get involved with people he worked with. Putting his life on the line and watching each other's back was one thing but putting his heart out there . . . He'd already learned that lesson.

Before long, the city turned into farm roads and fields of cattle south of Houston.

"Where are they going?" Jonas asked.

"I don't know," O'Conner said. "They're heading west now. This isn't the right route."

"She said he's avoiding traffic." Jonas studied his Google map. "You know the area. What would you do?"

"This isn't avoiding traffic."

Jonas pounded out another text, knowing he shouldn't jump to conclusions, but he already had.

you're not going the right way.

He stared at the phone, waiting for a response.

"Can you still see her?" Jonas asked.

"They're still three cars ahead."

give me an update.

He stared at the phone as if that was going to make her answer. Irritation mushroomed. She was a seasoned marshal who knew what she was doing, but that didn't change the fact that they were after a man desperate enough to kill to ensure his escape route.

i can't see you.

She'd been there a second ago.

driver heard from barrick.
plans changed. taking me to
south. think he's spooked.

where?

driver doesn't know.
giving directions as we go.

This was what he'd been afraid of. Barrick had managed to stay one step ahead of them, and now he was switching routes again. And if he thought Bianca was leading him into a trap—like she was—the man was going to run.

"What's the plan now?" O'Conner said.

"We keep following her, but we need to find out where they're meeting."

But that was impossible at the moment. Barrick could be planning to meet and drive to a dozen different airports in order to leave the country.

Unless he was trying to take Bianca out of the equation.

"What if he's planning to leave Bianca behind?" Jonas asked O'Conner.

"I don't know. Six million dollars is a powerful motivator, but I don't see them anymore."

where are you?

No answer.

Jonas grit his teeth. "Something's wrong." And this time it wasn't just his worrying. "She's not answering."

Suddenly his phone was ringing. His heart sank as he answered, putting the call on speaker. "Where is she, Patterson?"

"I've lost both tracking devices."

"You've got to find her."

"Give me a second."

"We don't have a second," Jonas said. "She's on her own. I need something."

"I'll find her." Patterson ended the call.

Jonas slammed his hand into the dashboard. "Stop the car."

He jumped out and stood along the side of the road, trying to spot the car, but all he could see was fields.

"Okay," Patterson said. "I've got a signal."

Jonas leaped into the passenger seat, while

Patterson gave him directions. "Go back to the last road and take the next farm road to the left. Looks like she's a quarter of a mile ahead. You're right behind her."

"Are you sure?" O'Conner asked.

"Positive. Both GPS markers are back online. She must have gone through a dead zone."

O'Conner pushed on the gas as they flew down the deserted two-lane road. Here, beyond the city, there was nothing but cattle and open fields and a sprinkling of trees. She had to be out here. And Jonas was convinced Barrick was as well. They had agents ready to intercept the man at both airports in case he did decide to escape, but as far as he was concerned, six million was too big a pull to give up on so easily.

Jonas focused his eyes on the path ahead of them. There was no way they'd come this far to lose Barrick.

Or to lose Madison.

His gut twisted and dragged him back to a place he didn't want to go.

They'd stood ready for the point man to initiate the raid. Something they'd already done three times that morning. Nothing was left to chance. Every decision was planned down to the minute detail of what could go wrong. But until they actually stepped into that house, they never knew for sure if the suspect was holding a gun or if there were hostages. A split-second decision was made. They were trained to avoid confrontation to avoid fatal mistakes.

Felicia hadn't died that day, but everything she'd known was ripped out from under her and she was never the same. She lost her leg and he ended up losing her.

And now Madison . . .

I don't want to lose her, God.

His knuckles whitened as his fingers formed into fists, every muscle on alert. Every action they took was a risk. It was why they trained and prepared. But sometimes, even the most thought-out plan went wrong.

His gut gnawed at him. He'd somehow managed to make this too personal and wasn't thinking clearly. He couldn't afford clouded judgment. He needed to focus on finding her—safe—and then he'd deal with whatever was messing with his head when all of this was over.

Barrick was a target.

Madison was the victim.

That was all. Nothing more.

O'Conner had slowed down. He looked down a gravel road that led to a farmhouse and barn, but the place looked quiet with no sign of the car.

"Tell me what to do, Patterson," Jonas said.

"You've still got another couple dozen yards."

"Pick up your speed, O'Conner."

"She should be near the road," Patterson said. "Not more than twenty feet."

"Stop! There's the car!"

O'Conner slammed on the brakes. Jonas jumped out before they'd come to a complete stop. He ran toward the black car. The driver's side door was open as well as the passenger's.

Madison's bag was still in the back, but she and her driver were gone.

"Where is she?" O'Conner asked, running up beside Jonas.

"I don't know." He stepped around the side of the car and something caught his eye. Madison's phone was on the ground, smashed into a dozen pieces. His stomach reeled. Had the driver found out he'd picked up the wrong woman? He shoved back the panic. No. She had to be safe. He couldn't lose her.

Madison ducked behind the tractor as Tyler fired off two quick shots. Their plan had backfired. From the one-sided conversation she'd overheard in the car, Barrick's uneasiness prompted him to ask one too many questions. Maybe six million dollars sitting in Bianca's account wasn't enough motivation to drag her along, or maybe he'd found a way to access the money without her. Either way, the man must have sensed that he'd been compromised and decided to run.

From her vantage point behind the tractor, Madison eyed the partially open door into the barn. Beyond the two-story wooden structure was an open field that would give her no cover. Her team might not be able to track her phone anymore, but she still had the GPS device in her shoe. Jonas couldn't have been that far behind her, and she needed a place to hide until he got here. Decision made, she ran as fast as she could for the door. She could hear her pursuer swearing as he stumbled after her. As soon as she stepped inside, she slammed the sliding door shut behind her.

It was dark inside the large, open barn, with only a few narrow streams of light filtering through holes in the wood. Madison bowed behind a wall of hay bales as Tyler slid open the door and fired another shot in her direction. Heart hammering, she kept moving, knowing that getting trapped inside was a possibility.

Where was Jonas?

"It's over!" Tyler shouted from the middle of the barn. "There's nowhere to run. I know you're not Bianca, so who are you? FBI? Houston PD?"

She crouched in the far corner of the room, ready to spring into action if needed.

"It doesn't matter. I have my instructions." From the sound of his voice, Tyler was making his way around the barn in a large circle, trying to figure out where she was. "What's funny is that you're both going to disappear. Except while he's getting ready to fly off to some tropical paradise, you'll just disappear."

She scooted another couple feet along the wall, needing to make sure he couldn't see her. But with nowhere to run, it would be hard to stay hidden for long. She glanced around her. To her left was a row of tools hanging on the barn wall. They might not be guns, but they might be enough to hold him off until Jonas came.

She inched over, then pulled a long-handled shovel slowly off its perch, trying not to make any sound. A floorboard beneath her creaked as she took a step away from the wall. She froze, but the scuffling of feet told her she wasn't the only one who had heard the noise.

She gripped the shovel in her hands, trying to stay hidden behind the hay as long as she could, gauging when she needed to move by the sound of his movements. He rounded the corner of one of the bales. She leapt forward and swung the shovel with all her might, hitting him directly in the chest. She was fast, but he was stronger. He pushed her over, knocking her off her feet before slamming her onto the hard, wooden flooring. Her head ached from the impact. She had no idea where his gun was now, but his hands were wrapped around her neck. She fought to shove him away. Fought to breathe. Fought to get out from under him.

She managed to fling her hand behind her, reaching for the shovel that had fallen. Where was it? Panic set in. Her lungs were burning. She was desperate for air. She heard voices. Jonas was here. Tyler looked toward the barn door, momentarily loosening his grip and giving her the distraction she needed. She found the metal bar and wrapped her fingers around it. With a grunt, she managed to shove him away and stumble to her feet. He lunged for her again, but this time she was ready. Madison swung the iron handle as hard as she could and heard the sickening crack of his skull. Tyler slumped to the ground.

Her own chest heaved from exhaustion as she stumbled backward.

THIRTY-THREE

M adison?" Jonas called out to her.

"I'm here." She stumbled away from the downed man, toward the light streaming from the open door.

Jonas ran over, quickly checking the man's pulse. "He's dead."

She nodded, allowing some of the emotions of her escape to wash over her. She'd served dozens of arrest warrants for her job and had been shot at more than once. She'd been in raids where a fleeing suspect was killed and twice where a fellow marshal had been fatally wounded next to her. She'd been trained in tactical formations, as well as taking every precaution possible to ensure both the officers involved and the fugitives got out alive in every single case. But this time . . . a few more seconds and she wouldn't have made it out alive.

Jonas's gaze surveyed her body. "Did he hurt you?"

"He tried. He would have killed me if you hadn't shown up."

"You're bleeding. Your forehead."

She touched her head and winced. "I must have hit it when I fell."

He brought her outside into the light, shouting for O'Conner to find something to clean her up. She could tell he was trying to hide his worry as he helped her sit down.

"You've got a few scratches, including the one on your forehead," Jonas said. "And your neck—there are bruises on your neck."

She raised her hand to rub the tender flesh. "He tried to strangle me."

But she was alive.

"Does anything else hurt?"

"I don't think so."

Jonas pulled her up and into his arms. She could feel her legs shaking as she leaned against him. "Why would he do this? Why couldn't he have just disappeared without having her killed?" Jonas said as he released her.

She squeezed her eyes shut for a moment. "Barrick got nervous and started asking the driver lots of questions. He figured out I wasn't Bianca somehow."

"Did you get anything out of him?" Jonas asked.

"He said something." She searched her memory. "Something about flying off to a tropical paradise."

"So Barrick's definitely leaving the country."

"I think he decided to run with or without

Bianca, and now that she's in custody, he doesn't have a choice."

"So he's leaving without the money. Maybe he never planned to take her at all."

"Maybe." She took a step back and leaned against the barn wall, taking a few deep breaths. She willed her legs to quit shaking. "Everything Barrick has done has been to distract us. All of this was simply misdirection. A game of illusion. The cabin in Wyoming. The bomb scare. I don't think he ever left IAH, Jonas. Never went to Hobby. He's still there. I'm sure of it."

"We can keep searching, though we've checked his name against every flight leaving out of Hobby and IAH, and he's not on them."

"We need to get back there." She forced her mind to work. "Maybe there was a second passport?"

"Why would you think that?" O'Conner asked.

Madison shrugged, then winced at the sharp pains. "He could have paid for a second one in case the first was compromised."

As soon as they made arrangements for someone to handle Tyler's body, they were back in the car and Jonas had Patterson on the phone. "Talk to Yuri again. We're on our way back to IAH. We think there's a good chance that Barrick's still there and that he's got a second passport. We need another name."

They were less than five minutes out from the airport when Patterson called back.

Jonas put the call on speaker. "What have you got?"

"Yuri's not talking. Either there really is no other passport, or he's lying, but we're not getting anything out of him."

Madison reached up and touched her bruised neck, her mind scrambling for a solution. "Even with every law enforcement officer at the airport looking for him, we're talking about what . . . five terminals, a hundred-plus gates, restaurants, shops, and clubs. And without being able to flag his name, the odds of him slipping onto his plane without being noticed are pretty high."

"So what are you thinking?" Jonas asked.

"We have to find a way to get him to come out of hiding." She turned and caught Jonas's gaze as a last-ditch plan began to form. "What's the one thing we know Barrick cares about?"

"The money in Bianca's account."

"Exactly. And while he might assume we have Bianca, he can't be certain. So what if she calls him and says we had nothing to hold her on and had to let her go. But she's terrified and needs to meet him. That she still wants to go with him."

Jonas shook his head. "He'll never buy it. He'll just think it's another trap."

"That's possible, yes, but if he thinks there's even a remote chance he can get his hands on that money, I think he'll risk it."

"I'm still not convinced it would work. We'd also have to convince Bianca."

Madison knew it was a long shot, but as far as she was concerned, it was their only chance. And at this point, she was willing to try anything. "All we need is for him to take the bait."

When they arrived back at the airport, Bianca was still sitting in the room where they'd left her. She had her hands folded in front of her, but her face was streaked with tears. Someone had brought her a sandwich and a drink, but she hadn't touched either one.

Jonas and Madison entered the room and sat down in the seats across from Bianca. They looked at each other since she wouldn't meet their gaze.

"We don't have a lot of time." Jonas slid his phone toward her. A photo of Tyler's dead body lit up the screen. "If you didn't completely believe that Barrick was lying to you before, maybe this will convince you."

Bianca's eyes widened. "Who's that?"

"Your driver. Barrick's plan was never to meet you. Instead he arranged for you to disappear. This was going to be your ride out of here."

"He attacked me," Madison said. "Said the real

plan was for me to disappear so Barrick could escape without two marshals on his tail."

Bianca shook her head. "I don't believe you."

"See these bruises on my neck? What if you had been there instead of me? Do you think you could have fought him off?"

"No, but—"

Madison leaned forward. "He would have killed you and left you in some shallow grave."

"Damon wouldn't have set that up."

Jonas looked directly into her eyes. "Then how do you explain what this man did to my partner when he thought it was you."

Bianca let out a sharp breath. She turned toward the wall and stared straight ahead. The emotions that had previously been etched on her face so clearly were gone now. "What do you want me to do?"

"We need you to call him," Jonas said. "We think he's still in the airport. You'll tell him that we had to let you go because we had nothing to hold you on. That you didn't know we were sending someone in your place and that you're terrified and still want to go with him."

Bianca nodded. "And he'll agree because of the money. Not me."

Jonas felt a sliver of pity for the woman. "I'm sorry."

"I guess that's the price I pay for being a

foolish old woman. I never should have believed he wanted me for more than my money."

"Not every man is like that," Madison said. "Barrick is very good at what he does."

Bianca shook her head. "He won't believe me."

"Then you're going to have to make sure you sound convincing."

Five minutes later, Madison and Jonas were settled in front of screens at the airport's communication center, where they could watch Bianca on the security cameras. Bianca had made the call to Barrick, and he'd agreed to meet her. Now they just had to wait for him to show up.

Madison watched the screen. Over a hundred thousand passengers traveled through this airport every day, but they only needed to find one. One who had been aggravatingly elusive over the past few days. She glanced at the clock on the wall. Another few minutes had passed and there was still no sign of Barrick. Frustration mounted as the seconds ticked by.

"What if he figured out this is a trap?" she said finally.

"Let's give it a few more minutes. We'll find him," Jonas said. "Whatever it takes."

Whatever it takes.

She blew out a huff of air. For all they knew, he was reclining in some business class seat, well on his way to South America.

Movement on one of the screens caught her attention. Madison leaned forward as a man slowly approached. He stopped again and glanced around him, clearly hesitant, but the camera caught his face. There was no question of who it was.

Barrick.

He looked at Bianca, stepped forward, then turned around.

"We need to move now," Madison shouted. "Something spooked him, and he's running."

The team moved into high gear. Madison and Jonas ran down a narrow hall toward the terminal with one of the airport police officers, who could stay in contact with the communication center by radio.

"Where is he?" Madison asked.

"He's taking an escalator."

"Where does it lead?"

"Out of the concourse to ground transportation and parking. But we're not far and I think we can get ahead of him."

Madison's heart raced. After six days of chasing this man across state lines, they nearly had him in their grasp. They sprinted down the terminal, through the airport, then toward the parking area.

As they burst through the final exit to the outdoors, Madison caught sight of Barrick running toward them with two officers on his tail. They turned the corner and Barrick grabbed a roller bag from a passenger, throwing it at his pursuers to try to slow them down.

He turned back around, still running, but it was already too late. Jonas slammed into Barrick with his shoulder, completely taking him off guard. He wrestled him to the ground and three more police officers from the Airport–IAH Division surrounded him, their weapons aimed at their target.

"Cuff him," Jonas said, taking a step back from the man and breathing heavily. "It's finally over."

Madison watched as Jonas rubbed his shoulder. "Are you okay?"

"Oh yeah." His smile widened. "Exhausted, but that felt really good."

"We got him." She smiled back. "Let's get out of here."

THIRTY-FOUR

Twenty-four hours later, Madison pulled Danielle into a big hug on the front porch of her sister's house, then took a step back. "I'm on my way home finally, but I had to at least stop and see you. I'm so sorry you got involved in this."

Danielle squeezed her hand. "None of this was your fault."

She shook her head. "Except it is. All of it."

"I figure as long as he's behind bars, we're safe. Still . . . I was so worried that something was going to happen to you. You could have died."

"I know, but I didn't and it's over. Barrick is safely behind bars, the threat to your life is over—"

"And the next time you go after some felon who wants you dead . . ." Worry lines appeared on Danielle's forehead as she motioned Madison inside. "I'm sorry. I know you're tired, but at least stay long enough for a glass of tea. I've missed you and the kids are actually all asleep— which means I might get about fifteen minutes of quiet."

Madison laughed. "Sounds perfect."

She followed her sister through the cozy house with toys scattered across the hardwood floors, between car seats and a stroller.

Danielle pulled a pitcher of iced tea from the fridge and poured them each a glass.

"Daddy's still here and wants to see you," Danielle said, "but I wanted to talk to you first. There's something you need to know."

Danielle set the two glasses on the kitchen table, then sat down.

"What's wrong?" Madison took the chair across from her sister, soaking in the forested view of their backyard from the kitchen table.

"Remember how Daddy went to the doctor's a couple weeks ago? They ran some tests that day, and we finally got the results back."

Madison nodded, not sure she wanted to hear what was coming next. "And?"

"You know how he's been forgetting things. Dates, names—"

"Yes, but he's almost eighty. Isn't that normal?"

"For the most part, but this is more. He's forgetting basic things like putting his laundry in the dryer after he washes it, taking out the trash, and leaving the oven on sometimes."

"I knew he was getting repetitive with his questions, but how did I miss all of this?"

"The changes have been subtle. I'm not sure any of us really saw it. While you were gone, he went on a walk in my neighborhood and forgot where he was. You're busy with your job and I want you to know that's okay, but this isn't going away."

A sinking feeling spread through her. "What are you trying to tell me, Danielle?"

Her sister hesitated before answering. "Madison, the doctor diagnosed him with Alzheimer's."

"Alzheimer's?" Madison shook her head. "They have to have made a mistake. Memory loss is a part of aging. Daddy lives on his own and has always been able to take care of himself. He still mows the lawn and—"

"Physically, the doctor said he's in great shape. And while I know this is scary, we have to deal with reality."

"Okay . . . I'm sorry, I just—Daddy's the rock of this family. He's always there. Always. What are we supposed to do?"

"We have some time, but we'll need to move him." Danielle took a sip of her tea. "Ethan and I are talking about letting him live with us. We have an extra room we could fix up for him."

"With two kids and a baby? How are you planning on doing that?"

"We want to. He's been having problems sleeping, and the doctor said he's going to need a safe place to live. And he'll need some structured activities and someone to ensure he's eating well. We're thinking about eventually bringing in someone to help out a couple days a week. Just to make it manageable. For now, I think we can make it work. The doctor also talked about some drug interventions we can discuss that can slow his decline as well as different strategies we can start putting into place. I have a lot to learn—"

"*We* have a lot to learn." Madison squeezed her sister's hand. "We're in this together. He still has a lot of life left in him, and we can help keep his life as normal as possible for as long as possible."

Danielle nodded. "I know."

"What about the house? Daddy will never leave the house. He lived there for forty years with Mama. We grew up there. How does he walk away from that?"

"With us being there for him every step of the way. I'm going to need your help talking to him about it, because it will be a hard transition, and I'm expecting some resistance."

Madison nodded, trying to wrap her head around what she was hearing. Trying not to let the guilt engulf her. She'd always tried to stay involved in her family's life, but somehow . . . somehow she'd missed this.

"Don't feel guilty for being gone so often," Danielle said. "It's okay."

"I can take some time off until he's settled—"

"I'm not asking you to do that."

"And I can't ask you to do this on your own."

"I'm not. I have Ethan, you, our church family, and Daddy has some money for extra care when it comes to that. We'll get through this. Besides, you've always been a part of his life. That won't change. And . . ." Danielle leaned forward. "That cute fixer-upper you like is still on the market. I called today, just because I was curious."

Madison laughed. "Just because you were curious."

"It would be perfect for you."

Madison's phone rang, and she pulled it out to check the caller ID.

"Do you need to get that?"

"No, it's fine." She slid the phone back into her pocket. "We'll figure things out, but I need you to promise me that you'll keep me in the loop, let me know what I can do. Anything."

"I will, and we'll get through this."

Her father walked into the kitchen, wearing his favorite blue plaid sweatpants and a black T-shirt.

"Hey, Daddy." She got up and gave him a hug, breathing in the familiar scent of Old Spice. "I missed you."

"I missed you too." His smile over seeing her faded. "I heard you were in a plane crash."

"I'll let the two of you catch up while I go check on the baby," Danielle said.

"Thank you." He hugged Madison again. "I guess no matter how old you are, I'll always worry about you. Are you sure you're okay?"

"It was a really tough week, but I'm okay. I promise."

"I always worry about you."

"You had the same job I do."

"I know. And I know we all have to die at some point."

"What if you're not ready to say goodbye?" she asked, instantly regretting the question.

"You never are." He followed her to the kitchen table and sat down next to her. "I wasn't ready to say goodbye to your mama, but all I could do was be grateful for the years the good Lord gave us together. And now . . . not a day goes by that I don't miss her."

She studied her father's face. Wrinkles indicated eight decades of life. His hair was now snow white. Age spots marked his face and hands. And yet to her he was still her daddy. The man who'd helped her become who she was today. At the moment there was no sign of confusion in his eyes or in his words. He was simply the man who had always been there for her. Teaching her how to drive at fifteen, walking her down the aisle at her wedding, and encouraging her to join the Marshals Service.

"I know about the doctor's diagnosis," he said.

"The Alzheimer's."

Her father nodded. "I'm slowly forgetting. It's little things now. Places. Words. Things that used to be easy. I'm afraid I'm going to lose her forever if I can't remember her."

Madison shook her head. "No. Mama will

always be right here." She placed her hand against his heart. "She'll always be there."

"Maybe . . . I'm just so afraid I'll forget her. She was so beautiful."

"You were a handsome couple."

He reached out and took her hand. "What about you, Maddie? You're young. You need a second chance at love."

"I'm fine, Daddy. I don't have to have someone in my life in order to be happy. I'm learning that. I have you, Danielle, and her family—"

"Yes, but I know what it's like, losing your soul mate. It's like a part of you is lost forever. I hate that you know what that feels like."

"Me too. But I'm okay. I really am."

"Losing a spouse." Her father shook his head. "We shouldn't have that in common."

"It always helps to have someone who understands. And this next step . . . We'll get through this as well."

He squeezed her hand. "Where the parent becomes the child."

"You took care of me for all those years. We'll walk down this road together, every step of the way. I promise."

Relief flooded Madison as she drove into the attached garage of her house and went inside, shutting the door behind her. The stress of the past week had worn her out. She hung up her keys and headed toward her bedroom. The black rose she'd found several days ago was still lying on her bed. She needed closure. A way to end all of this. To once and for all find the person behind this. But not tonight. Right now, she was going to take a long bubble bath and go to sleep for the next twenty-four hours.

Then after that she'd deal with reality and find out who'd left the rose.

She dropped her bag next to the bed, then peeled off her jacket. The last time she'd had a hot shower was thirty-six hours ago. The last time she'd had a decent meal was just as long.

Jonas had offered to take her out to dinner, but she'd told him to stop worrying about her. That she'd probably end up falling asleep before their meals came and would be horrible company.

Something creaked inside the house. A shiver slid through her as she pushed away any concern. The house was thirty years old and often made noises in the wind. It was nothing but fatigue that had her keyed up and her imagination working overtime.

Still . . .

She pulled her weapon out of her holster and cleared the house, room by room, making sure all the windows were shut and locked and the blinds closed. She checked the closets in both her room and the guest room. Nothing looked out of place from when she'd left. There were no signs that anyone had been here. Only an extra layer of dust and the milk in the fridge was spoiled.

Five years had passed, and there had never been any open threat. Just the black rose. Someone who wanted to try and scare her but didn't have enough courage to face her. It was nothing.

She picked up a photo off the fireplace mantel, remembering the moment the camera had frozen this image in time. A younger version of herself and Luke grinned back at her. She set the photo down. Grief had no time limit. She knew that. No one could tell you how long it took to move on. Was it progress when she didn't cry as much anymore? Or when more than an hour went by between the resurfacing memories? Or when the day came that she met someone else who made her pulse race unexpectedly and made her wonder what it would be like to fall in love again?

It's time to move on, Madison. No one will ever replace Luke, but there's someone out there who can love you just as much as he did.

Like Jonas Quinn.

The thought took her off guard, because falling in love again terrified her more than hunting down a fugitive. She shoved the unwanted thoughts to the back recesses of her mind. She wasn't going to go there. She might fall in love again one day, but not with Jonas Quinn. He'd told her of his concerns, and he was right.

Besides, happiness didn't dictate that she have someone in her life. She could be just as happy spending time with her family and friends. Being single didn't mean she was alone, because in the end, if she couldn't be happy by herself, another person couldn't fix that. Not Jonas. Not anyone.

She set her weapon on the counter, then started pulling ingredients for a protein shake out of the freezer, hoping it would help her get her energy back and feel somewhat normal.

The sound of movement behind her pulled her out of her thoughts.

Madison spun around, reaching for her gun.

"I wouldn't do that if I were you."

Madison hesitated in front of the unfamiliar woman. Her weapon was on the other side of the counter, at least six feet away, leaving her at a huge disadvantage. "Who are you?"

"You should know."

The woman was thirty, maybe thirty-five, long brown hair pulled back, nondescript clothes—but there was nothing familiar about her.

"I'm sorry, I don't know who you are or what you want, but if you put the weapon down, I'm willing to listen to whatever you have to say."

"So now you're playing the part of the negotiator. I expected as much. It's your job, after all, but I can honestly say that there isn't anything you can say or do that will change the outcome of what's about to happen."

"What is going to happen?" Madison asked, trying to plan out her next move.

"We'll talk a few more minutes, then I'm going to shoot you."

A piece of the puzzle clicked into place. "Like you did to my husband?"

"Would you like me to say I did? It would make you feel better, wouldn't it? Finally finding the person who shot him. The person who was there when he said his last words. And who watched him take his last breath. So many unanswered questions. It drives you crazy, doesn't it?"

Madison pushed back the emotions. She needed to keep her talking. Needed to find a way to disarm the woman. She could rush her. Try to take the gun away from her. But she was still standing too far away.

Madison took a step forward. "Why did you kill him?"

"I wouldn't take another step if I were you. As for your husband . . . it's complicated."

"Then why are you here? What do you want?"

"To know why you never found me. I'd like to think I was that good, but you're a marshal. It's what you do day after day and yet you couldn't find me. You weren't even up to the challenge."

"So this is some kind of . . . game?"

"You could call it that. I thought the note I left on your sister's porch might get your attention."

Madison's stomach clenched at the revelation. None of this made sense. "What do you want me to do?"

"It doesn't actually matter anymore. I'm done playing."

Madison frowned. Talking wasn't working. She had to make a move.

She lunged forward to stop the woman, but instead felt the impact of the bullet followed by a numbing then burning sensation as she fell to the ground. Her head hit hard against the tile. She tried to scream, but nothing came out. Tried to move, but she couldn't. A wet sensation bubbled around her midsection where she'd felt the bullet rip through her.

She'd just found her husband's killer and now she was going to die.

THIRTY-FIVE

Jonas walked up the sidewalk in front of Madison's house with its row of pink and yellow begonias growing along the front, hoping she wouldn't mind the unexpected visit. He knew he shouldn't worry, but he'd tried calling several times to make sure she'd gotten home okay. But he'd only gotten her voice mail. Though after all she'd been through the past week, both with chasing down Barrick and the added drama with her family, he understood her need for downtime. Michaels had insisted they both take some time off. Jonas planned to spend the next couple days fishing on Lake Washington, but first he wanted to bring Madison dinner and make sure she was okay.

He stepped onto the porch with carryout from a local Chinese restaurant and was about to ring the doorbell when a gunshot yanked him out of his thoughts.

"Madison?"

He pulled his weapon out of his holster and, without hesitating, used a front kick to drive the heel of his boot into the door. Wood splintered as his target took the impact. His heart raced. He had no idea what had happened, but he knew he had to get inside.

"Madison!" He shouted for her, then automatically prepared himself for a second kick to the side of the keyhole, the weakest part of the door. Then a third time. His mind raced with a dozen explanations for what was happening inside. None of them were good. He aimed one more powerful kick and the door made a loud buckling noise as it broke open. Something was definitely wrong. If she was able to come to the door, she would have already been there.

He ran into the house, shouting her name. A feeling of dread swept over him. The living room was to his right. A hallway to his left. The kitchen straight ahead . . . Where was she?

He ran around the kitchen island, gun held steady as he worked to clear the area. She lay on the floor in a pool of blood, a scarlet stain on her abdomen spilled onto the cream-colored tiles. Her gun was on the counter, and the back door had been flung open. Seconds slowed as he ran across the tiled flooring. What had just happened? Someone had been here. Someone had shot her. Had she known the person? Let her guard down? Or had she been taken by surprise?

He pulled his phone out of his pocket, automatically dialing 911. He turned it on speaker as he set it on the floor next to him, crouching at her side.

"Madison, can you hear me? Talk to me. Please."

He ripped off his hoodie and pressed it against her skin where a bullet had slammed through her side. He felt her wrist. No pulse.

"911. What's the location of your emergency?"

Jonas worked to pull up her address from memory, then gave it to the woman.

"I need an ambulance. My partner's been shot."

"What is your name, sir?"

"Jonas Quinn." He cupped her face. "Madison . . . Madison, I need you to wake up."

"Jonas"—the 911 operator was talking to him—"is she breathing?"

"I don't think so." He leaned closer to her face, praying that he could feel her breath against his cheek. Nothing. "No. She's not breathing."

"I have police and ambulance on their way now. Are you alone?"

"Yes."

"Can you find something to put pressure against the wound to stop the bleeding?"

"I've already done that."

His mind raced. She couldn't be dead. He'd just seen her a few hours ago. They'd survived a plane crash together. Managed to track down a convicted felon and survived the last week with barely more than a scratch. And now she was going to die on her kitchen floor? It didn't make sense.

"Jonas, do you know CPR?"

"Yes, I'm a US Marshal." He drew in a breath, forcing himself to keep a clear head. "I'm starting it now."

Still no breathing; no pulse.

He started the compressions, his mind automatically reverting to his training. Thirty chest compressions. Open the airway. Two rescue breaths.

"Come on, Madison." He resumed the compressions. "I need you to wake up and breathe."

He kept up with the chest compressions, then once again pressed his lips against hers in order to breathe for her. He'd thought about kissing her. Wondered how she'd react if he told her he was interested in her. And now . . . if he lost her . . .

She gasped for a breath like a guppy out of water.

His heart raced as he reached for her wrist and found a pulse. Weak, but steady. "Madison . . . Madison, can you hear me?"

Her eyes fluttered open and she groaned.

"Madison, you're going to be okay. I just need you to hang in there. You've been shot, but an ambulance is on the way."

He pressed his sweatshirt firm against the gunshot wound. Where was the ambulance?

She tried to move, then winced in pain.

"Don't move."

"I need to go."

"You need to stay right where you are and don't move." He focused now on putting pressure on the wound. He wasn't going to let her bleed out on her kitchen floor.

Sirens whirred in the distance.

He let out a whoosh of air, but then an icy thought brought him back to the moment as something caught his eye. A black rose sat on the tile beside Madison. Someone else had been in this house, and that someone had shot her. But he couldn't worry about who. Not now.

How was he supposed to do this?

What if I lose her?

The unanticipated question followed by a surge of unrestrained emotions surprised him.

All that mattered now was saving her.

Three hours later, Jonas paced the floor of the empty waiting room, anxious to hear from the doctors. Madison's sister had arrived shortly after he had, but he had little information to share with her. All he really knew was how much blood Madison had lost and how unresponsive she'd been. And as far as he was concerned, it was going to take a miracle to save her. Seeing her lying motionless on the floor had shaken him and left him to untangle a string of emotions he wasn't sure how to interpret. But the bottom line was that the thought of losing her had left him reeling.

Felicia's face flashed in front of him, pushing the present away for a moment. He could still hear her voice. Telling him she didn't want to see him again, no matter how hard he pleaded with her. For weeks he'd done everything to convince her he didn't want to lose her. That it didn't matter to him that she'd lost her leg. Nothing could change how he felt about her, but eventually, he'd had no choice but to accept defeat and simply walk away.

This situation, though, was different. Madison was just a friend. A colleague. One he had no problem trusting with his life, but he had no intentions of giving her his heart. Besides, he'd seen her face when she talked about her husband. No matter how many years had passed, she was still in love with him.

"Jonas?" His mom stood in the doorway of the waiting room. "I thought you might need someone to talk to."

He crossed the room and gave her a hug. "Thank you. Though I didn't expect you to come down here."

"I was worried. About her, about you. What happened?"

"Presumably it was a home invasion. She was shot in the abdomen. She's in surgery now. And I . . . I still don't know if she's going to make it."

Saying it out loud made it seem even more real.

"Is it somehow connected to the case you were working?" his mom asked.

"I don't know. I went to see her at her house . . . heard a gunshot . . . and when I got inside, she was bleeding out on the floor."

"I'm so sorry."

"So am I." Jonas fought back the emotions he was used to keeping shut off. "I trained her a few years ago, and we just spent the past week together tracking down a fugitive."

His hands were shaking in front of him, so he shoved them into his pockets, then sat down in one of the cushioned chairs.

His mom sat down next to him. "I know this has to dredge up a lot of old memories."

He blew out a sharp breath. He'd almost lost Felicia and now . . . It was as if life was repeating itself. A nightmare he couldn't wake up from, because he was already awake. Maybe that was why his reaction seemed so intense. Why he couldn't shake the terror over finding her dying.

"I don't know what to do," he said.

His mom took his hands and squeezed them. "We pray."

Ten minutes later, Madison's sister stepped into the room. Prayer had given him a calmness he hadn't felt before, but a layer of anxiety still lingered.

Jonas stood up. "Danielle. How is she?"

"The bullet hit the right upper abdomen, and the CT scan showed a liver laceration. No injury to her lungs. The next twenty-four hours are going to be crucial. She lost a lot of blood, but the surgery went well."

"Wow. I'm so glad." He let her words sink in. "So she's going to be okay?"

"It will take some time, but the doctor believes at this point that she'll make a full recovery." Danielle clutched the strap of her purse. "I need to warn you, though, she's having some memory issues. But she's awake, surprisingly talkative, and asked to see you."

Jonas hesitated. "What kind of memory issues?"

"Mainly, she doesn't remember who shot her. But the doctor is confident that the memories will return. Just keep your visit short."

He nodded. "Thank you."

"Of course. You saved her life. I'm grateful."

He said goodbye to his mom, then walked into Madison's room a moment later, pausing for a moment at the end of the bed. Her face was pale, and she looked tired, but she was alive.

"Hey . . . ," he said.

She offered him a weak smile as he sat down on the edge of the bed. "Hey."

"How do you feel?"

"Groggy. And like I've been shot. Like my rib cage was crushed."

He offered her a weak smile. "That would be me. You weren't breathing when I found you, and you didn't have a pulse."

"The doctors said you saved my life—that you were there, at my house."

"I knew the past week had been tough on you. I just wanted to make sure you were okay and decided to stop by."

"It's a good thing you did. Because if you hadn't been there . . ."

"Let's not even go there."

"Agreed."

He waited a moment before continuing, knowing she was tired, but also wanting to know what had happened in that house before he got there. "Danielle said you were having some memory issues."

She blinked back tears. "I can't remember who shot me. They were in my house and I can't remember what happened."

"Madison, it's okay." Her heart rate elevated on the monitor and he squeezed her hand. "Don't worry. We will find them. The police are there, trying to figure out what happened as we speak, and they will. What matters right now is that you get better."

"All I remember is hearing a noise. And then . . . and then nothing. No matter how hard I try I can't remember."

"It's okay."

"No. It's not. The doctor told me it's amnesia caused by a severely stressful event."

"Getting shot is pretty traumatic."

"Yes, but I'm a US Marshal. I've faced dozens of traumatic and violent situations. This isn't supposed to happen."

He held on to her hand, worried that she was getting too upset. But he couldn't blame her. "This was also personal. It's best not to try to force yourself to remember. Just focus on getting better right now."

He wanted to tell her about the rose, knowing she'd want him to tell her, but something made him hesitate. Her body was under enough stress and didn't need any more piled on top of it. Besides, at this point, the authorities were handling things and there was really nothing they could do.

"You were there at the house. Did you see who shot me?"

He shook his head. "They were gone by the time I got there."

She caught his gaze. "But there is something you're not telling me."

"Madison, there's nothing—"

"Just tell me. Please."

His jaw tensed, but he knew she wasn't going to take no for an answer. Even in her groggy state, she was too stubborn for that.

"I found a black rose on the floor next to you.

It was definitely the same person who's been leaving the flowers."

"Who killed Luke." She closed her eyes and drew in a deep breath. "I have to remember."

"You will." He squeezed her hand. "But you don't need to worry about anything right now. We'll find out who did this."

"Whoever shot me killed my husband, Jonas."

"I know, but don't try to force it. Right now you just need to rest more than anything else. Though this might change your moving date," he said, struggling to change the subject.

She tugged on the end of the sheet. "I've been thinking I might stay, actually."

"Really? What changed your mind?"

"I don't know. Things I talked about with my dad. Things you and I talked about. The realization that I don't have to leave or start over to move forward and that it doesn't matter where I am, but who I'm with. And maybe most importantly the reminder that I don't want to leave friends and family."

And me.

No. Jonas shoved back the thought. She wasn't staying for him.

"My sister found me this fixer-upper a couple weeks ago," she continued. "I went to see it, and while I didn't really say anything to her, well . . . I'm still thinking about it. It's still on the market. Or maybe it's more me not wanting to put up with Danielle's constant nagging about my well-being and needing to be close to her and her family." Madison laughed, then groaned at the pain. "Anyway, it was built in 1950, has the original hardwood floors, plus these large picture windows and mahogany woodwork."

"So with all your spare time, you're going to fix it up?"

"Are you any good with a hammer?"

"Are you implying you need my help?"

She laughed. "My sister's husband is a contractor and could do most of the work. I'd end up with a discount and a great house."

"Are you trying to convince me or yourself?"

She pressed her lips together. "Jonas, I can remember the hardwood floors in that house, my sister telling me our father has Alzheimer's, but not who stood in my kitchen and shot me."

All that matters is that I didn't lose you.

He swallowed hard and forced an easy smile. "You'll remember."

He needed to go but didn't want to leave her. Not yet. "There is another thing I hope you haven't forgotten. We made a deal. I would try your cream cheese hot dogs if you try a bowl of chowder."

"We did, didn't we?" She smiled. "I'd like that, though it might be a few days before I can handle an outing."

"Take as long as you want. I'm just grateful you're alive."

"Me too. You're my hero. I owe you."

"If you're staying, then you just might get the chance to pay me back. Looks as though we'll be working together a lot."

She yawned. "I'd like that as long as we never repeat last week."

"I agree." He smiled at her, but he couldn't forget how close she'd come to dying. Couldn't help asking the what-ifs. What if he hadn't been there at that moment? What if he'd decided not to go see her? There was another question, though, that he couldn't let go of. What would happen if he told her right now what he was feeling? Because when he'd found her lying on the floor of her kitchen, he felt a piece of himself dying when he thought he was going to lose her. And now, looking at her, all he could think about was kissing her.

"What are you thinking?" she asked.

Jonas avoided her gaze, thankful she couldn't read his mind. "A couple things. One, I need to go so you can get some sleep."

"I do need to sleep." Her eyes started to flutter shut. "It's getting hard to stay awake. What's the other thing?"

Besides the fact that I'm falling for you and don't know how to stop myself?

He shoved aside the thought and squeezed her

hand. "We're going to find who shot both you and your husband. I promise."

She nodded. "I'm sorry . . . I'm so tired."

She closed her eyes, and Jonas watched her sleep for a moment, before slipping out of the room. He would find a way to keep his promise to her, and maybe, just maybe, find a way to give her his heart as well.

ACKNOWLEDGMENTS

I'm so grateful to those who have worked with me behind the scenes to bring this story together. Andrea Doering and Robin Turici, my wonderful editors at Revell, along with the entire marketing and publicity teams. Ellen Tarver for her eagle-eye editing input and my sweet husband who continues to tirelessly support me through brainstorming, lots of coffee, and constant encouragement.

ABOUT THE AUTHOR

Lisa Harris is a bestselling author, a Christy Award winner, and the winner of the Best Inspirational Suspense Novel from *Romantic Times* for her novels *Blood Covenant* and *Vendetta*. The author of more than forty books, including the Nikki Boyd Files and the Southern Crimes series, as well as *Vanishing Point*, *A Secret to Die For*, and *Deadly Intentions*, Harris and her family have spent over sixteen years living as missionaries in southern Africa. Learn more at www.lisaharriswrites.com.

Books are produced in the United States using U.S.-based materials

Books are printed using a revolutionary new process called THINKtech™ that lowers energy usage by 70% and increases overall quality

Books are durable and flexible because of Smyth-sewing

Paper is sourced using environmentally responsible foresting methods and the paper is acid-free

Center Point Large Print
600 Brooks Road / PO Box 1
Thorndike, ME 04986-0001 USA

(207) 568-3717

US & Canada:
1 800 929-9108
www.centerpointlargeprint.com